*The
Heart
Is
Half
a
Prophet*

The Heart Is Half a Prophet

Ruth Tessler Goldstein

Macmillan Publishing Co., Inc.
New York

Collier Macmillan Publishers
London

Macmillan Publishing Co., Inc.
866 Third Avenue, New York, N.Y. 10022
Collier Macmillan Canada, Ltd.

Library of Congress Cataloging in Publication Data
Goldstein, Ruth Tessler.
The heart is half a prophet.
I.   Title.

PZ4.G64145He   [PS3557.042]   813'.5'4   76-10720
ISBN 0-02-544590-1

First Printing 1976

Printed in the United States of America

To the memory of my mother

But *his word* was in my heart as a burning fire shut
up in my bones . . .

The Book of the Prophet Jeremiah

And the Lord said, "Because the cry of Sodom and
Gomorrah is great, and because their sin is very grievous;
I will go down now and see." . . .

And Abraham drew near, and said, "Wilt thou also destroy the righteous with the wicked?

"Peradventure there be fifty righteous within the city:
wilt thou also destroy and not spare the place for the fifty
righteous that *are* therein?" . . .

And the Lord said, "If I find in Sodom fifty righteous
within the city, then I will spare all the place for their
sakes." . . .

And Abraham answered and said, "Behold now, I have
taken upon me to speak unto the Lord, which *am but* dust
and ashes: Peradventure there shall lack five of the fifty
righteous: wilt thou destroy the city for *lack* of five?" And
he said, "If I find there forty and five, I will not destroy
it." . . .

"Oh let not the Lord be angry and I will speak: Peradventure there shall thirty be found there." And he said,
"I will not do *it*, if I find thirty there." . . .

"Behold now, I have taken upon me to speak unto the
Lord: Peradventure there shall be twenty found there."
And he said, "I will not destroy it for twenty's sake." . . .

"Oh let not the Lord be angry, and I will speak yet but
this once: Peradventure ten shall be found there." And
he said, "I will not destroy *it* for ten's sake."

The Book of Genesis

Winter
1936

1

Snow fell while she slept. The sidewalks have vanished. Stoops have become slopes. Drifts block storefronts almost halfway up. The gaunt tenements, their rows of ecru window shades still pulled down, their faces scarred with fire escapes, lean against each other festooned in white ribbons and garlands, like sleeping drunkards adorned by urchins.

The only footprints Esther can see from her bedroom window lead to or from her house. Who but her father's regulars would come out so early on a Sunday in such weather? Esther rubs her hands along the sleeves of her nightgown and hopes at least nine men came—nine plus her father make a minyan. She puts on her new bathrobe, a present from her brother, Ben. She can't remember a morning without a minyan downstairs, but she worries anyway— ever since Ben told her that they pay hardly any rent because her father takes care of the synagogue. She'd asked him why her father makes such a fuss about getting the ten men, sometimes going to people's houses to get them or even bringing in strangers from the street. Ben said you have to have at least ten men or else, they say, the Divine Presence isn't there when you're praying and, while God wants you to pray anyway and he's supposed to help you if you do, some prayers are too sacred to say if He's not there, and you have to leave them out. So people might start going to a different shul if there was no minyan, and after a while there'd never be one. And if there were no minyans, there wouldn't be a shul to take care of, and they'd have to move out. Where would they go? Her father never seems worried, but her mother does. Esther can't recall ever seeing the rabbi who owns their house, but her mother doesn't like him; she calls him a "pruster mensch." So he can't be anything like her father's Rebbe—her mother likes *him*. It's hard to imagine a rabbi being coarse, but even if he is, he wouldn't throw them out in the street. If her father can't get minyans here, maybe he could do it in the rabbi's new house in Crown Heights. That's a much nicer neighborhood than Williamsburg, and the house is probably a lot nicer too. But if the house is still nice, the rabbi would want to keep living in it and not move out like he did from here. So where would they live? Esther hugs herself; the heating system doesn't work, and the house is cold. She'll just finish watching Mr. Lieberman, then she'll get ready for Hebrew school.

Across the street one strip of shoveled sidewalk shines blue-black against the faintly night-purpled whiteness. It leads to the narrow entrance of the store where a solitary yellow light bulb behind the glass casts into silhouette the large letters centered on the upper half of the window, I. LIEBERMAN—TAILOR, and the smaller letters on the lower left, Cleaning and Pressing. Mr. Lieberman is already back from the synagogue and, with his white shirt-sleeves rolled to his elbows, is already raising and lowering the big pressing machine. Esther thinks she can hear the thumping and hissing of the steaming press. Over and over again Mr. Lieberman raises it, lowers it, and holds it down. Esther knows that when the garment is pressed to his satisfaction, Mr. Lieberman will put it on a hanger, hook the hanger to the end of a special long pole, and then he will lean back and reach up with the pole to hang the fresh-pressed garment on the bar high against the wall of his store. She's waiting to see if when he leans back and looks

4

up, his yarmulka will fall off the back of his head. Mr. Lieberman leans back, looks up, hooks the hanger on the bar, and the small black yarmulka stays in place. She shivers with relief, with awe at the mystical affinity between Mr. Lieberman's head and his yarmulka, and because she is cold. As she pulls her bathrobe tighter around her, she sees that Mr. Lieberman is sweating. He takes a large white handkerchief from his pants pocket. First he mops his forehead, and then he mops his neck under the small black beard.

Mr. Lieberman sweats more than anybody she knows. She used to think it was the steam from the pressing machine that made him perspire so much, but it's the same everywhere. Even on freezing cold nights, when all the other men in the shul sit as close to the oil stove as possible, Mr. Lieberman sits in his same seat way in the back and sweats. One freezing cold night the oil stove went out and the other men had their overcoats on and were shivering. Mr. Lieberman had no overcoat on and his face was glistening. And it can't have anything to do with his beard. Melnick from the grocery store is fat and has a real long beard, a red one that covers his chest, and Melnick doesn't sweat. She looks up the street to the grocery store; the snow is piled high against the door. Melnick is probably still in the shul, shmoozing over cake and shnapps, enticements her father uses now and then for the less reliable ones. Pants from the tailor you can pick up already, Esther thinks, but if you needed butter or milk for breakfast, you'd still be waiting for Melnick to open up. Maybe that's why, under his big red beard, Melnick doesn't sweat.

Turning abruptly away from the window, Esther knocks over the nagel vasser. She forgot to use it.

Every night before he goes to bed, her father places an empty basin and white enamel pitcher filled with water beside their bed so that Esther and her sister, Lila, can perform the ritual of purifying themselves upon rising in the morning. One is supposed to pour water three times over each hand into a vessel. If not, her father says, the unclean spirits which entered the body during sleep, when the holy spirit departed, would not be entirely banished and your body would not be ready to receive the spirit of the Creator. You had to be careful to pour the water over the nails because when you wake up, the unclean spirit leaves the rest of your body, but does not leave your fingertips. When she asked her father why she couldn't just wash at the sink, he said the sink was not a vessel and, besides, it was too far away; one is not permitted to walk four cubits without having washed his hands. She knew it would be a waste of time to ask why it had to be into a vessel and no more than exactly four cubits because he'd only say, "It is so written in the Shulchan Aruch." And it would be clear that he didn't want any further questions. She isn't sure whether there's no better explanation or her father just doesn't know one. Or whether it's true, as he keeps saying, "One must not question. One must believe."

The water, spreading across the linoleum, soaked her felt slippers. It feels awful. But luckily the noise didn't wake Lila. Esther picks up the pitcher and runs quickly through the dark, drafty hallway to the bathroom. She fills the pitcher, runs back to the bedroom, bends down, pours the icy water three times over each hand and reaches for the towel on the hook beside the bed. After she wipes her hands, she wipes the floor, being careful to leave a part of the towel dry for Lila to use. Not that it matters, she thinks. Lila doesn't use the nagel vasser anyway; she just pours it right into the basin. She saw her do it once when Lila thought she was asleep.

Esther looks at her sister curled up on her side under the thick feather comforter with the flowered cotton cover. Lila can sleep as late as she likes on Sundays because she's three years older and doesn't have to go to Hebrew school. Her wavy hair is a blond puddle against the white pillow, her cheeks are pink, and her wine-colored mouth is pouting, with the moist inside of her lower lip showing a little. She looks glossy. Such a pretty girl in an ugly metal bed with peeling brown paint. Lila doesn't fit with the bed, with this room, with this house. Lately, Lila doesn't even seem to fit with the family. Her name doesn't seem right either. She picked it herself. She even went by herself to the principal's office and told them that Leah was only her Jewish name, that her real name, her English name, was Lila, and they believed her and changed the name on her record. Lila really has nerve! Of course, she doesn't say anything when Mama and Papa call her Leah, but if I do or anybody else, she gets real mad.

When Esther goes to the bathroom again, she remembers to tiptoe across the room so the floorboards won't creak and maybe wake Lila up. Why does Lila have to get so angry if she's awakened? She's angry a lot lately. If she isn't being angry, she just doesn't seem to be paying attention. Like last week, while she was getting ready to go out, I was telling her about that terrible thing that happened at Millie's house. And all the time she kept looking in the mirror, turning her head this way and that way, fixing all those little curls into that cluster she wears on her forehead, and when she finished fixing her hair, she walked out. Without saying anything. As if she hadn't heard a word. As if I wasn't even in the room. Oh, who cares about Lila anyway?

The hall, insulated from sunlight, is like an icebox; a cold draft comes up the steps, plunges into the blinding dimness, and then darts about as though looking for a way out. Esther hurries into the bathroom. While she sprinkles salt on her toothbrush, she wonders if they'll ever be able to afford toothpaste. How did her mother know that salt was just as good as toothpaste when she didn't even know

7

about toothbrushes until Lila told her? Lila said she had to have one because her teacher said that teeth that aren't brushed every day get rotten. Even Lila's teacher agreed that salt was okay. Her mother and father still just rinse with salt water, but Ben has a toothbrush too.

Esther takes off her bathrobe. She washes her hands and face, then lifts her nightgown and, with more speed than scrupulousness, washes her underarms. If only they could have hot water, it wouldn't be so bad. The cold baths in summer are okay once you get yourself in. When she used to take them with Lila, it was fun. Her mother would get annoyed by all the water they spilled. "It will leak through the floor and drip into the shul and ruin the ceiling," she'd tell them. But somehow it never did. A hot bath is a real bother. They have to heat kettles of water on the kitchen stove two floors below in the basement and carry them up the steps past the stoop floor to the top floor. When the bathroom is too cold, her mother takes both of them along to the mikva where, besides the little pool ladies dip themselves in, there are bathtubs. Her mother still worries about getting her money's worth, but now she lets them wash themselves. When they were little she must have imagined that the longer they soaked and the harder she scrubbed, the longer it would last, and they'd come out with shriveled fingertips and sore backs.

On the way back to her bedroom, Esther is again especially careful when she passes Ben's door. She does not want to wake him. Not that he'd get angry; he just seems so tired all the time. He was different when he was still going to school, and he'd come home and play punchball with the boys on the block. He could run faster than anybody else. His wiry body seemed to hardly touch the ground. And when he'd come back in, he'd be sweating and excited, and he'd sprawl in a chair, smiling and kidding around, with his tzitzis hanging out from under his shirt tails. Now Ben is quiet, as if speaking requires energy he doesn't have or doesn't think it deserves.

The black walnut chifforobe squeaks when she opens it. Luckily that doesn't wake Lila either. Besides the bed and chifforobe, the room has a dresser with a mirror above it. Esther decides once more that the dresser makes the room look much nicer, with Lila's things laid out on top—the fancy comb and brush set Ben gave her for her birthday, the gold-framed picture of Fred Astaire and Ginger Rogers that she won at the movies, her jar of Mum, and the cigar box for her curlers that she pasted over with the flowered paper she got free from Mr. Greenberg, the painter. Esther begins to get dressed, trying not to feel the confusion of love and hate, longing and disappointment and dismay that possesses her whenever she thinks about her sister. *Sometimes, I wish Papa never stopped making us take a nap on Shabbes,* she admits to herself.

Esther's father, interpreting the commandment to rest on the Sabbath in the ultimate literal sense, had imposed a decree that everyone in his household was to nap on Shabbes afternoon, unless he was "learning Torah." Under the pretense of that absolution, Ben was able to leave the house after the noonday meal. The girls had to go to their bedroom and nap. After the big Shabbes meal with the tzimmes and the fish and the chicken and the kugel and the stewed prunes, they were pretty sleepy anyway, and in the winter when it was cold both inside and outside, Esther and Lila used to love stripping down to their underwear and crawling under the thick comforter and whispering together. And often they fell asleep. But on warm afternoons when the smell of the sun-drenched streets and the voices of their friends floated through the open windows, they didn't want to go to bed. So when they had chanted the Grace after Meals, they would go dutifully upstairs, take off their shoes, get under the covers with their clothes on and lie very still, listening for their father's snoring to sound through the wall. It didn't matter whether their mother was asleep because they knew she'd pretend not to hear them. Then they would sneak out of the house. They wouldn't play stoopball or jacks because it was Shabbes, but they would sit on the steps of their high stoop with their friends and play Ghost or Movie Stars. Their father's bedroom faced the back and they kept their voices low, so they didn't wake him. And when it was almost the time their father generally got up, they'd go back inside and up to their bedroom, mess up their hair, and then greet their father stretching and yawning, barely awake.

How glad she was when she didn't have to nap anymore! It was right after Simchas Torah. All of them, her mother and Lila, she and Ben had walked the bridge with her father to his Rebbe on the East Side to watch the Hassidim dance and to see the Rebbe dance with the Torah. The shul was packed with people—some came to sing and dance, others to listen and see. Children stood on the benches; parents put the smallest ones on their shoulders to see better. The singing swirled and surged and soared and throbbed. The circle of dancers rocked and twirled and swayed and stamped. The same two Hassidim, Elya and Velvel—both small and dark, one fat and one skinny— became excessive in their ecstasy, leaping and jumping high into the air, throwing their bodies about violently, convulsively. Her mother turned away and muttered, "Tzvai mesheguyim. A shandeh." Two crazymen. A disgrace. Then suddenly it was quiet, and her mother was shushing her, and the Rebbe came out and danced alone with the Torah. So many times she's recalled the Rebbe's delicate face with its silken amber beard, his black velvet shtreimel with its border of fur glowing like a halo around his head, his long slender caftan. He kept his feet close together, his eyes closed, and danced with small, barely perceptible steps, turning from side to side, hugging the Torah close to him, as though she were his sweetheart or his bride.

Everyone was quiet on the way home. It was the next morning that Lila, with a glint in her blue eyes, presented her father with irrefutable evidence that the Almighty did not require one to sleep on the Sabbath; Rivka, the Rebbe's daughter who was her age, had told her that she never had been required to take a Shabbes nap. Her father colored a little, but did not speak. The following Saturday, he went straight to his bedroom without reminding them to go to theirs. How glad they were! They went out to play in the autumn air and were still sitting on the stoop when he woke up. Not a word.

Now, Esther is not glad. She ties the sash of her dress and thinks of the good times she and Lila used to have, whispering and giggling and sneaking downstairs. Now, I hardly do anything with Lila, she says to herself, except on Sundays if Ben gives us money for the movies; and she only goes with me because all her friends go on Saturday when she can't go. Esther looks in the mirror to comb her hair which is thin and pale and straight, just like the rest of her. Lila is the beauty of the family. Even the most stolid of the synagogue regulars have at some time openly expressed admiration of her sister. The only one she can remember saying anything nice about *her* is Mr. Lieberman. She had stopped in with her mother to pick up their cleaned spring coats; Mr. Lieberman stood back looking at her while he said to her mother, "When you look into those eyes, you see wheels turning in the head." She didn't understand what he meant, but her mother smiled and patted her shoulder, so she knew it was something good. Afterwards, she went up to her bedroom to look in the mirror. She couldn't see any wheels turning, but that day she decided she had nice eyes.

The sun has come out. The room will be warmer soon.

Not that Esther minds the cold as much as her shivering seems to indicate. She cannot articulate, even to herself, just why and when she began to accept physical discomforts with a stoicism that bordered on affectation. It might have been on that sweltering July day when her father sent her, with an old rattan baby carriage, to bring home a block of ice because it was cheaper than having it delivered. She did not want to do it. Why couldn't he send Lila? she asked. "Because you're younger," her father said, and she was certain she was going to look foolish and pathetic. But as she pushed the baby carriage with its block of ice under a burlap sack through the streets, she became determinedly unashamed. A small boy pulled at his mother's dress and pointed to her; two girls she knew slightly from school nudged each other and snickered; people looked at her a little too long. She kept her head high. She felt beads of sweat on her forehead, but did not wipe them away. They trickled into her mouth, and she relished their taste. She suffered exultantly and ostentatiously, seeking favor only in the eyes of her omnipresent God who would love her for her courage and goodness.

Now, possessed by a sudden need to atone, not only for forgetting to purge her body of unclean spirits in preparation for him, but also for knocking over the water designated for the ritual—an act that might be construed by her omnipresent God as one of willful, disdainful desecration—Esther postpones putting on her sweater until after she has said her Modeh Ani. Growing solemn and speaking softly but clearly, she recites the morning prayer: "I give thanks unto thee, O King, who livest and endurest, who hast mercifully restored my soul unto me; great is thy faithfulness. The beginning of wisdom is the fear of the Lord.... Blessed be the name of his glorious kingdom for ever and ever."

Yes, she does fear him. When she was little, she memorized the Modeh Ani and recited it by rote. Her father had explained the significance of the act, but not the meaning of the Hebrew words. Nevertheless, she feared the Lord. Now that she knows the meaning of "Rayshis huchma yiras Adonai," the fear is reinforced. But she is troubled by the incongruity of enjoying her fear. Maybe Millie is right; maybe she *is* crazy. And God isn't watching all the time, caring whether you do this or that dumb thing. Oh, how would Millie, with her mother and father, know anything about God anyway?

Still, there must be something wrong with that peculiar, good feeling she gets, not only when she's too hot or too cold, but even when she's sad. Like when they were still living on the East Side and the other girls went to the pool in Pitt Street park and she and Lila couldn't go. "The daughters of Zalman Hirsch do not bathe in other people's filth," her father announced, as if the whole world was listening. And that was not the only thing the daughters of Zalman Hirsch did not do; they did not wear shorts, or sunsuits, or even beach pajamas in the street; they did not eat popsicles—"poison," her father called them. Even though she was too little for the big pool and would have had to stay in the wading pool, she wanted to go so much. And when all the girls came home with their hair wet and their towels under their arms and told her what a good time she missed, she felt bad. Yet, she remembers, that she felt a little good too—about not being just like everybody else. Esther buttons her sweater over her dress, feeling delight, but also apprehension, in her individuality.

When she looks out the window again, Mr. Lieberman is not at his pressing machine. He must be in his apartment behind the curtain. Mrs. Lieberman is probably giving him breakfast on the little table with the oilcloth cover. If a customer opens the door a bell will ring, and Mr. Lieberman will come out, maybe still swallowing. She puts another bobby pin in her hair to keep it neat and is still unhappy with how she looks in the mirror. When she was younger, she looked so different, and she felt different too—lighter, much lighter. When she ran, she was sure that for at least a minute, she had flown. Everybody laughed when she said she could fly. But she still thinks she did. Now, ungainly, approaching pubescence, Esther can't imagine herself flying.

The hall is still like an icebox. As she walks down the steps to the first floor, it begins to smell brown and musty and brackish. The aroma of snuff, of old wood and wax, of crumbling, yellowed, tear-stained parchment seeps from under the synagogue door, which is closed to keep out the cold. She hears the men's voices, some soft, quavering, others—Melnick's above the rest—resonant, pontifical. All reluctant to leave the warmth and conviviality inside for the cold outside. They are, Esther supposes, her father's friends, like Millie and Angie are hers.

At the end of the landing, she turns and continues downstairs. The basement rooms are partially underground, and the small, high windows of the dining room are completely blocked by snow. Esther walks carefully across the wobbly, wooden door lying between the dining room and the kitchen, where the floor has rotted away. Her mother is standing by the range, stirring oatmeal in a blue enamel saucepan, and does not stop or turn around. Esther goes to her mother and reaches up on tiptoe to kiss her quickly between her neat brown bun and her plump sweatered back. Her mother continues to stir the oatmeal, but a shy delight filters through the brusqueness as she speaks. "Sit down, the oatmeal is getting hard and lumpy."

Esther sits down, with her back to the coal stove, to eat her oatmeal, which is neither hard nor lumpy. She does not expect her mother to return her kiss or to make further conversation. With her mother, there is a time for everything. Kisses are for special occasions—to accompany the Gut Shabbes or Gut Yontev after the lighting of the candles, or for an unexpected demonstration of "menschlichkeit," a good deed, an advance toward maturity. Conversation is for when one's work, for the time being, is completed—like late Shabbes afternoon. In the summer, her mother puts her folding chair on their high stoop, and women from the neighborhood come, and they sit and talk. Her mother does not sit on someone else's stoop or join the line of folding chairs in front of another building. Her mother stays at home, and women come—Mrs. Lieberman, Mrs. Melnick, and sad Mrs. Koopitz with her strange, shy daughter who looks older than Ben, but still wears Mary Jane shoes and white anklets. In the winter when her mother stays inside, women hardly ever come. Often there are just the two of them, she and her mother sitting by the window in the shadowy twilight with the flames from the oil stove dancing on the dining room wall. And her mother's workworn hands, with their fingers like carrots, are folded in her lap as she tells Esther stories of the past. She tells about her girlhood in Kishinev. How she and her sister hid in the hayloft whenever the Cossacks rampaged through the village. How there were just the two of them, she and her sister, because the Cossacks had killed both her brothers. About her uncles who were landowners and killed by the revolutionaries. Why her father had only one eye—because her grandmother did not want him to serve in the Czar's army, so she put out his other eye. Over and over again, she tells of her departure—of crossing the border in a blizzard, holding one small son by the hand and the other in her arms, and how the one holding her hand let go and was lost in the snow, and how when she found him he was frozen, dead. She tells about the two friendly peasants who helped her bury her eldest son in a strange place in the snow, and how she doesn't know where her son lies buried. She tells of the list of places and people Esther's father had sent her, and how she followed the list across Europe until she arrived in Antwerp where the ship was waiting. She tells of the voyage on the ship, and how

15

warm mysticism for arid scholasticism, and whose God wishes, above all else, to be worshipped sincerely and joyfully, with singing and dancing.

Zalman Hirsch worships sincerely and sings joyfully. But when he attends services or celebrations at his Rebbe's, which in recent years is not as often as he likes, he does not join the circle when the other Hassidim dance. Some, in their fervor, become unseemingly wild, and, although he defends them when his wife calls them "a disgrace," his own distaste and the concern for his dignity prevent his participation.

There are other deviations. Often he is troubled that his wife does not wear the obligatory wig, but he loves to look at her own lovely brown hair. He himself has not let his beard grow long. For years he did not have even a mustache, worrying that it might make him less pleasing to look at and to kiss. He observed the prohibition against shaving with a razor by using the permissible depilatory. When he grew a mustache, his wife didn't seem to care one way or the other, so he grew a beard—but a trimmed one, small and becoming. Zalman Hirsch is a jolly, earthy man with a vigorous body and a roguish eye, who has frequently felt compelled to discomfit the smug and the prudish by reminding them of King Solomon's seven hundred wives and three thousand concubines and of King David's similarly lascivious inclinations. But Solomon and David are, in truth, small comfort to him. They were, after all, kings of Israel; he is an ordinary man. Zalman suffers from his sins of vanity, sensuality, and his concern for worldliness. Perhaps, he thinks, that is why the Lord, in his wisdom, has chosen to chastise him—to make him mindful of his imperfections. So Zalman does not complain about his lot in life and tries to be compensatorily devout in his own way. He prays with not one but two pair of phylacteries, and, because he also is not a learned man and his ignorance worries him, he is inordinately rigid and zealous in adhering to the dogma and rituals he does observe.

Even his colors and contours are inconsistent and unsubtle. Thick curly white hair covers his titanic head, while the substantial mustache and the small sculpted beard under his full red underlip are black. And he comports himself not only like a man with a fierce faith in the Almighty, but as one with equally powerful faith in himself, taking his Sabbath stroll with his head high and his thumbs thrust into his armpits. His voice is voluminous, his wit relentless, and his temper explosive. And with his unquenchable optimism, he has managed for many years to maintain his family at a level of high expectancy.

The excesses of Zalman Hirsch are legendary. No one can drink more glasses of both hotter and sweeter tea at a single sitting. His bath water would scald an ordinary person. Any innocent, who accepts his smiling offer of one of the red peppers he is popping merrily into his own mouth, finds himself gasping while Zalman roars with delight. And included in his avidity for the spices of life is a clamorous sexual appetite. He adores his wife Malka—Malkela he calls her more often than she likes. If she doesn't adore *him*, what can he do? Cry to the world? To what purpose? As long as she doesn't shame him before people. . . .

Well-worn stories about Zalman Hirsch go back many years. Zalman did not come to America as the conventional steerage passenger; he came as a stowaway. And so concerned was he with concealing himself on a ship that he chose the wrong one; its destination was not New York but Buenos Aires. Zalman spent a year working in the wheat fields of Argentina, where he picked up the Spanish accent that distinguishes his broken English from that of his cronies. The next time he stowed away, the ship brought him to the right America. But even the right America, it turned out, was different from the image which had pulled him away from his small Russian village, from his pregnant wife standing in the doorway and his small son playing on the dirt floor. Nectar did not flow in the streets. But it did lie, shimmering and sweet in clandestine corners, emanating a discreet smell.

Zalman's sharp nose was equal to his sweet tooth. He sniffed around and found things out. Then he set about ferreting out old friends, landzleit, his cousin Sam Gittleson who started out selling shoelaces on a street corner in New Jersey and now was a big suit manufacturer in New York—one of the biggest. Zalman presented them with propositions. Some gave and some did not, but Zalman borrowed enough to begin investing. He bought first one building, then another—decrepit ones, but it didn't matter; immigrants were poor and had to live someplace. He paid back the friends and the relatives with interest. Now he could put up security and began going to banks for first mortgages and to brokers for second ones. Credit flowed freely and Zalman swam with the tide. Before long he owned buildings in blocks, even one that housed a United States Post Office. (He still likes to refer to Calvin Coolidge as his old tenant.) God was good to Zalman who, in turn, became known for lavish ways and a generous spirit. He brought his wife to a fine house with thick carpets and satin draperies and a maid to serve her. She wore silk dresses and golden jewelry. He brought his two sisters and four brothers to America, cousins, nephews, nieces, old friends. He was proud of his good fortune; if you were a relative or friend of Zalman's, you expected for your wedding present nothing less than a grand piano. He gloried in his family—his handsome wife, his two little girls, and, above all, his Benjamin, before whom sages sat in wonder. Remarkable mind, they said of him. Brilliant. So Zalman dreamed of greatness for his son; a distinguished scholar, a rabbi, a teacher of men he would be. Zalman praised God for his goodness.

Then came the crash. Tenants couldn't pay. Mortgages were foreclosed. The Great Depression had begun. Business associates jumped from office windows and lay in shattered heaps on the sidewalks. Zalman Hirsch became penniless, but remained whole—firmly rooted in his faith. It was bashert. It was God's will.

From uptown, they moved down. One by one the trappings of affluence vanished, except for the Queen Anne bedroom set with its triple-mirrored dressing table, the dark mahogany dining room furniture with the brocaded chairs, the elaborate Passover silver and crystal and china, and the gold locket watch with the diamond in the center that his wife continues to wear on special occasions—if it is not burrowed between the banjos on the pawnbroker's shelf. And on top of the buffet in the dining room, their blue and gold bindings still impressive, there is the set of The Books of Knowledge he presented to his son when he was five years old and arrived with his mother in America. And there remained his irrepressible spirit. Flanking the bureau in his bedroom are monuments in testimony to that spirit. On one side, crates of aspirin reach ceiling-high from the time he planned to put Bayer out of business. On the other side, cartons of vanilla and almond and lemon extract rise in ambrosial columns. Zalman Hirsch is still undaunted—there is still room against the bedroom wall.

But recently, the expectancy level of his family has become much lower, and his own spirit more difficult to sustain. He prays more fervently than ever in the holy language he only vaguely understands. How else to vent his feelings, his desire to please and praise God? How else to strengthen his hopes and quell his confusion?

The synagogue has emptied out. The oil stove is out of oil, he is out of cake and shnapps, and all the men are gone. But thank God, they had a minyan. Even without Benjamin. Zalman sits down—for just a few minutes—

before going downstairs for breakfast. His anxieties are taking their toll—even his appetite is not what it used to be.

Can he blame Benjamin? Can he blame him for lying in a warm bed asleep and unconcerned while his father shivered by the window, looking to see how many would trouble themselves to come on such a morning? He stared out at the snow until his eyes almost left his head. But he did not dare go up and wake his son. Perhaps, it is possible, Benjamin might have yielded—a terrible snowstorm, a special circumstance. But if he had not, who knows what would have ensued? And his son has had enough; he has been chastised enough. But why, Lord? Tell me why! All right, you're entitled to chastise me. But why my son? Do the sins of the father warrant such punishment? True, the boy was beginning to stray; the Yeshiva Yitzhak Elchanan no longer suited him. He wanted instead to study at Schechter's seminary, to become what they call a Conservative rabbi. What did I not do to dissuade him? I screamed, I hit. The boy was stubborn. But was he so terrible that you should keep him from studying at all? And what does that accomplish? My son only strays further away. He refuses to go to the mikva any longer—now he takes showers at the YMCA. I wonder if he still wears his tallis koton under his shirt? Or is he afraid the goyim will see his fringes and make fun of him?

Zalman starts to rise, but stops. Once again, with despair, he recalls that night. His son waited till after sundown so as not to mar the sanctity of the Shabbes. If he has to go to work, he said quietly, it is enough if he davens with the minyan on weekdays and Shabbes; on Sundays he is going to sleep as late as he likes. The eyes and lips quivered, but the voice was firm and sharp. It tore Zalman apart. The pain he felt! A boy who could do what he could with a blatt Gemara, a boy whom sages called "brilliant," and his father, after all the carrying on, could not send him to study *anywhere*. All he could do was send him to work as a shipping clerk. And as if that wasn't enough, they had to hide him in the closet whenever the Home Relief investigator came snooping around. Go tell the Home Relief that a family cannot live on a son's twelve dollars a week! "He went away. We do not know where he is," they told the investigator. Oh, that it should always have been a lie! Sometimes it was and sometimes it was not.

But that night, when Benjamin told him, did pity for his son move him to act like a father? No. His own miserable plight moved him to act like a madman. The other times were as nothing compared to that night. He still hears his voice reverberating in the room, hurling itself back at him, at his need and his humiliation. He needed his son to make up the quorum for prayer and he needed him to make up for his own inadequacy. Again and again he struck him. With each blow, he felt his son thrust further away—from his faith, from his home—even, God forbid, from the world. But he could not stop. Not against his son was he pounding, but against his own terror and confusion. Yet it was his son's body he bruised.

To strike so heartlessly at one's own flesh and blood is evil. The Lord does not condone this! He sent an angel to stay the hand of Abraham when it rose to slay Isaac. Will the Lord send an angel to stay *his* hand? He must pray. He must sing God's praises. He must rejoice in his faith. He must wipe from his mind the flinching of his son's flesh, the pleas of his wife, the horrified faces of his daughters. Leah ran out of the house. Esther's eyes were wide with disbelief and fright. And what did it all avail him? Finally he gave in.

3

Esther kicks at the snow to clear a path up the steps to the iron-railed enclosure outside the basement windows. In the little court, the snow comes almost to the tops of her galoshes. She makes footprints out onto the sidewalk, then turns to look at them. The deep hollows look enormous and significant. All about her, snow blushes pink and new. The only sound is the scraping of shovels far up the block where two small figures bent dark against the sky move slowly toward her, clouds of snow flying up beside them. The buildings with their raised shades and their windows glistening like opened eyes look freshly awakened and washed. The cold air tingles her cheeks, the sun caresses them. Still feeling the warmth of her mother's good oatmeal, Esther presses her books close to her chest. She feels good.

Across the street, the Riccios come out of the building where they live above their fruit store; they are going to church. Angie and her little brothers are wearing the same coats they wear every day, but Esther knows that underneath, Angie has on one of her two Sunday dresses, and the boys are wearing blue suits and white shirts with red ties. Instead of her kerchief, Mrs. Riccio is wearing her black hat with the velvet flowers. Their store stays closed on Sundays, but Mr. Riccio doesn't go to church. According to Angie, he thinks his wife is religious enough for both of them; her prayers will save his soul too. The older boys stay home like their father, and Angie says that whenever her mother tries to make them go to church, her father says not to bother them, that they're good boys and someday they'll marry girls who will pray for them too. Esther has heard her father tease Mr. Riccio. "Whatsa matta, Joe?" he says. "Why you so lazy? Why you no go to church? You a lazy bum, you!" And Mr. Riccio laughs and says, "Church is for da women. Da men take care a da family in thisa world, da ladies in da next." And they would both laugh.

Esther waves to Angie who waves back. Angie is one of her best friends, but she's never been inside Angie's house. She doesn't know exactly why. And Angie has never been in her house. They just wait for each other to come out and play. She can understand why Mrs. Riccio and her mother don't sit and talk together; Mrs. Riccio can't speak Yiddish and her mother can't speak Italian, and neither one speaks English well enough. No one has *told* her not to go to Angie's house, so why doesn't she go? She imagines it's very different from her own, but doesn't know exactly how. Maybe they have crosses on the walls. Maybe they have some with Jesus bleeding on them like the one she saw through the open door of the church. She hated the way it looked—it frightened her. Maybe that is why she doesn't go to Angie's house.

Crossing the street, she comes face to face with Mr. Lieberman's window. He's still not there, and she's disappointed. Mr. Lieberman always notices her; he doesn't actually wave, but he throws his head back slightly and smiles. The empty store window feels like an affront. Turning the corner, she becomes subdued and walks with her head bent, staring down at her galoshes. They look funny, like fat black puppies sniffing the snow and coming up with smudged noses. Esther smiles at them and forgets about the empty store window.

At the end of the next block, she sees Millie huddled in the doorway of her apartment house, all bundled up in her squirrel coat and shivering. Even in the brisk morning air, Millie's round face is sallow and mournful; the only thing cheerful about her is her red beret.

"Hi, Esther," Millie whimpers.

"Why are you standing in the doorway?" Esther asks.

"Why do you think? It's cold!"

"Not in the sun, it isn't. Wanna walk me down?"

Millie doesn't have to go to Hebrew school. Her father is a free thinker. "An apikoris," Esther's father calls him; and then he hurls a "Ptuy!" at the floor.

"No, it's too cold. I'm going upstairs soon anyway. Can you come over later?"

"Sure. I'll call for you when I finish eating. Maybe we can make a snowman."

"Maybe," Millie says, "if it gets warmer."

Esther leaves her friend standing in the doorway and, as she trudges along to the Talmud Torah, wonders why Millie who is fat and wears a fur coat shivers so much. Maybe because she lives in a new apartment house with hot radiators steaming all day, she isn't used to the cold.

As she approaches Myers' Candy Store, Esther forgets about Millie. The air smells of malt and vanilla and chocolate syrup and spearmint, even with the glass partition above the sidewalk counter closed. The width of the storefront has been shoveled all the way to the bench by the curb. The green newsstand is heaped high with stacks of *News*es and *Mirror*s and *Journal American*s, their colored comics flagrantly provocative; while in the rack behind them, their somber Semitic faces scowling, *Jewish Morning Journal*s, *Forward*s, and *Day*s stand like censorious sextons. No one is sitting on the bench, but two men with slick hatless heads and upturned overcoat collars are already at the stand, reading their *News*es. Soon other men with brilliantined hair will join them, and boys in club jackets blazing with Rex, Lancers, Avalons, Amiks. Natie, the Myers' CCNY college boy, is inside behind the counter. Later on, women will come in, with deeply-ringed mascaraed eyes, and lean on the counter and ask Natie for a pack of Luckies or Camels, and afterwards they'll sit on the stools and smoke, and stare. Even when they speak to each other, they stare straight ahead as if at something discernible only to themselves. And sometimes, they stare at the muscles in Natie's arms. While outside, their babies, stuffed in their carriages, sleep in the sunshine.

Esther likes these women. She likes them better than the young girls who dangle about the boys in the club jackets, giggling and snuggling and assiduously indifferent to her. The women talk to her once in a while, and they're sad and funny. They don't smile much, but they might suddenly laugh real loud. And when the weather is nice and they sit outside, one of them might holler in a deep hoarse voice all the way from the bench by the curb, "Hey, Natie! Make me a malted!" If she talked to her mother about them, her mother would probably say they are prust, but Esther finds in them a redeeming pathos and she likes them.

Crossing the street, she comes to Spiegel's Plumbing Supplies with toilets and sinks and spigots set out behind a dirty window. (She doesn't like this block.) After Spiegel's, there's Dominic's, Shoes Shined—Hats Blocked. Esther quickens her pace. She doesn't know why Dominic's has a bad reputation, but once she went inside with Millie to pick up her father's shoes, and the men sitting up high in the shoeshine chairs, in their pin-striped suits, and their shiny pointed shoes, and with their legs spread out, looked scary. They were the same kind of men, with insolent eyes and insinuating smiles, that sit outside Marty Feldman's pool room, leaning back in the folding chairs with their legs spread out, and their cufflinks catching the sunlight. As she hurries past Dominic's, Esther feels her face get hot. She is suddenly very anxious to get to Hebrew school.

When she sees the red-brick building with TALMUD TORAH gleaming in gold on black over the entrance, Esther runs to it. She pushes open the door and immediately is enveloped by the friendly smell of damp wool and warm bodies mingling with steam heat. The tile-floored, marble-plaqued vestibule rings with voices clanging back and forth between the gold-engraved names of memorialized dead on one wall and living benefactors on the other. Irving Greenhouse and Albert Siegel are leaning against the inside door with the sign pasted on it, "PLEASE DO NOT LEAN ON THE DOOR. IT IS DANGEROUS." At eight-twenty-eight, the doorknob turns, the boys spring away, Mr. Spiro, the principal, emerges, and the crowd cheers. Mr. Spiro smiles uncertainly; he senses something equivocal—his appearance is somehow incommensurate with such spirited acclaim—but you can never tell. He does not see Irving and Albert on either side of him, clasping their hands in victory high above their heads.

It is not that they do not like Mr. Spiro; they worship him. With his small waxed mustache and his pearl-gray spats, he is their Adolphe Menjou. And every day, except Friday and on Shabbes, he comes to them all the way from Ocean Parkway with its doormen and canopies and manicured shrubbery. You can see the Parkway from the trolley car window on your way to Prospect Park—it's the most elegant street you pass. Even his fingernails are glossy and perfect. But such urbanity cannot go unchallenged by full-blooded boys, in high spirits, bursting to display their courage in whatever meager feats of bravery they can muster. And the envy tempering their esteem eggs them on. But they want only to counterpoise, not to conquer. No one wants Mr. Spiro to be different. Nobody wants an *ordinary* principal!

Mr. Spiro looks down at his watch, and there is quiet. At precisely eight-thirty, he looks up and in modulated, mellifluous tones, speaks. "Good morning, boys and girls. I hope you have enjoyed a good and restful Shabbes and are refreshed and ready for work. Please proceed quietly through the corridors to your classrooms. If your teacher is not yet in the room, open a book and read silently."

Stationing himself on the inside of the door, Mr. Spiro smiles benignly at the students as they pass slowly before him into the dimly lit hall, their heads intentionally hanging down, to resemble yoked oxen. Once out of the principal's view, they break into a run. Not because they long to read silently. Nothing released creative energy more effectively than a teacherless classroom. They thought of everything—spit ball throwing and snorting, face-making and belching, and often there was high drama, like choking to death or belly-clutching expirations from bullet wounds. Mostly the males performed while the females stood guard, giggled, screeched, or looked disgusted. But this morning, Mr. Podoloff is already there, so Esther and her classmates file to the coat hooks on the back wall, deposit their coats and hats and galoshes, and, on the way to their seats, the boys take yarmulkas out of their pockets and put them on.

Mr. Podoloff is small and spread-out with a pale bald head, a pasty face, little yellow teeth with gaps between them, and a speech defect which, while it doesn't sound too bad, makes him spit a little when he speaks, especially when he gets excited. He sits at his desk, staring at his students until they have settled into their seats.

"We will begin with dikdook," he says as he turns and writes on the blackboard the infinitives of four verbs to be conjugated in all tenses. The class groans responsively.

"I'll have none of that!" Mr. Podoloff snaps. "Open your machberohs and begin!"

The notebooks appear and are opened with ostentatious slowness. Esther moves as reluctantly as the others, careful not to let on that she likes to conjugate; sometimes, she comes across lovely sounds like "ahni hispalalti," I have prayed. Is she peculiar, she wonders. Some others must be faking too.

"When your conjugations are finished and marked," Mr. Podoloff announces, "begin the Chumish assignment for tomorrow, which I will put on the blackboard." He turns and writes on the board, "SKIP page 26. Read and translate pages 27 and 28."

About half the class is still conjugating when Esther returns to her seat, clutching her notebook with her new 97 percent. She doesn't care about getting a hundred anymore, not since the day she ran into the house screeching that she got a hundred on a history test and Lila sniffed down at her and said that any test, especially, for God's sakes, history, on which anyone got a hundred was babyish. Ninety-seven does have a certain dignity to it, she decides, and as she opens her frayed and faded blue Chumish, she decides that it is also babyish to care about not getting one of the rebound maroon ones that looked brandnew and that she so coveted when books were distributed.

The last Chumish assignment was about the destruction of Sodom and Gomorrah. Esther is still not clear about the terrible things that went on there, but she squirms at the recollection of Lot's wife turning into a pillar of salt. The next page is 26, to be skipped, with "SKIP" underlined twice. She wonders why Mr. Podoloff seems to worry more about what they skip than what they read. She knows better than to raise her hand and ask why page 26 should be skipped. Irving Greenhouse asked him just last week why they had to skip a page, and Mr. Podoloff glared at him as if he were being purposely fresh, and then said nastily, "Because it isn't important." Esther had trouble believing Mr. Podoloff; everything in the Bible was supposed to be important. So when she got home, she read the page Mr. Podoloff told them to skip. And it really didn't seem very important, or very clear—something about Sarah telling Abraham to go into her servant, so that Abraham who had no children could have some. She decides to read page 26 anyway; something about skipping pages bothers her.

She reads: Lot's daughters, who were living alone with him in a mountain cave after the destruction of Sodom and Gomorrah, are having a conversation. "And the first born said unto the younger, 'Our father is old and there is not a man in the earth to come in unto us after the manner of the earth. Come, let us make our father drink wine, and we will lie with him, that we may preserve seed of our father!' " There begins to form in Esther's mind the vague outlines of a generalization—anytime the Bible talked about someone going into someone, or coming into someone, it wasn't important and was to be skipped. She doesn't understand why the girls wanted to make their father drunk and how lying with him would preserve his seed. She continues reading: The first night after Lot's daughters had this conversation, they made their father so drunk he didn't even know when the firstborn daughter lay down with him and when she got up. And the second night, they again made him drunk, and the second daughter lay down with him and got up, and he didn't know about that either. Then each of the daughters had a baby.

Esther stops reading. Again, going into or coming into has to do with getting a baby. Esther looks up from her Chumish, her face flushed. Lila was right! She *is* a dumbbell! When she told Lila that she knew babies grew in the mother from a seed planted by the father, Lila smiled in that annoying way of hers and said, "All right, show-off, what does the father plant the seed *with*? His *hand*?" She thought it was a pretty stupid question. What else? But whenever Lila got that look on her face, it turned out *she* was the one who was being stupid. So she asked, "Isn't it his hand?" And Lila said, "No, dumbbell, with his *thing!* He puts his thing in the mother's thing." Lila kept looking at her and laughing so hard that she was sure Lila was only teasing. Now, she is not sure. All that skipping pages! She's pretty sure the right name for the thing is penis, because Millie said her cousin who goes to Hunter College told her, but Esther can't say that word—it sounds dirty. Even Lila doesn't say that word. There are other words for it too; she has seen them printed on the toilet walls in school, even in Hebrew school: "MORRIS FISHBEIN HAS A BIG DONG," "RUBIN EPSTEIN HAS A TINY SHMECKEL," and she couldn't believe it when she saw "EVELYN ROTHMAN PULLS PRICKS!" No one had actually ever told her what the words on the toilet walls meant; she just *knew*.

But how could Lot's daughters make him do that to them? Disgusting! That's what it is. Disgusting! And even Abraham? And Sarah told him to put his thing in her servants'. . . . Esther searched for the word. Her mother called it a perishka; she's heard other mothers call it a krepl. She still doesn't know what the English word for it is. When she saw on the toilet wall in public school "ROSE KOSLOWSKI HAS A BUSHY CUNT," she thought that might be the word; but when she looked it up in the dictionary, it wasn't there. She still doesn't know. She doesn't know *anything!* She doesn't *want* to know! Knowing makes you feel sick. Knowing spoils everything. They make you skip pages so you wouldn't know, because if you knew, you wouldn't think much of the Chumish. They make you kiss the Chumish if you accidentally drop it, but if you knew everything in it, you wouldn't want to kiss it. Mr. Podoloff must know everything in it, or he wouldn't be able to know what we should skip. Esther is appalled at the conspiracy going on to keep her from knowing. She suddenly remembers the story of Adam and Eve and the tree of knowledge of good and evil. God forbade them to eat from that tree. Mr. Podoloff told them it was so man would not learn evil ways. But that doesn't make sense. How would they learn *good* ways? Maybe God didn't want them to know *anything*, to just leave everything to him. He would let them know only what he wanted them to know, just like her in Hebrew school. A terrible possibility dawns on her—that knowledge might be inconsistent with belief in God.

God warned Adam and Eve that they would die if they did not obey him. Is that why everyone has to die? But what if you stayed dumb or you did everything God told you? Would you live forever? Is that why her father tries to make her do everything right?

Her mother and father did *it* too—or else she wouldn't have been born. Doing it *can't* be dirty. But still, the first thing Adam and Eve noticed after they ate from the tree was that they were naked. And they got upset about it, and they made aprons out of leaves to cover themselves— *there*. You're supposed to be ashamed of those things. Maybe that's why there are so many crazy names for them and people write about them in toilets. But if men and women didn't do that with their things, they wouldn't have children. There wouldn't be people. There wouldn't be a world! Her head hurts, and an enormous nausea is taking hold of her. Everything is too hard. She doesn't understand *anything*. She is going to stop trying. From now on, she's going to read only the assigned pages, and translate them into English, and that's all. She won't try to understand *anything*. It make her feel too sick.

Esther turns to the first assigned page and reads: "... that the Lord visited Sarah as he had said, and the Lord did unto Sarah as he had spoken. For Sarah conceived and bore Abraham a son in his old age ..." The *Lord* did unto Sarah? The *Lord*? God *himself*? Resolutely, she erases crazy images forming in her head and hurries on. Sarah is telling Abraham to cast out her servant, Hagar, the Egyptian, and Hagar's son, Ishmael, who was also Abraham's son. How awful! And when it was all her idea in the first place! But God saves Hagar and Ishmael from dying in the wilderness. Esther is glad; God seems more like God again. She goes on. The Lord is speaking, "Take now thy son, thine own Isaac, whom thou lovest, and get thee into the land of Moriah, and offer him there for a burnt offering..." Esther crosses her arms over her stomach and presses hard. "...and Abraham built an altar there, and laid the wood in order, and bound Isaac his son, and laid him on the altar upon the wood. And Abraham stretched forth his hand, and took the knife to slay his son." She can't believe it! She hears Mr. Podoloff announcing to close their Chumashim, the discussion of the text assigned last week is going to begin. Esther cannot close her Chumish yet. She reads on until the angel of the Lord appears just in time and stops Abraham, and how Abraham lifted up his eyes and beheld a ram caught in a thicket by its horns, and killed the ram instead of Isaac. She closes her Chumish. Mr. Podoloff has asked something, and hands are being raised all around her. She cannot raise her hand; she has not heard the question. Her head is reeling. Why did God have to ask Abraham to do such a horrible thing? And even if Isaac stayed alive, how could he ever forget being tied up by his father and looking up into the wild eyes of an old man with a knife in his hand raised and ready to slit his throat? Everything is all crooked and jagged. She hates them all—Abraham and Sarah and Lot and his daughters—all of them! She hates God. She thinks she has a perfect right to. But if she hates God.... Esther is frightened.

"Why did God destroy Sodom and Gomorrah? Esther?" Mr. Podoloff's voice reaches her as though from a great distance.

"What?"

"Didn't you hear the question, Esther?"

"I'm sorry. I was—"

Mr. Podoloff rises to the occasion with relish. "Excuse

me, Miss Hirsch," he croons. "I apologize for waking you up."

The class titters.

"I—I'm sorry. I—"

But Mr. Podoloff, with as much of a flourish as he can manage, turns disdainfully away and calls on Gladys Suretsky, who speaks up promptly. "God destroyed Sodom and Gomorrah because the people there were wicked and sinners." Mr. Podoloff smiles approvingly.

That's a stupid answer, Esther mutters to herself, typical of Gladys. And now Gladys has that satisfied smile on her face because she knew the answer and I didn't. I can't stand Gladys! And it's not just because she doesn't like me. And that really was a stupid answer. It doesn't *mean* anything. What were the wicked things they did? *How* did they sin? And why should Lot and his daughters have been saved after what *they* did? What was good about *them*? And why should God turn Lot's wife into a pillar of salt, just for turning around? He isn't fair! Her heart pounds. Her mind is uttering blasphemies. It is speaking the unspeakable! The dazzle of her dialectic is replaced by the glare of her irreverence and engulfed in the darkness of impending doom. She will be punished. She must stop before something terrible happens. The Torah is holy! The Chumish is part of the Torah! Everything in it makes sense! She just doesn't understand, but everything in it is right. God is good!

But Mr. Podoloff is horrible. He studiously avoids calling on her again, although she raises her hand as high as she can, obviously entreating redemption. The history lesson is over. This was her first encounter with Mr. Podoloff's sarcasm, and the first time the class laughed at her. With a little effort, she convinces herself that the class had not really laughed at her but at the threadbare quality of Mr. Podoloff's wit. She hates him.

There is a knock on the door. Mr. Podoloff hollers, "Yes?" The door opens. Mr. Ehrlich is standing on the threshold, asking silently if he may come in. Mr. Ehrlich comes only on Sundays, to teach them songs and to sing with them. In every visible way, he is the opposite of Mr. Podoloff. Mr. Podoloff is always projecting his voice as if the small classroom is a packed stadium and is always sniffling or snorting, or squeaking in his chair as if constantly requiring some reassuring sound of his existence. Mr. Ehrlich makes only pleasant sounds and no unnecessary noise. Mr. Podoloff is squat and unassembled, with his jacket always open and his tie spread apart. Mr. Ehrlich is tall and lean and neat, with a smooth olive complexion, orderly features, and silvery gray hair combed close to his narrow head. His lips are deeply hued, and his eyes are soft behind rimless glasses. He moves carefully, like a man cognizant of the worth of his humanity. If there is anything disproportionate about Mr. Ehrlich, it is his love of music. He was first described to the entire Talmud Torah student body by Mr. Spiro in assembly not only as the imminent "modern addition to the up-to-date curriculum," but as a distinguished graduate of a great music conservatory in Europe who would not be with them if not for Hitler over there and the depression over here. Then Mr. Spiro said something about every cloud having a silver lining, and no one knew whether to smile or look solemn. But the skepticism which naturally greeted any such glowing assessment of an addition to their curriculum was obliterated after Mr. Ehrlich's first visit to the classrooms. Even the most bumptious boys succumbed.

Mr. Ehrlich's silent query on the threshold is met with Mr. Podoloff's effusive "Hello! Hello! Come in! Come in!" as he scrambles about his desk in a show of clearing a large space for Mr. Ehrlich, who requires so little. There is a brief silence before Mr. Ehrlich says softly, "Shalom, Chaverim," and the students respond gaily, "Shalom, Mr.

Ehrlich." The song sheets are distributed and the singing begins.

The first attempt at the plaintive "Yerushalayim" is too energetic; the second more subdued; the third time they approach something of the spirit of the song, and Mr. Ehrlich smiles warmly at them, undoing all sorts of psychic knots hidden about the room. Esther forgets to keep hating Mr. Podoloff. Next, they are roused into the vigorous "Korebombuli." Eyes brighten and smiles break forth; they love the sound they make. Then, organized into groups for a round of "Zum Gali Gali," they try to concentrate on their parts, but it takes two unsuccessful attempts before the final "zums" flow together just right, and they heave a collective happy sigh. Mr. Ehrlich smiles again and tells them how sorry he is the time is up. He bids them farewell and leaves the room to the accompaniment of pleasantly discordant shaloms, "Shalom, Mr. Ehrlich."

At once, Mr. Podoloff bounds out of his seat in the back of the room, where he has been squeaking all through the singing period, and lurches down the aisle, sputtering "All right, all right, let's settle down now. The fun's over!" He yanks down the big yellow map of Palestine and, jabbing at it with his pointer, starts splattering rivers and mountains and borders all around the room. His face is not pasty now; it is blotchy red. It gets that way after every singing period and stays that way through entire geography periods. And the better they've sung, the blotchier Mr. Podoloff gets, and the more saliva he works up. He stops pointing and hurls a question at Irving Greenhouse who, because he is a troublemaker, sits right under Mr. Podoloff's mouth.

Irving looks up and says, "Just a minute," then fishes in his pants pocket, brings forth a large white handkerchief, and makes a great show of mopping his face. The class howls. Mr. Podoloff's hand shoots up and out and comes down hard against the side of Irving's head. The class winces and falls silent. Irving's jaw quivers, but otherwise he doesn't move or make a sound. Mr. Podoloff stands over him, breathing heavily and bareheaded—his yarmulka has fallen off. His bald head with the red blotches is like an animal's with its fur ripped off. He looks up at the class. His eyes are bloodshot and wet. In a voice so small, they can hear it only because the room is so quiet, he says, "Class dismissed." He picks up his yarmulka, puts it on his head, sits down at his desk, opens his rollbook, and stays bent over it. He stays that way, not moving, while the students shuffle to the back of the room, put on their coats and hats and galoshes and, with eyes averted, file silently past him. None of the usual jabbing or punching. Not a single "Shalom, Mr. Podoloff." No one says anything to anyone.

It isn't the first time a boy was hit in Hebrew school, but it's the first time it got them dismissed early and the first time Esther has seen a teacher with wet eyes. As she hurries down the hall with the others, she feels an urge to go back and look in her desk as if she'd forgotten something. Not even one person said "Shalom" before walking out. The loneliness of the ugly, unhappy little man touches her. But she pushes it away, remembering how he licked his lips when he called her "Miss Hirsch," as if anticipating the deliciousness of her embarrassment.

Outside, the girls are huddled together, watching the boys crowd around Irving.

"You really got it that time, Irv!"

"Gee whiz! Does it hurt?"

"I gotta hand it to ya, Irving. You got guts!"

"I wouldn't let'm get away with it," David Kligman says heatedly. "If I were you, I'd tell my father."

Irving has been enduring them, like a trapped lion, until he growls back at David, "Big joke! You know whose side *he'd* be on!" Then, his face threatening to dissolve into tears, Irving breaks from the circle, his hand goes up to the side of his head, he cries out, "The big prick!" and stalks away. The boys and girls look at each other; they don't know if he means Mr. Podoloff or his father.

The sun has disappeared. Hunching over her books against a chilling wind, Esther walks home. Thelma Halperin catches up with her.

"It was awful, wasn't it?" Thelma says through trembling teeth.

"Terrible," Esther agrees. But she isn't sure which part of the morning she is talking about.

"S—such language," Thelma says.

Esther pretends, her own teeth chattering, to be too cold to talk, and doesn't respond. When their paths part, she manages to say "So long," and as she watches Thelma scurry down her block, all scrunched up, with her legs pressed tight together like any minute she is going to pee, something gives way inside her, and she is convulsed. She laughs until she's afraid she'll be the one to wet her pants, and the idea makes her laugh more. She isn't quite sure why she is laughing. It just feels good.

When she quiets down, she feels much better about everything. Irving's obscene epithet begins ringing in her ears; she finds it excruciatingly titillating. She tries to say it softly to herself, but can only form it soundlessly. She remembers her arrangement with Millie and hopes it will stay cloudy and be too cold to play outside and they will play inside, in Millie's house. Wantonness, unfamiliar and pleasurable, is undulating inside her and stands more chance of being sustained in the steam-heated opulence of apartment 4D high up in an elevator building than in the snow or in the ascetic atmosphere of her own house. Sidewalks have been cleared and the snow banked along the curbs. Esther climbs up and walks home along the tops of the snow hills, warming herself with recollections of lovely afternoons in Millie's house.

The Brenners' living room is soft and shimmering—

with satiny furniture and plump pillows, and glowing tables with slender legs sinking into the deep nap of the oriental rug, and dark red draperies that billow at the bottom. In Millie's room there is a soft green rug on the floor, and they lie on the soft rug with the radiator hissing beside them and Monopoly spread out before them, and they buy and sell and mortgage the whole afternoon away. When they finish a game, they stretch and are thirsty, and they go into the kitchen with its cherries and apples on the wallpaper dancing around them, and Mrs. Brenner is sitting at the table, bending over a magazine, with her cigarette and her cup of coffee and her long red fingernails and her hair still smelling from the beauty parlor. She gets up and takes a package of chocolate cupcakes out of the flowered breadbox. Even though her mother says cake you buy in the store has no taste and her father says it's poison, Esther gets fluttery inside at the sight and sound of the dark, velvety cupcakes rustling around in their cellophane wrappers. Then Mrs. Brenner opens the refrigerator with all the wonderful colors and shapes inside, and she takes out ice cold milk and the jar of Hershey's chocolate syrup. First she pours the milk into tall glasses with red and blue bubbles swirling around them, then she pours a thick stream of syrup into the milk, and she stirs them together with a tall spoon that tinkles against the glass. They eat their cupcakes and they sip their milk slowly through striped straws. And all the time the kitchen is filled with the good smell of coffee bubbling on the stove. Even if it's after five o'clock there isn't anything else on the stove— just the shiny percolator bubbling softly. Sometimes the telephone rings, and, after talking for a while, Mrs. Brenner tells the other person that she has to go put up some potatoes and throw a steak—or it might be a chop— in the broiler, Sam'll be coming home any minute. For Mrs. Brenner, cooking is throwing in and putting up. But since Millie says her father spends even less time eating a meal than her mother spends preparing it, you can hardly blame Mrs. Brenner; even if she spent hours making an appetizer and chopping up vegetables for a pot roast, Sam would probably chomp it all down in two minutes and go running back to the store.

Esther wonders if Millie ever eats anything for supper besides steak or chops and put-up potatoes. Esther doesn't know how they come out, but she is sure that "put-up" potatoes and a steak or chop thrown in the broiler must taste as delicious as everything else does in Millie's house. She asked her mother once why they never had steak—adding "thrown in the broiler." Her mother stopped grating the radish that was going to be mixed with chopped onion and melted chicken fat for the evening's forschpeiz, and spoke to the wall. "Steak, she wants? From the broiler yet! That's also a meal?" And nodding her head pensively, went on grating. Mrs. Hirsch had succinctly told her daughter that not only couldn't they afford steak, but only a lazy "Americaner" housewife would serve such a drab, unadorned piece of meat. Esther remembers how after a few minutes, her mother suddenly stopped grating and looked at her; even though she didn't ask, Esther assured her mother that she had never tasted steak in Millie's house, that everybody knew the Brenners didn't keep kosher, that all she ever ate there was Dugan's cupcakes straight from the wrapper with the "U" on it and milk in a glass. Her mother kept quiet, but Esther sensed she was holding herself back from saying something else about Millie's house.

Esther thinks she knows what it was her mother wanted to say and that afterwards made her begin grating the radish harder and faster. Even though all their furniture comes from Sloane's and they hired a decorator to be sure everything matched, there is something wrong with Millie's house. Millie's house is prust. And there is something more wrong with Mr. and Mrs. Brenner. It's odd to see

Mrs. Brenner always so dressed up—in winter with her mink coat—and never going anyplace, except to shop at the A&P or to get a fingerwave and manicure at the beauty parlor or to sit behind the glass partition in Brenner's—Men's Suits & Haberdashery—keeping the girls in the office company. Even if she does have a woman who comes in to clean the house, she ought to be able to think of something else to do besides sit in the store. Maybe, Esther speculates, she sits there to remind Mr. Brenner not to bite the bookkeeper. It's still hard to imagine Mr. Brenner doing it, but she was there when Elsie, the bookkeeper, ran out of the stockroom, holding her neck and screaming, "He bit me! The filthy bastard bit me!" Millie ran out of the store and Esther ran with her, and Millie wanted to go home and didn't want Esther to come with her. The next day, Esther found an excuse to go to the store to see if Elsie had teeth marks on her neck, but she wasn't there and she never came back.

Sometimes, though, Mrs. Brenner sets up a bridge table in the living room, and some ladies from the building come in to play cards. Once while the ladies were playing, she and Millie came in. Mrs. Brenner turned to her friends and said, "Get a load of that kid! The fella who marries my daughter is gonna get two things —a fat ass and a pot of gold!" Millie ran out of the living room into her bedroom and banged the door. She let me come in, but was so gloomy I wasn't sure she wanted me to stay. After the ladies went home, Mrs. Brenner came to Millie's door and asked if we wanted anything to eat, and Millie answered back very loudly, "No, thank you!" and that day I went home without milk or a cupcake. But Millie still eats a lot; she's always getting Hershey bars and candy buttons and malteds at Myers'.

It's hard to dislike Mrs. Brenner, even though she says mean things to Millie. She's always so nice to *me*. It's as if Mrs. Brenner can't help saying peculiar things. Like anytime she knows we're going over to my house, she calls after Millie, "Behave yourself! Remember!"

Maybe, since it's Christmas vacation, she'll be able to go back to Millie's house after supper and listen to the radio programs—first Jack Benny, then Eddie Cantor, and then Fred Allen. She can hardly wait. Jumping off the snow bank, Esther turns the corner into her block.

The people are set out like broken spokes of a wheel, dark against the snow. She hears wailing voices. Her eyes run along the jagged lines of people to where they meet in a thick hub—in front of Mr. Lieberman's store. She walks slowly toward them. Mrs. Melnick comes running out of the grocery store, holding her unbuttoned coat together over her housedress, stops at a cluster of people, and looks at them inquiringly. One of them speaks, and Mrs. Melnick thrusts her fist into her mouth and bites it. Esther begins to make out words. Geshtorben. Imgefalen. Dead. Someone is dead. She looks for her mother. She looks for her father. She doesn't see them. Tears spring to her eyes. Then she sees Ben standing on their stoop, stiff and shivering in only his shirt, his arms close to his sides and his hands in his pockets. She runs to him. "Ben—Ben, what happened?" He looks at her. Then, still shivering but not otherwise moving, he stares across the street and says, "Lieberman. Mr. Lieberman is dead."

4

———————

"What? What did you say?"

She heard Ben clearly, but cannot grasp the idea of
what he has said. How could someone *she* knows die? It
never happened before. What is she supposed to say? She
feels self-conscious and stupid. What should she do with
her face? It's like in a movie. She wants her face to perform properly, but her mouth moves perversely into, an
idiotic, pointless grin. She presses her lips tight to make it
stop. Mr. Lieberman is dead. It is terrible and sad—and
exciting. Her feelings are all tangled up; it's embarrassing. And it reminds her of that Yom Kippur when she and
Lila couldn't stop themselves from laughing right in the
middle of the saddest part of the service. They knew it was
the saddest part because there was that upsurge of wailing
in the women's section which every year sounded comical
to them and made them giggle a little. But that year one
of the women gave out with an unexpected embellishment,
and it broke them up. They had to wiggle their way to the
aisle, past fierce and horrified faces, and get out into the
street where they completed their desecration of the Day
of Atonement, laughing until their sides ached. She must
wipe that scene from her mind; it could easily set her off
again. She must concentrate. Someone *she* knows has
actually *died*. Someone who has been nice to her. Someone she likes. Someone she saw sweating just a few hours

ago. She should cry, but she can't. Even though she is really and truly sad.

As if he understands that she heard him but is not fully convinced, Ben says, "They found him lying on the floor by the pressing machine."

"Who found him?"

"A customer. He wanted his suit. When he didn't see him, he called. Then he went behind the counter to see if he was in the back room and tripped over the dead body."

"How awful!" Esther moans. She imagines Mr. Lieberman, all stiff and white and spread out on the floor, his mouth open, his eyes rolled up. His yarmulka has finally fallen off his head. He has stopped being Mr. Lieberman —he is something grotesque that she doesn't want to look at.

"When did he find him?" she asks.

"About half an hour ago. But he might have been lying there all morning. Nobody remembers seeing him after he left the shul."

"I saw him, Ben, when I got up this morning. He was working the pressing machine. But after I got dressed, he wasn't there anymore."

Could she have been the last person to see him alive? Could he have dropped dead a minute after she stopped looking? She can't *believe* it.

"What a crappy world!" Ben mutters.

"Yeah, it sure is!" Esther agrees eagerly. She is a little bewildered; Ben has never spoken to her this way. Her brother's misanthropic estimate of the world sounds mature and sensible—and confidential. Then, hoping she isn't going to spoil everything, but just to make sure their alliance is solidly based—that both of them are perceiving "crappiness" in the same phenomenon—she adds, "He could have been lying on the floor dying and all the time people went in and out of the store and didn't even look."

Ben says nothing.

45

"If that customer didn't want his suit real bad, maybe nobody would even know yet he was dead," she goes on, hoping Ben will say something more. Suddenly it occurs to her, "Where was Mrs. Lieberman?"

"Mama thinks she went to visit their son."

"Where does he live?"

"In Flatbush," Ben says, beginning to sound weary.

Esther can't remember ever seeing the son. She knows he's married and there's something wrong with his wife because she heard her mother say once to her father that if he could bring his wife, he would visit his parents. She remembers coming home with her mother from the dry goods store with the pink material for the dress her mother made her for the holidays, and meeting Mrs. Lieberman coming down the steps from the train station. Mrs. Lieberman was dressed up in her navy blue dress and her straw hat with the feathers. Her mother asked, "How did you find your son?" and Mrs. Lieberman answered, "Thank God." Esther wondered why her mother didn't ask about his wife, especially since she was the one who was sick. Right now, Esther thinks, wouldn't be a good time to ask Ben about that. She'll be quiet like him and just stand and watch what's going on across the street.

A man comes out of the tailor store all upset. "Can you beat that?" he says to a group of attentive listeners, "It's gone! The buck is gone! An hour ago, I come in. I wanna pick up my wife's dress 'cause we got a wedding tonight. The old man's not around. I holler but he don't answer. I see the dress hangin' so I take it. I'm in a hurry. I don't have change, so I put a dollar on the counter, figurin' maybe he's in the toilet, and I don't wanna be a crook or anything. I figure I'll pick up the change some other time. Well, I just looked on the counter, and the buck ain't there. And accordin' to the doc, he's been out for more than an hour. Can you beat that? Someone took the goddamn dollar! I don't give a damn about the money, y' understand.

I went in to see just for the hell of it. And it ain't there!"
The listeners cluck sympathetically.

"Oh, my God!" Ben groans, and goes into the house.

Esther follows and stops him inside the door. "Where's Papa?" she asks.

"He's out rounding up the Chevrah Kadisha," Ben says.

"What's a Chevrah Kadisha?"

"It's a holy brotherhood. They fix up the corpse for burial."

"What do they do?" Esther asks.

"Oh, they wash it, give it a fancy egg shampoo, clean the dirt out of its nails, and comb its hair real sharp. Then they dress it up in a white robe and put its tallis on."

Why should Ben sound as if he's teasing her? He's so strange. She watches him walk up the steps. She can't see anything exactly broken, but he seems a little like a cripple. He reminds her of the sparrow she and Millie found in the yard; it was so sweet-looking, and its wings felt so fragile. It was lying on the ground, struggling to fly, but couldn't. Millie said one of its wings was broken and wanted to bring it to a doctor. But they didn't know one who fixed broken wings. Millie took it home, but her mother made her drown it in the sink and throw it in the garbage because, she said, it was better off that way. Millie cried all the time she was doing it.

Esther doesn't want Ben to disappear into his room the way he does all the time, so she calls after him, "Where's Mama?"

"She went over to the station to meet Mrs. Lieberman when she gets off the train."

"How does she know when she'll get off the train?"

"She said Mrs. Lieberman always comes home in time to give her husband lunch."

"Where's Lila?"

"I don't know," Ben says as he disappears into his room at the top of the stairs.

Esther puts her books down on the cold radiator and goes outside again. She'll wait on the stoop until her father comes. He'll arrive like a boss at the head of a work crew, bellowing "Okay, you guys, let's get this job done!" He'll sound like Edward G. Robinson. The men will have their sleeves rolled up and go to work on Mr. Lieberman, whom Ben has already called an "it." She imagines Mr. Lieberman drooping like Raggedy Andy, but naked, while the men wash him and comb him and clean his fingernails and dress him up. It doesn't seem too bad to her, really a little like playing with a doll, except for the nakedness—the dangling genitals, with the hair around them. She remembers walking in once while her father was getting out of the bathtub; she saw *everything*.

She walks down the steps to hear better what the people are saying. The voices and gestures are intense and excited. The block has taken on a festive look; only on special occasions has she seen so many people standing in the street. There was the time President Roosevelt rode through the neighborhood; school was let out and everyone stood along the curb and waited for him, and the religious men like her father said a blessing over him when he passed. And when Mayor LaGuardia came to dedicate the playground they named after him. Now it is Mr. Lieberman who has drawn a crowd. Only they can't see him, so she wonders why they keep standing there.

In front of their fruit and vegetable store, Mr. and Mrs. Riccio stand apart from the others—by themselves. Mrs. Riccio is still wearing her hat with the velvet flowers. Mr. Riccio, short, muscular, with a mane of white hair, has his arms folded across his chest over his brown sweater. He hardly ever wears a coat and never looks cold. They seem to be the only people not talking or listening to someone. Everyone she knows likes the Riccios. Why aren't they mixing with the others? Mr. Riccio's English is pretty good, so that can't be why. She supposes it has to do with being Christian; maybe death is something religious to them. They're the only Italians on the block. There are a few other Christians, but they're Polish or Lithuanian. Esther doesn't see any of them. Until Crazy Mike comes staggering down the street. He is drunk already.

Crazy Mike is a janitor, and he lives in the cellar of one of the buildings on the block. When he's sober, he stokes the furnace in the building and sweeps the halls, and he fixes broken things and stops leaks and unstuffs stuffed-up toilets. But most of the times Esther has seen him, he's been drunk, like now. His nose and eyes are red and runny, and he doesn't seem to see where he's going. He's bumping into people. They get angry, until they see who it is, and then they turn away looking disgusted and ignore him. Sometimes he acts real crazy, like when he goes reeling through the streets, muttering and cursing and shaking his fist at the sky, and when he dances for the boys and they crowd around him in a circle clapping and whooping, "Shake it, Mike baby! Shake it!" and "How about a little bump and grind, honey? Let's have it, baby! Take it off! Take 'em down!" and one of the boys always sneaks up behind him and gooses him, and sometimes they even try to pull his pants down. But she still finds it hard to believe those stories about how he'll pay a boy a quarter to pee in his mouth.

Crazy Mike stops and tugs at a man's overcoat sleeve. "Whassa matta? Wha's goin' on?" he asks.

The man pulls his arm away and keeps talking to someone else. Crazy Mike tugs at his sleeve again. The man says impatiently, "The tailor died," and turns away.

Crazy Mike tugs at the sleeve again. "You mean the little fella," he says, holding his hand out shakily waist high.

"Yeah, the little fella," the man says, and then angrily, "Now, scram, Mike! Beat it!"

Mike doesn't scram. He keeps standing there, and tears begin to roll down his cheeks, and snot streams from his

49

nose onto his coat. No one looks at him. Esther feels sorry for him, but she thinks he looks repulsive too.

She can hear Melnick talking to little Mr. Shleeman— gentle, diffident Mr. Shleeman who feeds his family by steering a large unwieldy pushcart laden with onions and potatoes and carrots through the whole south side of Williamsburg, and even through the treacherous north side where vicious children call him "mocky Jew" and throw rocks at him. Even now, he has a bruise on his left cheek. He is listening to Melnick with his head turned away a little, as though fearful of being singed by the grocer's flaming beard. Melnick from his greater height appears to be haranguing the peak of the gray tweed cap that Mr. Shleeman is wearing along with his bluish double-breasted suit jacket and olive green pants. Underneath the bluish suit jacket, he has on a brown button-down sweater, and Esther is sure that underneath that one, there are more sweaters, and then his shirt, and then finally probably a union suit like her father wears. And he might have on two pairs of pants. If he were pushing his pushcart, he'd have on a lumberjacket too. She has seen him in the summer so she knows he is skinny. In the winter when he has to be outside in the cold all day, he looks very very fat. Melnick is explaining to him whose fault it is that Mr. Lieberman is dead.

"The son is to blame. For years that momzer has been pushing his father into the grave. And let me tell you, the Liebermankeh pushed a little too."

Esther can't believe it. What is he *talking* about? She wonders why Melnick and Mr. Shleeman aren't in there starting to clean up Mr. Lieberman. Do they have to wait for her father? Maybe they're scared to be in there alone? Or, maybe they aren't holy enough.

Melnick goes on, sententiously, punctuating his rhetoric with rhythmic flourishes. His voice swells and swaggers.

"First, there is no Jewish girl that suits him; he has to present his father with a shiksa for a daughter-in-law. But is that enough? No. He has to go be a sport and give his father yet another present—a counter for his store. Whattsa matter, the plain table his father used for years is not good enough? And with it yet, because he's a gantzer cnocker, a big shot, he wants his father's store should have a cash register too. Let me tell you, a drawer in a table can hold just as much money as a cash register. But that jewel of a son—whose father already would not look at him—wants everything should be fancy-shmancy. Why? So, maybe, if someday he brings his shiksa to the store, he shouldn't be ashamed in front of her. Does Lieberman want all this chozzerei? No! But the wife, she wants. And who prevails? The wife! Of course! She nags and nags until he gives in. And what has she accomplished? Now she has a dead husband. Who knows how long he was laying on the floor hidden from the world behind the counter so nobody could maybe call a doctor, an ambulance—something. Even a glass water no one could give him! As long as the store was fancy-shmancy!"

It is difficult to tell whether Melnick's logic has impressed Mr. Shleeman who neither responds nor changes his woeful expression, but only seems to have moved a few barely perceptible inches away from the grocer's vigorous voice. Esther thinks it all sounds crazy. Maybe because it's Melnick, and he has that annoying way of talking. Even if the things he said about the son might be true, it's hard to imagine Mr. Lieberman not wanting to look at him. And it's pretty mean of Melnick to talk that way about Mrs. Lieberman. Especially now. Anyway, at least she knows what's wrong with the son's wife. She isn't sick; she's a shiksa.

Suddenly, it is quiet, and everyone is turning and looking in the same direction. Esther sees what they've been waiting for. Holding on to her mother's arm, Mrs. Lieberman comes into view. Her coat, despite the cold, is pulled open and crooked. Underneath, she is wearing the same blue dress she had on the last time Esther saw her coming from her son's house, only the collar is torn away on one side. Her black hat is askew on her head, and the veil is ripped from the brim. Her bun has become undone, and dark gray hair is strewn over her coat. It's as if she had tried to tear herself apart. The outlandish disarray comes dangerously close to being ludicrous, but is saved by her awesome absolute silence. And Esther's mother is at her side, glaring fiercely at everyone.

The crowd makes way, and Mrs. Lieberman, holding firmly to her friend's arm, enters the tailor store. Only when the door has shut behind her and she has disappeared behind the flowered curtain, do they hear, through the cloth and the brick and glass, her enormous, horrible wailing.

As though they have seen and heard what they were waiting for, people begin to disperse—studiously mournful, yet somehow looking stimulated and comforted by Mrs. Lieberman's misery, as if their lives have been enhanced, and their better luck is evidence of their greater morality and wisdom.

Most of the people are familiar to Esther. She imagines they have known the tailor and his wife for years; they have traded and talked and prayed together. Their faces seem sad, and she hears sighs. But nowhere does she see a single tear. And she notices that her own eyes are dry. The only one who cried was Crazy Mike.

Some weeks later, on one of those Shabbes afternoons, Esther and her mother will sit together in the dining room with the setting sun embroidering the wall, and Esther will catch in her mother's eyes the same fierce glint she carried into that crowd, and it will make her ask her mother why she went to the station to wait for Mrs. Lieberman. And her mother will look out the window and say, "Better she should spend her grief in the toilet of the station than she should cry out her heart before them. False! All of them! A falshe velt." A false world.

5

Wispy remnants of the crowd keep dawdling in the street, as if purposely spoiling a respectful starkness. The block is returned to insignificance. Esther is getting tired of waiting for her father. She lost track of Melnick and Mr. Shleeman and wonders if they are inside the tailor store or if her mother is still in there alone with Mrs. Lieberman and the dead Mr. Lieberman. She feels lonely and superfluous. Until she realizes, all at once, that Millie may not know, and how upset Millie will be because she's always hugging Mr. Lieberman and calling him zaydeh, and even though he's not her real grandfather he almost is because he used to be best friends with her father's father who died in Europe, and her father used to be religious and was a boarder with the Liebermans before he got married and now he was Mr. Lieberman's biggest customer—all the suits that came creased from the manufacturer went straight to Mr. Lieberman for pressing. She runs all the way to Millie's house.

She can hear the chimes sound inside 4D, but no one comes to the door. Millie doesn't like to stay in the house alone—probably everyone's at the store. She pushes the "Down" button for the elevator. A family from the fifth floor is already inside—one of the women who plays cards with Mrs. Brenner, her husband, and her two children.

Esther has seen the children outside but never talked to them. They all act as if they don't know her, so she acts the same way. All of them are dressed up. She breathes in the woman's perfume and the man's hair lotion. The boy is wearing a navy blue coat with very shiny silver buttons. The girl's coat has a white furry collar. Esther decides they are going uptown to the Roxy or Radio City. They remind her of Shirley Goldblatt in her class whose father is a furrier and who has a beige coat with real beaver collar and cuffs. Shirley is forever talking about the shows she sees uptown and about the hotels in the mountains with their casinos, while Esther keeps trying to imagine what uptown or a casino or the mountains look like. She feels an urge to shatter the equanimity of this stylish, aromatic foursome. She wants to scream out "Do you know that Mr. Lieberman, the tailor, is lying dead on the floor around the corner?" just to see what happens. But she doesn't say anything. And as she walks behind them out of the elevator, she notices that her coat is fraying and her fingernails are dirty.

Outside, the sky is leaden and it is colder. She trudges toward Broadway. Her galoshes feel heavy. Unexpectedly, all of a sudden, she is exhausted—as if the tumult of the entire day has surreptitiously been draining her. Does she have to tell Millie now? She'll find out pretty soon from somebody. Esther wants to go home. But she doesn't feel ready for Mama fresh from Mrs. Lieberman's wailing, and Papa might smell funny from washing a dead person. She passes Elite Cleaners—A. Coppola, Prop. John Coppola is in her class. He told her that his father wants him to be a priest when he grows up. Their store is closed. She comes to Brenner's, with the handsome dummies in the windows dressed in "Ready-Made" and "Custom-Tailored" suits, and one in a tuxedo.

The glare of the store lights after the gray sky and the

deep shadows of the elevated tracks makes her squint. Mr. Brenner, his wavy red hair meticulously barbered, his face pink with exertion, is kneeling on the black and white linoleum, measuring a customer's inseam. He ignores her. Beside the door, in the glass-walled office area, the new bookkeeper is bent over a ledger. Esther remembers that she works Sundays instead of Saturdays because she's orthodox. Mrs. Brenner is sitting on a high stool nearby, wearing her mink coat and looking into space. When she sees Esther, she calls Hello and that Millie is in the toilet and will be right out. Millie appears promptly and tells Esther she was just going over to her house. "Mr. Lieberman died!" Esther announces. Everyone stares at her. "They found him on the floor by the pressing machine," she adds.

"What? What?" Mrs. Brenner stumbles out of the office, wrapping her coat tighter around her. She clutches Esther's arm. "What are you saying?" she breathes into her face.

"Mr. Lieberman, the tailor, is dead," Esther repeats.

Mrs. Brenner's hand flies to her chest. "Oh, my God!" she croaks.

The bookkeeper comes out too, looking startled. Millie keeps staring at Esther and not moving, until she turns and runs back into the toilet. Mr. Brenner has stopped measuring the man's inseam. "Terrible. That's terrible," he says. Then looking heavenward, he heaves a sigh and intones, "For God's sake, what the hell am I gonna do now? A whole load of suits comin' in tomorrow!" Then with a look of persecuted resignation on his face, he bends down, muttering, "I guess I'll have to send 'em to the wop," and continues measuring the distance from his customer's ankle to his crotch. The bookkeeper goes back to her books. Mrs. Brenner returns to her seat, folds her mink-sleeved arms over her stomach, and, speaking to no one in particular, says, "They'll probably have the funeral tomorrow. I

hope they have nice weather." Esther keeps waiting for
Millie to come out until Mrs. Brenner tells her not to bother
because who knows how long that crazy kid will stay in
the toilet.

6

When she reaches her block it is empty. A sunless sky
and a biting cold wind have brought everyone to terms.
The shoveled sidewalks look like blackboards with the day's
lesson erased. Esther peers into the window of the tailor
store. The steam-stained walls, the fresh-pressed garments,
and the pressing machine with its gaping mouth stare back
at her. She remembers when they put in the counter, but
she never really noticed the cash register before. The
flowered opaque curtain is closed.

She crosses the street to her house. No one is home. In
the dining room the tall chairs, their more tenacious
threads glittering in the dimness, stand guard over the
candelabrum in the center of the table. The Sabbath candles have dripped down their holders and left wax puddles
on the rims. Esther leans over and begins lifting the wax
with her fingernails, eventually settling the candelabrum
on a torn paper bag and going to work with the end of a
spoon. She finishes by rubbing a towel over the smudges
until the candelabrum gleams. She notices, for the first
time, that it is bent, and wonders if it is real silver. On
her way to the kitchen to get something to eat she trips
over the door lying across the rotted floor and falls. She
hurts her knee. She presses it to stop the pain and feels
her eyes grow wet. Why doesn't someone come home? The

house is so empty and silent. She knows what she'll do! She'll just go upstairs and get into bed and sleep until someone comes home.

On the way up to her bedroom she stops at the open synagogue door, hesitates for a moment, then goes inside.

The golden lions embroidered on the red velvet curtain covering the Oren Hakodesh shine, the crown glistens; everything else in the synagogue is either encrusted or worn out. The lectern holds a Siddur with its cover and pages shredding; tea-colored flakes litter the floor. Esther sits down on one of the benches.

Each Friday before sundown she has the job of sweeping and dusting the synagogue. There is a special brush for the velvet curtain of the Oren Hakodesh and after she has whisked off the lint, she fluffs up the nap with her fingers, then she smooths it, and fluffs it up again and again until finally she stops. Once, in irresistible defiance of her father's instructions, she drew aside the velvet curtain and saw the Torah glowing softly in its dark recess. Reaching out, she ran her hands over its satin cover and fondled the gold fringes; the bells in their filigreed minarets tinkled, and an extraordinary sensation bloomed inside her. She wonders if she can recapture that feeling and is tempted to draw aside the curtain again. But she is too tired to get up right now. Cracks stagger across the ceiling and along the walls, which are painted dark green half way up and light green the rest of the way. Her eyes follow one jittery line after another, and she wonders why she never saw them forming—only the final cracks. She selects one that resembles the profile of a woman with a short broken nose. It is unfinished; the woman has no chin. She stares fixedly at the end of the crack, waiting for a chin to materialize. She becomes confused; she can't tell if the face is developing or disintegrating. The longer she looks, the more panicky she becomes. She shuts her eyes. Gradually the panic subsides, and she is asleep.

The synagogue is full of worshippers because it is Pass-over. You hardly notice the cracks in the walls. Sunshine is streaming through the long windows, gliding down the silvered slopes of the men's voluminous prayer shawls, flowing over the maroon and royal blue dresses of the women whose warm bodies release a scent of crushed flowers moistened with buttermilk. Yellow holiday dresses and shiny patent leather pumps have turned little girls from moths into butterflies who dart in and out and around. And above all of them, the lyrical voice of the Baal Tefilah rises to tremulous heights. The Baal Tefilah is Mr. Podoloff. He is too small to see into the prayer book on the lectern but his voice rises high above it, sending the butterflies soaring into the air where they hover, quivering, until his voice descends, when they swoop down and swarm around the worshippers. Mr. Podoloff's voice surges. Esther is the only butterfly who hears. Her yellow dress billows about her, splashed by the sunshine with red and pink and gold. She streaks upward. A crack in the ceiling becomes a grinning mouth, beckoning to her; it opens and grows wider as she ascends higher. She strives with all her strength to descend, but Mr. Podoloff's voice thrusts her up into the blackness of the mouth, where she hovers and quivers alone, peering down onto the heads of the worshippers, hoping someone will look up and see her. The mouth begins to close over her. She searches for her mother and father. She sees them and calls to them, but they do not hear her. Their heads stay bent over their prayer books, and they become smaller and smaller until they vanish. There are two empty places. Mr. Podoloff's voice stops, and Esther falls.

She awakens clutching the bench. Downstairs a door has been closed, and she hears her parents speaking to each other. Tears are trickling down her cheeks. She wipes her eyes and nose with the hem of her dress. Stiff with cold, she leaves the synagogue and goes downstairs.

In the doorway to the kitchen Esther stops. Her mother is standing by the sink, washing vegetables. Her father is sitting bent over the table with his overcoat on, his black hat pushed back on his head, and his hands pressed to his temples. He looks miserable. She feels sorry for him—his friend is dead. No. It can't be just because of Mr. Lieberman. Most people would look like that because their friend died, but not Papa. Papa makes jokes, even about dying. He says to old Mr. Koopitz, whose hands shake so much he keeps dropping the Siddur, "Don't worry, Koopitz. Soon you'll have nothing to do but lie and smell the green grass above you. And your hands will be so quiet, it will be a pleasure." Papa acts like dying isn't even sad—or scary. But now her father's hands fly away from his head and he begins rocking back and forth and intoning. He is not speaking to her mother or to her or to the Almighty with whom he often has conversations; he is speaking to the dead Mr. Lieberman. "Oh Lieberman, Lieberman, you played us a fine trick! You bequeathed us a puzzle. For a sage a puzzle. Lieberman, five years now you cast him from you. Five years he has not entered your house. Shall we now invite him in like an honored guest? Call him up, the mother begs. Otherwise, she will go herself to telephone, even if she falls in the street from grief. But you, Lieberman, what do *you* want me to do? For five years, you have refused to look on him! But he is a *son*, and the mother cries for him. Give a sign, Lieberman, a sign!"

Zalman looks about as if, indeed, there would be a sign—something to enlighten his ignorance. "The Torah, what does the Torah say? I do not know. If I could talk to the Rebbe.... But where is the Rebbe? In another city. At a wedding yet. His brother's daughter. Even if I could reach him.... To cast a pall over so joyous an occasion? God forbid!" Zalman paused for a moment and then his voice rises. "Master of the Universe, what shall I do?"

Malka Hirsch turns to her husband. Her voice seethes. "The Master of the Universe hears you like Haman hears the grahger! Listen to me. Call up the son! What kind of foolishness is this? The mother cries out her heart for her child, and you look for a sign from the dead father. Don't worry, he'll forgive you. He won't want his only son to say Kaddish over him? What happened has happened. Enough already!"

"But what if Lieberman has already said the Kaddish over his son?" Zalman asks.

"The Kaddish he did not say. To forbid him to enter the house is one thing, to mourn him as dead another. This he did not do."

"How do you know?"

"I know."

"Everything she knows!"

Esther sees her mother's shoulders rise. Are they going to have one of those terrible arguments? Are they going to begin calling each other names? She waits. She'll go outside if they start. But her mother turns back to the sink and starts peeling a cucumber.

"And the shiksa he'll also bring? To honor his father?" Zalman says.

"The shiksa he won't bring. Believe me. A son is a son. He must be told."

Esther enters the kitchen and stands by the stove. No one speaks to her. She watches the deft movement of her mother's hands. The green slivers fall swiftly one after another. The cucumber has been peeled. Her mother reaches for a towel, wipes her hands, takes a piece of paper from her apron pocket and points it at her father like a knife. "Here is the telephone number. Go call up!" she commands.

Her father rises and takes the piece of paper. "All

right," he says, grudgingly, "I'm going to the drugstore. I'll call up."

The door shuts behind him.

Her mother places on the table a buttered piece of bread and two bowls, one with cut up cucumbers, tomatoes, and scallions, the other with sour cream. "Here," she says to Esther. "Eat."

Esther sits down. As unobtrusively as possible, she re-arranges the bowls on the table to conceal the whirly black pits worn into the white enamel. Sometimes, close up, they look ominous. She ladles sour cream onto her vegetables. So it's true about Mr. Lieberman and his son. Still it's hard to believe. How could anyone who seems so nice be so mean? But maybe he wasn't exactly mean. Maybe he felt terrible about doing it but thought he had to. She is glad her mother won about calling up. But she cannot tell her. It would be like speaking against her father, and this is not permitted. Her mother may get angry with him, insult him, call him awful names, but never behind his back, never to them. And they must never say anything bad about him. Even that night, after he hit Ben all over—it was horrible and Mama kept begging him to stop—when she couldn't help herself anymore and she said that Papa acted crazy, Mama said, "Be quiet! What do *you* know?"

7

Malka Hirsch does not love her husband. Malka does not like her husband. She never has. She feels for him only compassion. Poor, miserable person, how he has borne his loveless lot! He jokes, he laughs, he hollers, he prays to God; he comes to her in the night with passion and tenderness; he tries to arouse her, to cajole her. Nothing. She submits. But she feels nothing—only obligation, compassion.

From the first day they brought him to her, with his big head and his eyes like saucers and his red lips and a new suit that didn't fit—unlearned, poor. He slurped his soup; he smacked his lips over the fish; he made jokes. A buffoon! A buffoon with burning eyes. Distasteful to her. How much kinder to have refused him! But how? An orphan with no dowry. Only a pretty face, a small waist, and big ideas. Big ideas they told her she had when she told them, "No!" He was not what she wanted. Who was she to say what she wanted? And he? He persisted. Oh, how he wanted her! Nothing could dissuade him—her disdainful looks, her caustic remarks, her silences. So she married him. And what did he not do for her? Like a queen she was! But still—nothing. Even after a child had been born and she was big with a second child and he had gone to America to find for her all that was good and sweet and beautiful, she did not miss him. Money arrived regularly.

Never was she in need. He wrote her to come, everything was ready. She did not want to go. She told them to write that she was not coming. Only her sister was silent. The others berated her. "Evil woman!" they called her. "Is this how a Jewish daughter behaves?" they asked. But she insisted, and they wrote to him. His letters kept coming, bewildered, pleading. They read them to her. "What has he done to deserve this?" they asked. "And what are you? Even your own letters you can't write. Nahr that you are!" They were right. She was and she remains a fool. She still cannot write a letter. In shul she sits without a Siddur—she cannot read.

Oh, what a plague is her ignorance! Like a baby she is! She cannot go by herself on the subway. Her little Esther knows more about the world than she does. Why? Why did she let it happen? In Europe, an orphan, no one cared—what could she do? But in America, what could she *not* have done in those young years? But she was a great lady, the wife of Zalman Hirsch—with a maid and a big house. She should be a *schoolgirl*? Stupid fool that she was! And now, too late. Who has the strength? So much to bear.... The poverty is heavy. But it is not his fault. Perhaps, it is her punishment. The unhappiness she brought him! And even now, what does she do for him? She comforts him like one comforts a starving dog. Children. What do they bring? Heartache. You carry them under your heart, you nurse them, you clean them, you cry over them. But when they need you, can you help them? No. What does she do for her son when his father is crushing his bones? Nothing. She wants to claw at the father, to rip his arms from his body, to tear his tongue from his mouth, to cut his eyes from his head! But she cannot; her heart knows his helplessness and his need and his rage—and her guilt. Her hands do not hurt him, only her words. She speaks. She pleads. She reviles! Between them there are no blows to the body, only words that pierce the heart. The good moments they have had together she has fondled so long in her mind, they are like silk that has lost its luster. The bitter quarrels survive, the filthy epithets. Who would believe? A pious man and a daughter of Israel. Why? Oh Lord, why have you constructed us of such flimsy stuff— fit only for *small* mitzvos, for easy rituals that even the most flawed and simple person can perform? To light the Sabbath candles, to separate the meat from the dairy utensils, to avoid the meat of the pig.... For the *large* mitzvos you have not equipped us. We are only people! He wants from me what I cannot give. I want him to be what he is not. What are we to do?

Everything in excess with him! Perhaps if he had loved her less, his emptiness would not have been so great. So great that only the Almighty could fill it. And so full has he become with love of the Almighty, that there is not enough room for his son. And our son is sick. It is sickness to disappear for days and be found dirty, twisted, tied up with ropes. Under the steps, like an animal, they found him. They were still living on the East Side, so how old could he have been? Only a boy. The whole building was in the hall, looking. The gypsies kidnapped him, he said. They tied him up. Who believed it? No one. Who is to believe such a thing when it happened yet a second time? Sick. Sick. He will do it again. He is sick. The way he goes for days without speaking. He needs doctors. He needs help. God, protect him! Keep him from hurting himself!

And her Leah, her beautiful Leah, where did she see her? By the candy store, smoking a cigarette and pasted against one of those bums. Like a whore. When she saw her mother, she ran away. Talk to her? Talking to Leah is like talking to the wall. Tell Zalman? He will go mad with shame and rage. Have hope. How? He—he has hope. How weary she is of listening to him, "Meh tur nit zindigen." But one must be made of iron not to complain! *He* doesn't complain; he only screams and hits like a crazy-man. And then he sings his nigunim and jokes with the world. She understands nothing. She goes to the Rebbe to unburden herself, for enlightenment, comfort. A good person, a wise man. His lips spoke hope. In his eyes she saw that his heart was weeping.

"Did you speak to him?"
Zalman is still holding the paper with the telephone number in his hand. "I spoke to *her*."
"Why? Where is he?"
"He? He is playing ball."
"What are you talking about?"
"Ball! She said he is playing 'hendball'—in a 'club'."
"What is hendball? What is a club?"
"I know? I should know from troubles like I know what she's talking about."
"So, did you tell her?"
"I told her. She said she was sorry. Sorry shmorry, everyone is sorry. In America, as long as one says he is sorry...."
"Will she find him? Will she tell him?"
"Don't worry. She'll find, she'll tell." Zalman is weary. His voice sags.
"Go upstairs and lie down. Rest," his wife tells him.
"Rest? Who needs rest? The Almighty will give me plenty of time to rest."
"All right, *don't* rest."
Zalman looks at his wife. His head nods resignedly. "I'm going over there. I'll wait for the son," he says. And he leaves the house.
Esther brings her dishes to the sink and wipes the crumbs from the table. "Who will tell the others?" she asks her mother.
"Others?"

"The other relatives."

"What relatives?"

"Brothers, sisters—I don't know. Cousins. . . ."

"There is no one."

"No one? On both sides?"

"Not in America, in Europe. But who knows what has happened to them there." Her mother soaps the dishes and holds them under running water. "Alone," she sighs. "Everyone is alone."

Lila comes home. Esther is glad to see her. She waits impatiently while Lila takes off her hat and coat and galoshes. Finally, she asks, "Do you know what happened?"

"I know," Lila says.

"About Mr. Lieberman?"

"About Mr. Lieberman."

"Isn't it terrible?"

"It's terrible."

"You don't even sound like you care."

"What am I supposed to do?"

"I don't know. You just sound like you don't care."

"Do *you* care?" Lila looks straight into her eyes. "*Really?*"

"Of course."

"Good for you!"

"For God's sake, Lila, what's the matter with you?"

"Nothing's the matter with me. I can't see why I have to get hysterical just because an old man dies. *Everyone* has to die."

"Mr. Lieberman wasn't very old. And besides, what about his wife?"

"What *about* his wife? She'll survive. She's not the first one."

"You really are peculiar, Lila."

"There's nothing peculiar about me. Everyone has to die sometime."

"I know. But still. . . . "

"Still nothing. When are you going to grow up and be a realist?"

Esther isn't exactly sure what a realist is. She hopes Lila will keep talking so maybe she'll figure it out, and not have to ask her. She knows Lila is waiting to be asked. Millie once said that Lila acts mean sometimes because she's jealous. It's true that Lila doesn't get such good marks in school, but so what? She's pretty and has lots of friends. Maybe if Papa didn't brag so much right in front of her about my marks, she wouldn't mind so much. Even Mama, who never brags about anything, acts a little nicer to me than to Lila after we bring home our report cards and Papa explains to her what the marks mean. But that's not *my* fault. I'm sure it would make Lila feel good if I asked her what a realist is. But she's always sticking in big words when she talks, probably just to show me—just to make me look dumb. Well, I won't ask.

The sisters stand facing each other. Neither one speaks. Suddenly, Lila smiles.

"What's so funny?" Esther asks.

"You," Lila says, and goes into the kitchen.

"Mama," Lila stands by her mother, hesitating. "Mama, I have to eat early tonight."

"Oh? Why?"

"I have to go someplace."

"Where do you have to go?"

"Someplace."

Her mother says nothing. She gives her attention to the stew on the stove. She tests the meat with a fork and then pours in chunks of potato.

"All right?" Lila asks.

"Where is this someplace you have to go that is so important? You just came in."

"A friend of mine is having a party. I promised I would help her."

"Ooh—a party? Which friend?"

69

"Florence Hollander."

"That one. That is truly a fine friend you've chosen for yourself."

Lila's color rises, but she pretends not to notice her mother's sarcasm. "Can I go?"

"You're asking *me* if you can go? Since when do you ask *me*? Did you ask me if it was all right to stand in the street with that—" Esther has come into the kitchen. Her mother looks at her and stops speaking. Lila keeps standing by her mother, who does not look at her. Her mother stirs the stew as she speaks again, "You'll eat when it's ready."

"I don't care if I eat at all!" Lila shouts as she storms out.

"All right, *don't* eat," Malka says softly. She keeps stirring the stew.

8

"Don't stay out long," her mother calls after her. "It's cold."

It is beginning to get dark, but maybe she can catch a glimpse of the son. Esther waits on the stoop. Her father is outside too, waiting in front of the Liebermans' store.

His coat is just like Mr. Brenner's, tan and a wraparound. Millie says her father's is camel's hair and very expensive. It looks a lot better on the Liebermans' son; he's tall and handsome, like Allan Jones—the same curly brown hair. He must be the Liebermans' son because when her father saw him, he rushed forward, slapped him on the back, and sang out "Hello doctor!"

As they enter the store, Mrs. Melnick is coming out. "Good," she says to the son. "It's good you're here. I must go give my husband supper. But I didn't leave her alone. There are people."

The Liebermans' son looked bewildered when Papa greeted him—he was upset and Papa was smiling, and probably also because he's not a doctor. He doesn't know that Papa calls almost *everybody* doctor, especially if he wants the person to like him. Lila told her that when she was in the sixth grade and Papa came to her class Open School Week, he called Mr. Benedetto doctor. Then he gave him a whole card of his aspirins in all those little wax paper envelopes; Lila thought she'd die! Nobody else gave

the teacher a present—and aspirins yet! Esther remembers
he did the same thing in her class. He didn't call Miss Callahan doctor, but he brought her a whole bag of his ex-
tracts. Miss Callahan became confused and began fussing
with her hair and suddenly looked younger. Papa's eyes
were looking straight into hers and shining, and his smile
was big and white and his mustache and beard looked so
smooth and black. Miss Callahan was blushing when she
looked away and took the bottles out of the bag and put
them on the desk; there were four of each—lemon, vanilla,
and almond. Some of the girls began whispering whether
their mothers should have brought presents too. On his
way to the back of the room where parents were supposed
to sit, Papa stopped to kid around with anybody he recog-
nized, like Millie, and the whole class had to wait. It was
so embarrassing. Finally, he took off his big black hat and
sat down with the other parents. He was the only father,
probably because the others had to go to work. Some of
the kids kept turning around to look at him; it was strange
to have a man with a yarmulka on sitting in the classroom.
Afterwards, he asked Miss Callahan, "What do you think
of my Esther? She's a smart girl, no?" Then *she* almost
died. But that must have pleased Miss Callahan just like
everything else about Papa. Even now, Miss Callahan stops
her in the corridor and asks, "How is that *wonderful* father of yours? You're lucky to have a father who thinks so
well of you."

A lot of people seem to like Papa—more than like Mama.
Mama doesn't laugh and talk so much and crack jokes.
Mama wouldn't bring a teacher a present, especially since
you really aren't supposed to. Once Mama came for Open
School Week. She didn't say a word; all she did was smile.
When she came in, she smiled at Mrs. Todd and sat down
in the back of the room. Before she left, she went to say
goodbye like the other mothers. Mrs. Todd said how pleased
she was to meet her, and Mama nodded and smiled. Mrs.

Todd thanked her for coming, and again Mama nodded and smiled. She never came again. She's probably ashamed because she can't speak English.

Esther goes back into the house. Her mother is leaving, carrying two covered pots. She is bringing food over to the Liebermans. If Ben comes in, Esther is to tell him to wait; she'll be back as soon as she can and give him supper.

Esther ate supper alone that night. It was so quiet she kept hearing herself chew. Not that eating alone was unusual. Except on Shabbes, whenever you're hungry, if your food is ready, Mama serves. But this time, it felt different. When her mother came back from the Liebermans, she immediately asked if Ben was home. That wasn't unusual either. Her mother is always asking if Ben is home. Esther knows why. Ben was not home. An hour later, her mother asked her if Ben had said anything about not coming home for supper. Esther said he hadn't. Her mother finally fed Lila and let her go out without saying anything; Esther said she would wait for Ben. The minute her father walked in, her mother said, "He is not here." Her father said, "What are you worrying about? It's early." Esther became hungry and had her supper. Her father said, no, he wasn't hungry, but half an hour later, he ate too. It's almost nine o'clock. Her mother has not eaten yet.

Esther wishes she had gone to Millie's, but she felt funny about asking tonight. By now the radio programs are over anyway, and Millie will probably still be upset about Mr. Lieberman. She finds her library book, *My Antonia*, and settles down at the dining room table to read. Even though Antonia's parents are a lot like hers, poor and they can hardly speak English, they seem more American. Is it because they live on a farm or because they're Christians? Maybe both. She doesn't like Mrs. Shimerda, but Tatinek, Antonia's father, is a kind man and so sad. Antonia isn't like anybody she knows. She wonders if Antonia and Jim will still be just friends when they grow up or if they'll fall in love. Or maybe she falls in love with him, but he can't marry her because her family's so different and everything. The book is real good and she'd like to keep reading, but she's too sleepy.

The bedroom is freezing. Esther hurries out of her clothes into her nightgown, slides gingerly onto the icy sheet, and hugs herself under the comforter. It's much worse when Lila isn't in bed. Her teeth are trembling so, she can barely form the words of the Krias Shema. "Blessed art thou, O Lord our God, King of the Universe. . . . May it be thy will O Lord my God and God of my fathers, to suffer me to lie down in peace and to let me rise up in peace. Let not my thoughts trouble me, nor evil dreams. . . . O lighten mine eyes lest I sleep the sleep of death. . . .

"Hear O Israel: The Lord our God, the Lord is one. Blessed be his name whose glorious kingdom is forever and ever. And thou shalt love the Lord thy God with all thine heart, and with all thy soul, and with all thy might. And . . ."

She awakens shivering worse than ever—it was a ghastly dream. She was in this huge kitchen with a low ceiling. It looked bleak and desolate; all it had in it was an old wooden table in the center and one chair, and there was a sink against one wall. Crazy Mike was at the sink doing something. A woman who seemed to be his wife was sitting on the chair. She had long gray hair, a bulbous red nose, and brownish broken teeth; she looked like a drunken witch. The woman reached out and grabbed her and began to swallow her. It didn't hurt; she was just being swallowed. She was disappearing!

Her heart is pounding. She can still feel the chapped hands on her arms. Lila is in bed beside her. She wishes she could hug Lila. What's *that*? What's that thing at the window? Mama! Papa! Help me! Something white with wings! I'm *awake*! *I'm not dreaming*! It doesn't move. It looks like—like an angel! Esther shuts her eyes and very very slowly opens them again. It's her mother, her mother in her long nightgown with the big sleeves, and her hair hanging down, standing by the window with her arms raised and her hands pressed against the pane; she is looking out into the street. Esther wants to call to her, Mama, you frightened me! What are you doing in the cold and dark looking out the window? But she doesn't. The light from the street lamp forms a halo around her mother's head; she looks holy. Esther lies wide-eyed, barely breathing. Suddenly her mother shudders. Esther hears a moan, a broken sob, and softly, "Thank God—thank God." Her mother moves noiselessly across the room. Through the wall, Esther hears the springs whine as her mother gets into bed. A few minutes later, there are footsteps on the stairs—Ben's. The door of his room closes.

9

Esther sleeps late the next morning and awakens to a sore throat and the sound of rain. Lila is gone. Bunched in front of the tailor store are big black umbrellas, and in the street is a long, black hearse. Yesterday's white snow mountains are dingy and cracked. Thin gray rivulets run down their sides. There is dirty slush everywhere—as if the snow has been chewed and spit out. How fast it all changed, Esther thinks. It's hard to tell who everybody is under the umbrellas. She recognizes Mrs. Brenner's mink coat—the bottom is getting wet and matted. Mr. Brenner is there too, and Millie, huddled under her father's umbrella. Angie is standing in the doorway of her father's store. Esther would like to get dressed and go out, but her throat hurts and she feels wobbly. The bedroom doesn't seem cold—she feels hot. Some of the other people outside are familiar, but she doesn't know their names. The door of the tailor store is open and people keep coming out. The Melnicks come out and stand with the others. Mrs. Melnick can hardly fit under the umbrella with her husband; she's getting wet. The rain is coming down hard.

Esther gasps. She has never seen a coffin before. Four men, two on each side, her father, Mr. Greenberg the painter, the man her father calls "the hungarisha," and Beryl Miller from the dry goods store are carrying the coffin. It is covered by a dark blue cloth with a white Mogen

David in the center. It looks very long, much too long for little Mr. Lieberman. Mr. Lieberman is really in there! Great tears of rain splatter the cloth. The people make room. Behind the coffin Mrs. Lieberman is leaning on her son and sobbing. A man comes out alone. Esther has never seen him before, but she can tell—the way he's dressed, the way he walks. The people make even more room. He must be a rabbi. Could he be the one who owns their house, the one her mother doesn't like? His stomach sticks out and he has a fat brown beard. Behind him are more people. Old Mr. Koopitz, all bent over, with his wife holding on to him. Her mother. Then Mr. Shleeman and two more men Esther recognizes from shul; one is "the Litvak," the other her father calls "the Galitzianer." A man steps out of the front of the hearse, walks around it, and opens the back doors. The coffin is slid inside, and the doors are shut.

Behind the hearse are two black cars with drivers at the wheel, then Mr. Greenberg's orange truck with "Painting & Paperhanging" under his name, then a blue car. Mrs. Lieberman is about to get into the first car with her son when she stops as if suddenly remembering something. She whispers to her son and hands him something from her pocket. He goes back to the store and locks the door. Then they both get into the first car. The rabbi gets in next to the driver, and her father gets in back with the Liebermans. Her mother gets into the second car with the Melnicks and Mr. and Mrs. Koopitz. Mr. Shleeman is leaving. Is he going to go out with his pushcart in the rain? Mr. Greenberg and two other men get into the front of his truck. Some people are getting into the blue car; Mrs. Brenner is trying to get in, but Millie is trying to get in too, and her mother keeps pushing her away. Finally her father pulls Millie away and Mrs. Brenner gets in. Millie looks like she's crying when she walks away with her father.

Esther leaves the window. Again, she forgot the nagel vasser. She bends down and pours the cold water over her

10

It is afternoon when Ben comes down. Esther is in her bathrobe, sitting by the oil stove in the dining room with her pencils and crayons and pad spread out on the table. Millie gave them all to her for her last birthday and said she hoped she would use them because she was talented. Esther looks at what she's drawn so far. It doesn't look like Mr. Lieberman. She's not good at drawing real people, especially men—they're hard.

"Why aren't you dressed?" Ben asks. "What's the matter?"

"I'm sick. My throat hurts," Esther says. "Mama left some cocoa on the stove, but you'll have to warm it. I turned off the gas."

Ben comes over and feels her head. "You feel hot," he says. "You ought to be in bed."

"I don't like to stay upstairs alone. Mama and Papa'll be home soon. They went to the cemetery."

"Did you gargle with salt water?"

"No."

"For cryin' out loud! Why do you have to wait for Mama to do everything for you? All you have to do is boil some water and put salt in."

She has never boiled anything. Her mother does everything. She wasn't even sure she should turn the gas off under the cocoa. "I don't know. I just didn't," she says. "I'll do it now."

"Never mind," Ben says. "Just stay there, I'll make some for you."

When the salt water is ready, Esther goes into the toilet next to the kitchen and gargles at the sink. Her throat feels a little better, but not much. Ben is eating breakfast. "I'll play dominoes with you after I finish, if you like," he says as she goes by.

Ben is so nice, she thinks as she clears the dining room table. But he can get real annoyed too—like just before. She wonders why he didn't come home for supper and where he was until so late. If she could be sure he wouldn't get angry, she'd ask him. Sometimes he tells about places he's been. Once he told her all about a play he saw—a Broadway play, he explained. And he acted out all the parts. He was so funny! And once she asked him about the YMCA where he takes showers. Wasn't it a Christian place, she asked. Wasn't he scared? He put his hand gently on her head and said it wasn't scary at all; it was just a place with friendly people where they had good hot showers. But lately, she doesn't like to ask him things. He seems different. He used to compliment her a lot on her drawings, but last time she showed him a picture she drew in school, he just said, "It's all right." And when she said, "Miss McKeon said it was the best one in the class—even though I know she doesn't like me." Ben said, "Yeah? Well, just don't get a swelled head."

She puts the dominoes on the table and sits down to wait.

Ben comes into the dining room. "Get up," he says.

"What for?" Esther asks.

"Don't ask so many questions. Just get up. You shouldn't be sitting like that with your feet on the drafty floor."

Esther gets up. Ben puts three dining room chairs together to form a small narrow bed. "Just your size," he says, smiling. "Get in. I'll be right back." He comes back with the comforter from his bed and spreads it over her legs. Then he removes a huge volume of Gemara from the china closet which they now use as a bookcase for Talmudic texts. He places the Gemara across her lap and pours the dominoes onto it.

"Papa'll holler if he sees us playing dominoes on the Gemara," Esther says.

"Don't worry about Papa," Ben says. "Let's play."

Esther wins the first game, and they are starting a second when Millie arrives. She is wearing a powder blue rubber raincape with a round white collar. Esther hears Ben admire it as he lets her in. The raincape *is* pretty, and Esther admires it too. But Millie looks sad and forlorn; her eyes are puffy. "What's the matter with you?" she asks Esther.

"I have a sore throat. Maybe a fever too."

"That's too bad. I'm sorry," Millie says.

"Millie, wanna finish playing dominoes for me?" Ben asks. "Esther beat me the last game. I wouldn't want her to do that again."

Millie smiles shyly at Ben. "Okay," she says.

When Ben has his coat on and is ready to leave, Esther asks, in a careful voice, the words significantly slow, "Will you be home for supper?"

Ben's narrow shoulders tense. It's like he's trying to hold himself together, Esther thinks. I hope he doesn't get angry.

Gradually Ben's shoulders relax. He looks at Esther softly, tenderly. "I'll be home. Tell Mama, I'll be home," he says.

After he has gone, Millie says, "You're lucky to have such a nice brother."

"I guess I am," Esther says.

"I don't believe anything I've—" Millie stops.

"You don't believe what?" Esther asks. Her heart is thumping.

"Oh, nothing," Millie says.

"What were you going to say?"

"It doesn't matter."

"It matters to *me*!"

"It'll only make you feel bad."

"So I'll feel bad. I'll feel worse if you don't tell me."

"I don't even know exactly," Millie says. "I just heard a friend of my mother's telling her she saw Ben someplace, someplace uptown."

"So? He goes uptown sometimes."

"I don't even know what she meant because I didn't hear the first part."

"What did she *say*?"

"She just said, 'You'd never believe it was the Hirsches' son. The way he looked—I almost didn't recognize him. And that person he was with. Friday night too!'"

Esther is quiet.

"Isn't he always *here* on Friday nights?"

"Of course," Esther says, "—except once in a while."

"Really! Where does he go?"

"How should I know? Let's play dominoes."

"I knew I'd make you feel bad. I shouldn't have told you."

"Who cares what that stupid woman said. Let's play!"

They begin to play. Esther, without looking up, asks "How do *you* feel, Millie?"

Millie matches a domino. "About Mr. Lieberman, you mean?"

"Yes."

"I'm okay. But you shouldn't have left the store yesterday."

"Your mother *told* me to leave. She said you might be in the toilet forever."

"My mother—you know my mother. You should have waited anyway."

They have stopped playing.

"It's when a friend is upset that she needs you," Millie says.

Only Millie would say a thing like that, Esther thinks. She's so—so *old*. No wonder girls don't like her. She's so serious, and she expects everyone to be perfect.

"Like when we're playing a game at my house," Millie goes on, "and we get into a fight. You always just get up and leave. I know sometimes it's my fault, but that's when you should stay and help me—help me be sensible."

Esther looks down at the dominoes and starts pushing them around any old way. What can you say to someone like Millie? She's my own age, and she makes me feel so bad and so dumb. Millie *is* smart. *She's* really the smartest one in the class. And she's so different from other girls— like when she brought us two rolls of toilet paper after she saw that we only had torn-up newspapers. And the time in the movies when I was crying so much at the sad part that my nose was running and I didn't have a hand-kerchief, Millie tore a piece off her petticoat and gave it to me to wipe my nose. I hope Mama doesn't find out that sometimes Millie treats me to the movies; she wouldn't like it. "I think you're right, Millie," she says, "but some-times it's hard. . . ."

Millie sighs. "I guess so. I just expect too much from people, don't I?"

"No, you don't."

"Yes, I do. And I act like a little old lady, don't I? My mother says I'm a little old lady."

"Come on, Millie, your mother doesn't mean that," Esther says. Her throat feels worse and she wishes they would change the subject. "My throat really hurts," she murmurs.

"Did you take any aspirin?" Millie asks.

"No. We never take aspirin in our house."

"Why not? Don't you still have a whole lot of it from when your father was in business?"

"We still have it. But my father won't let us take any."

"Why not?"

"I don't know. He says it's chozzerei."

"But if it's junk, why did he sell it?"

"How should I know?"

"It doesn't seem right to me."

"Oh, Millie!" Esther says wearily.

Her parents have come home. Esther hears them at the door. She sweeps the dominoes onto the floor. "Here Millie, quick!" she says, lifting the Gemara. "Put this back in the china closet. Hurry! *And don't drop it!*"

Millie doesn't know what's happening, but she does as Esther tells her. Then she stands against the china closet, her eyes wide and her mouth open. The way Esther screamed, "Don't drop it!" like it was made of glass or something. The things that go on in the Hirsch family are unfathomable to her.

"What's wrong?" Esther's mother is startled when she sees her in her bathrobe, all propped up.

"Nothing. My throat hurts a little. That's all."

"Look at her," her father says. "I think she has fever."

Her mother feels Esther's head. "She's burning," she says.

Her father comes close to her. "Stick out your tongue," he says.

Esther sticks out her tongue. "It looks nasty. Did you move your bowels today?"

She's glad Millie doesn't understand Yiddish. "No. I don't think so," Esther answers.

"We must give her an enema," her father says.

Esther groans. That's the first thing they think of whenever I get sick! She hates it—but it's not as bad as castor oil.

"You must get into bed right away. I'll bring up the little oil stove from the shul," her mother says.

Esther looks at Millie, and her mother's eyes follow. Her mother smiles when she notices Millie; she likes Millie. But she thinks she should go home now anyway and gently tells her so in a brief mixture of Yiddish and English. Millie puts on her things. "Come morgen," Esther's mother says. "She says you should come tomorrow," Esther explains.

"Okay, I'll see you tomorrow," Millie says as she leaves.

The enema was awful. She feels exhausted. Both her parents are looking at her with worried expressions. Finally, her father says, "I'm going now. I'm going to bring the Sayfer Torah over there."

Her mother shrugs her shoulders.

"It's a mitzva," her father declares.

After he leaves, Esther asks her mother what her father is going to do.

"He's going to take the Torah from downstairs and bring it over to the Liebermans."

"Why?"

"Because it's a mitzva, he says. For the seven days that a family mourns, it's a religious duty to pray there with a minyan. And, if possible, a Torah should be there too."

"Really?"

"Plenty of people mourn without a minyan or a Torah, but you know your father.... Did you gargle yet with salt water?"

"Yes. Benjamin made me some. And—and he said to tell you he'd be home for supper."

"He said to tell me?" Malka's eyes mist over. Her love for her son is a profound ache deep between her breasts. She turns away so Esther will not see her tears. "I'll go bring you some tea," she says.

Esther gets out of bed and stands by the window. She wants to see her father carry the Torah across the street.

It has stopped raining. People are coming outside to enjoy the sun. Jackets and overcoats are unbuttoned. Some women have brought out their folding chairs. Babies are being rocked in carriages. Even Choochie, the idiot, is having a good time, jumping rope with some little girls. Once the door of the ungraded class was open when she went by on the way to Assembly and she saw Choochie inside, weaving something. He looked up, and she waved to him. He looked down again—she couldn't tell if he didn't recognize her or if he was ashamed of being in that class. Angie is outside too, probably wondering where I am. Maybe she'll knock on the door and ask, and Mama will send her upstairs.

Everything stops. Everyone is looking toward her house. Esther presses her face against the glass. She sees them— her father and the Torah, wrapped together in sunlight. Its red satin blazes, the gold beading and fringes glisten, its filigreed minarets flare. The red and the gold entwine. The Torah is a flaming torch! Her father walks slowly, holding the Torah high, with both his arms around it. Holding it like it is an enormous jewel! Esther opens the window, just a little. She wants to hear the tinkle of the golden bells.

The people step aside as Zalman Hirsch approaches. His head is high. He turns from side to side and smiles. His eyes sparkle. Let them look! Let them see! Let them see the splendor of the Torah.

11

It is the fourth day of her vacation, and Esther is still sick. On the third day, Millie asked, "Why don't your parents call the doctor?"

"My parents never call the doctor," Esther told her. "Only once when I had double pneumonia—they thought I was going to die."

"Probably it's because they have no money to pay," Millie said.

"I don't think that's the only reason. They just know how to make me better themselves. I'm almost better now."

It's true. She is almost better. She doesn't have to stay in bed, but she can't go outside yet. The best thing about being sick was that Angie finally came over. They had such a good time. They played Dots and Guess the Number. At first Angie seemed nervous, but then she began to laugh a lot, and her brown eyes stopped searching the room and became soft and happy. Lila played two games of Casino with her after supper one night. Esther was surprised. She could tell that her sister was trying to be nice to her because she was sick and it was vacation and she couldn't go outside; Lila didn't seem to be enjoying herself at all. But when she was on her way out afterwards, and Esther called to her and thanked her, Lila smiled, and her eyes were wonderful—blue sapphires shattering into tiny dancing crystals.

By midafternoon, Esther has had three glasses of hot tea with lemon, played two games of Solitaire, read four more chapters of *My Antonia*, and wondered on and off what happened in Hebrew school when the class met again. Did Irving come back? Did his father have to come to school? Whose side did his father take? Even though she feels sort of sorry for Mr. Podoloff (imagine having to explain that you can't help spitting when you talk) she still doesn't like him. She's getting tired of staying inside and hoping someone will come to see her—when Willie arrives. She is happy to see him. Nobody in the family, no other relative, is like Willie. She likes her father's sisters and brothers who come from New Jersey to visit and bring her Hershey Bars and sometimes slip her half a dollar before they leave to "buy yourself a treat." But except for being richer and not as religious, they're not so different from her parents. Willie *is* different.

Willie Schneider is the least prepossessing of all the relatives—shorter, fatter, sallow, slightly pock-marked, and his large brown eyes look at you differently; he is somewhat wall-eyed. And when Willie walks into his cousin Zalman's house, the climate and color of the house change. He brings in the acrid smoke of his Raleigh cigarettes and the dissolute brownness of his nicotine-stained fingers. His thick graying hair is generally disheveled, his shirt collar loosened, his suit a little rumpled, and always there is a newspaper sticking out of a pocket. He smells of secularism, and before long, the air begins to crackle with his irreverence. Only Willie would ever come to Zalman's house, traveling from Brownsville, on the Sabbath. Zalman's face becomes stormy and Willie can see the bile rising in him, and sometimes he is afraid it will spill over, but it never has.

With his cousin Willie, Zalman Hirsch restrains himself. Willie is not only a cousin, he is the boyhood friend with whom he shared everything: the cramped bench in the village Cheder, the beatings of the melamud, running in the fields and plotting mischief in the tall grass. Willie, even then, had disengaged himself from rules he considered fatuous or unreasonable. When he concluded that Moshe Kalb, who it was well known was a miser, had more apples in his orchard than he needed, Willie climbed one of his trees and took some. And because stealth would have detracted from the assertion of his rights, Kalb saw him. Willie was a scrawny ten-year-old and Kalb was a hefty forty-five; a confrontation would have been unfair. Willie ran and Kalb chased him all the way to his own house where the adults were outside enjoying the summer air and sipping tea around the samovar. Willie looked behind him to see if Kalb was still coming and knocked over the samovar. He still bears the burn scar on his left hand. Willie is no longer a boy nor scrawny, but he is still asserting his rights, and his adversaries—the bosses, the capitalists—are still larger than he is.

Willie Schneider is a Union man and a Socialist. Both his father and his grandfather had been tailors, but in the new land you could become what you liked. So Willie took his wife, Clara, and their small daughter and came to America. In the daytime Willie stood over a cutting table and followed patterns for ladies' dresses, and at night he sat in school, squeezed between a small seat and a low desk, and followed the letters on the blackboard. He was still a young man, he could learn, he could study, he could become something. He learned to read from left to right, to form letters, words, sentences. He never got to paragraphs. By then he had two children and began taking home piecework. "On this you expect me to feed a family?" Clara had shrieked, throwing his pay on the floor. Willie stooped to pick it up (he had to crawl under the table for some coins), placed the money on the table and went out for a walk. The years had made Willie rounder, but not much taller; Clara, like all his adversaries, was bigger than he. Again, a confrontation would have been unfair. Willie needed allies; alone he was too little.

The very next week, Willie found himself in the Union Hall listening to a speaker who explained to him the meaning of the words pasted on the wall, "In Union There Is Strength." He was converted. The Almighty, Willie concluded, had been too passive in his behalf; he either didn't exist or he didn't care, Willie was not sure. But he was certain that there was more strength in Union than in God. Little by little, he doffed his old ways and learned new ones. The *Morning Journal* gave way to the *Forward*, and Willie became convinced that free enterprise must give way to Socialism. Religion? Rituals? For the fools. But fools were also entitled. If Clara would be ashamed before the neighbors, she could keep her separate dishes and buy Kosher. And when she wanted the children should go, like everyone else's, to Talmud Torah, he let. Poor woman, what else could he give her? Homely she was, even when he married her—mostly out of pity. She wanted him. Who else ever would? And she needed him. Willie had a kind heart. Go know she would turn out to have such a mouth! But he forgives her. Why should *she* be defenseless? Everyone needs something, some weapon against the world.

He did not want his children to go to Talmud Torah, but he also did not want to send them no place. He was not an assimilationist; he trusted the goyim less than he trusted God. Let the children be Jews. But must one fill their young heads with buba-meysehs, with fairy tales? With miracles and pestilence and an arrogant, vengeful God? Teach them what is meaningful, purposeful: the social justice of the Prophets, the living language of their people, not a dead tongue good only for pointless prayers. And in the Workmen's Circle School, they would learn Marxism too. But Clara was horrified. How would Yankele prepare for his Bar Mitzva? All her life she had been waiting to bake shtrudel for her son's Bar Mitzva. Did he think he was going to deprive her of this? He gave in with both children. And what did he get? His daughter, Ethel, is becoming a gantseh rebbitsin; still no more than a child, she walks around on Shabbes with her girlfriends, all of them with handkerchiefs tied around their wrists—they shouldn't desecrate the Sabbath by exerting themselves to carry a handkerchief! And what Clara is doing to Yankele is unspeakable! A chazzen she's making him into! Yankele Schneider, The Boy Cantor With The Golden Voice, and his picture in the paper with the big fancy yarmulka like an inverted bell on his small head. Already he's making almost as much money as his father, and Clara puts it away for him in his own special bank account—he shouldn't look like a pauper when the time comes; she already has her eye out for a worthwhile match. God in heaven, are you there? He is only fourteen years old!

It is not Shabbes, so Willie has a cigarette da his lips. To smoke in Zalman's house on Shab going too far. Zalman would have no choi does not want to be banished from his cou loves Zalman and Malka and all their chil not a fool, he is only wrong—enslaved by mysticism, and periodically, at each visit, out to him, and the dialogue begins. Bac Esther's head turning first one way th

Willie removes the cigarette and tak ling face between his hands. "Is that l me, Estherel, or have you forsaken me weet-heart?"

It is an old game between the es and shakes her head. "No, you are stil

"Good," Willie says. "You have d. If you forsake me for another, I will tear n my bare hands."

"Oh, Willie!" Esther says, laughing. "Why do you tease me?"

Malka greets Willie warmly, but is surprised to see him. "It's the middle of the afternoon. Why aren't you working?" she asks.

"I'm not working," Willie answers, "because I'm on strike."

"On strike? What does it mean—on strike?"

"Give me first a glass of tea and sit down with me, and I'll tell you."

While her mother prepares the tea, Esther settles into a corner of the kitchen to listen; Willie is fascinating. Someday, if he comes when nobody is home and she has the nerve, she's going to ask him about those unfair things in the Bible.

Malka places a glass of tea, a bowl of sugar cubes, and a plate of her rugalech before Willie and asks him again, "What has happened?"

Willie first stirs two sugar cubes into his tea, takes a few sips, exclaims over the deliciousness of the rugalech, and then slowly explains that the Ladies' Garment Workers are refusing to work unless they get more pay—and for less hours.

"*More* pay for *less* hours?" Malka is awed by such chutzpah. "How can you accomplish such a thing?"

"*I* cannot. But the *Union* can."

Malka nods her head. She has heard from him about the Union and follows his reasoning.

"But how will you live? The Union will feed your family?"

"The Union treasury will give me whatever it can. We'll live. And when we win, we'll collect from the bosses."

"You're so sure you'll win? They'll find others to take your place."

"Scabs, you mean. No. Scabs will not take our place."

"What means 'scabs'?"

"Scabs?" Willie takes another sip of tea. "Scabs are vultures who feed on the flesh of other workers. Scabs are a menace to all the people. A scab is a person who will take your place when you are fighting for a human being's right to live like a human being."

"But what can you do about them?"

"We do what must be done."

Malka's eyes grow wide. Esther sits very still, listening. "Willie, you don't...."

"I don't. But others do. Scabs learn very quickly not to interfere."

"I'm afraid to ask, Willie. What do they do to them?"

"Don't be afraid. We don't kill them. We only frighten them."

Malka is relieved. Esther is impressed. She has seen pictures of strikers in the paper. Yes, Willie could be one of them.

Zalman comes rushing in, upset. Mr. Shleeman has been badly hurt by a rock some momzer on the North Side threw at him, they might not have a minyan for prayers at Lieberman's house. He looks at Willie as if he were seeing the Messiah himself. "Such good fortune! God provides! Willie, this once you cannot refuse. A mitzva like this can't hurt you. Why else would you be here like this?"

"I am here like this not because God provides, but because God does *not* provide."

"What are you talking about *now*?" Zalman says. "Please Willie, don't start in."

"I'm not starting in. I'm just trying to tell you why I am here."

Zalman is silent now, waiting. Something is wrong. Finally, he says, "All right, so tell me why you are here."

Willie tells him and adds, "I thought I'd stop for a visit on my way home from picketing—to fortify myself before I have to contend with Clara's abuse."

Zalman is saddened. "God will help you, Willie. God will help."

Willie's glass clatters onto the table. "God! You and your God! God will not help! Dubinsky will help! People must help themselves!"

"Willie, Willie, who are we to understand?" Zalman is taken aback by Willie's fury. He tries to calm him and speaks soothingly. "God moves in mysterious ways. He will help."

"Whom? Whom does God help?" Willie smiles sardonically. "His chosen people, maybe?"

There they go again, Esther thinks.

"All right! We have not been chosen for lives of luxury! We have not been chosen for hedonism!" Zalman sympathizes with Willie's problem, but.is in no mood for his scoffing. "We have not been chosen to be wild goats running mindlessly through hills and meadows, or to be pigs rolling in the mud! We have been chosen to show the others what is most worthy in human beings. To suffer, to sacrifice ourselves for what we believe to be good—for God and for Torah. Without suffering, how would we feel for others? What would we understand?"

"But what do you accomplish with your understanding?" Willie asks.

"Those who have suffered not only grow stronger, but with their understanding will not cause others to suffer."

Malka sighs heavily as she places a glass of tea before her husband. He looks up and sees the accusation in her eyes. "For Klal Yisroel," he adds. "For Torah, one suffers —the fathers and the children and the children's children."

"To suffer for what is good, all right," Willie says. "But tell me, Zalman, how much time do you and your Hassidim spend contemplating what is good and how much worrying about foolishness: the right towel to wipe a dish, God forbid you should use the wrong spoon to stir your sour cream, and if you should get mixed up and recite the words of the Maariv service before the Mincha, what an offense to the Almighty!"

Her father has put a sugar cube between his teeth and is sipping his tea through the cube. Esther tries not to look at him or hear him; she wishes he wouldn't do that.

Zalman puts down his glass, impatiently. "Willie, Willie, what kind of foolishness are you speaking? You know as well as I that the rituals you speak of are not the essence; they are the reminders. We are only people. We need to be reminded or we will forget who we are. We are in galus, scattered among the Gentiles. How will we hold ourselves together?"

Willie heaves a disgusted sigh. "If these trivial concerns are all that can hold us together, God must truly help us, because we are not worth holding together."

"God *will* help! Because what you call trivial helps us to observe the larger mitzvos. God sees. He will help."

Willie explodes. "God sees? He sees what Hitler is doing? Do you know what is happening now in Europe? God is seeing. Do you remember what happened in Kishinev? God saw. Did God help?" He turns to Malka. "Tell me, Malka, did he help in Kishinev? Did he help your mother and father? When they cut open your father's belly and stuffed it with chicken feathers, God helped? Did he help your mother? When they pulled down their pants and climbed on her one after the other, and afterwards slashed her throat, did God help? He watches! He saw! Everything!"

The room is whirling. Esther sways in her chair. This! *This* was how they died! *This* was the death past what one could imagine! Oh God!

Malka presses Willie's hand and, with pleading eyes, inclines her head toward Esther. "Willie, the child, please," she murmurs.

But Willie will not be placated. "The child? She is not such a child! She should know truth, not fairy tales. How much older were you when you knew? You saw! You told me yourself how you watched from the hayloft. God did not even have the kindness to cover your eyes. And if the Cossacks had found you there in the hayloft, would they have done differently to you? *You* were a child."

"Willie please!" Malka begs.

Zalman is silent. Esther feels weak. She wants to leave, but she wants to stay. She cannot move. Her mother looks at her. "Are you all right?" she asks. "The first day out of bed you shouldn't be up so long. Maybe you should lie down now."

Esther's voice wavers. "No. I'm all right."

"Well, Willie," Zalman says, rising, "I know your stubbornness. You will not come to help us make a minyan."

"No."

"Then I must go and find someone else." Zalman is tired, his eyes are mournful. "Goodbye," he says, "I hope God will help you." He puts on his coat, and puts his hat on over his yarmulka.

Willie calls after him, "If God had not honored Shleeman with that rock, you wouldn't have to go out searching!"

Zalman bangs the door behind him.

Her mother looks at Esther, who is sitting by the stove and shivering, and insists she go upstairs and get into bed or she'll have a fever again. As she rises, Esther's legs feel weak. Her head is in a tumult. She stops before she leaves the room and says softly, "Goodbye, Willie."

"Goodbye, Esther. Be well," Willie says. As she goes upstairs, she hears him say to her mother, "Don't worry, the truth will not hurt her."

She undresses and gets under the comforter. She will not go down for supper. She will stay in bed, covered up and quiet, and think about everything. Maybe, if she just thinks hard enough, she'll understand. She must make herself understand. Otherwise, everything will be terrible and stupid. She will think her father is dumb or crazy or a liar—forever talking about God and what you're supposed to do and not supposed to do, and screaming and hollering. Esther draws the comforter up close to her chin. But maybe he screams and hollers and hits Ben because he really cares that we should do the right thing. If he was really mad at us or didn't care about us, he just wouldn't speak to us. Millie's father never tells her *anything*. He doesn't care *what* she does. Does Papa worry that if we're not religious, God will punish us? Or does he think God will punish *him* if he doesn't make us religious? Maybe, he's just afraid we'll embarrass him. But how could all that stuff about God be true when...? No, I can't think about Mama's parents. It's too horrible. How could Papa be right? No wonder they don't seem to mind being poor. Compared to the terrible things that happened in Europe, just being poor isn't so bad. What did Willie mean about what's going on in Europe *now*? And about Hitler. I keep hearing about Hitler but nobody ever really explains why he's bad. I think he's being mean to Jews, but what is he doing *exactly*? And who were the Cossacks? Why did they do those things? It must have happened to other people too, not just Mama's parents. I wonder if Lila knows about them. Maybe if she did, she wouldn't look so annoyed every time Papa says, "Dahnk Gott der fahr," and she wouldn't mutter under her breath, "Thank God for what?" Even Mama is always saying "Dahnk Gott" when anyone asks her how she is or how anybody in the family is. And all that stuff about suffering. I do get a peculiar good feeling sometimes when I think I'm suffering. Can it be for the reasons Papa talked about? But I never think about *those* things. I guess I just imagine that God is watching me and he'll like me better. Or maybe that I'll like *myself* better if every time I think I'm suffering, I don't act like a cry-baby. What I call suffering! I don't know *anything*! I'm glad I never met Mama's parents. At least I don't know how they *looked*. How could anybody do such things? I can't believe

12

Her mother kept changing her mind about taking her because she had been well for only a few days and it was freezing cold outside, but she made her bundle up real good in long winter underwear (which she hated—it itched) and pull her beret down over her ears and they all went to the mikva. Lila walked ahead by herself wearing whatever she liked and acting as if she wasn't with them. Esther noticed how Lila looked around furtively before darting into the basement of the decrepit little building.

Inside it was warm and steamy with great stains like spilled coffee running down the dun-colored walls. The same ancient attendant with her shrunken face and papery lips, her little black eyes glittering like bits of coal, was sitting on her chair under the low ceiling with the pipes twisting in all directions over her head. She was delighted to see them—patting Esther's head and crooning and clucking over her. Lila stayed as far away as she could from the old woman, like she was afraid of her. The hot bath felt good—she had been feeling smelly and it was hard to keep her fingernails clean. She washed herself, but her mother insisted on scrubbing her head and washing her hair.

Now, only a few days later, her hair has to be washed all over again. If they'd gone to the mikva today, her hair would still be clean for tomorrow when she goes back to school. All the way there, she kept bothering her mother about why they had to go on Thursday this time. Her mother said, "When you're older and the time comes, I'll explain to you why." Her father goes to the mikva every Friday, but her mother goes on different days about once a month. It could have something to do with the "monthlies" which will happen when she gets older. But then why wouldn't Lila have to go every month even in summer? Maybe only married women have to. But why? And Lila just takes a bath and washes her hair. After her mother takes a bath and washes her hair, she dips herself over her head in the small swimming pool they call the mikva and she says a brucha, so it must be something religious. Once when her mother was in the pool, she asked if she could go in too, but her mother said she wasn't supposed to. Her mother's face was all flushed and rosy and her hair was flowing over her shoulders, and she was naked with her white breasts hanging down like sacks of flour. Lila's breasts are different; they stand straight up and are much smaller and pointy. She wonders when she'll have breasts. Right now, she has nothing. Some of the girls in her class have tiny ones, like pimples under their dresses.

The reason her hair has to be very clean when she goes back to school is that she is going to be examined for nits. There are two big pots and a kettle of water boiling on the gas range. As soon as she finishes stoking the coal stove, her mother is going to scrub her head at the kitchen sink with Octogon Laundry Soap. It's going to be awful, but it'll be worse if they find nits in her hair. Last year Shirley Fogel had nits, and they sent her home from school to get her hair washed with kerosene. She smelled terrible for days, which was sad because Shirley has hardly any friends anyway—probably because of her mother. She saw Shirley's mother once in the Sunrise Cafeteria on Broadway, sitting by a table in front of the window; she had on bright red lipstick and rouge and was smoking a cigarette and her fat legs were spread out and her dress was so high up you could see her garters. She couldn't believe it was really Mrs. Fogel (she looked so different Open School Week). When she first heard about Shirley's mother—that she let men do it to her for money —she didn't know exactly what the men did, only that it was something dirty. Now she's sure she knows.

Esther turns to look at her mother who is moving briskly about the kitchen. She sees the clean apron, the work-bruised hands. Her mother stops to roll up the sleeves of her sweater—her arms, creamy and smooth and elegant, glow in the dim light.

When she is told to bend down over the sink, Esther complies without fussing. Shockingly hot water is poured over her head, but she doesn't let out her customary yelp. Her mother rubs the large bar of soap hard against her scalp and then scrubs with her strong fingers and it hurts. Esther remains silent. Mingled with the harsh odor of the brown soap is the smell of her mother's body—milky and good, and the full breasts brushing against her back feel so soft. When she is satisfied that she has routed any suspicion of uncleanliness from her daughter's head, her mother stands before her, rubbing a towel through her hair. Esther sees the set mouth, the eyes flashing with fierce determination. Suddenly, Esther reaches up and quickly kisses each moist cheek. Her mother looks surprised, but then she smiles—her blue eyes shimmer and her cheeks become shiny little apples.

13

The silver bells are still strung along the corridor walls, red and green streamers swing from the ceiling, and wreaths still hang on the doors. But inside the classrooms, children are peeling trees and stars and Santa Clauses off the windows. Christmas is over.

Esther unsticks her tree very carefully so it doesn't tear. She lays it on her desk, admires it for a while, and then slides it inside her notebook. Millie walks by her desk and mumbles, "I threw mine away." She would! Of course, Millie's right—Jewish kids shouldn't make Christmas trees in school, but it isn't so terrible; it's not like making a cross. It's funny.... Millie is the only one in the class who makes such a fuss about it and her family isn't even religious. Sometimes I think she's jealous because my family is—the way she's always asking about Hebrew school and about what happens at a Seder and how whenever she comes over, that noticeable way she stops at the door to kiss the mezuzah. Then there was the time she came over when Mama was making challah. She kept standing in the kitchen watching Mama's floury hands roll the long cords of dough, and braid them and brush them with egg white. And while the challah was baking, Millie kept saying how good the house smelled, and she kept going back into the kitchen asking if the challah was ready. When it finally came out of the oven, high and glistening and golden, Millie was so excited—like it was some kind of miracle.

Esther slides her Christmas tree out of her notebook and looks at it again. It's *so* pretty. But it really is a goyishe thing; she shouldn't bring it home. She folds it slowly, under her desk, over and over. On the way to Assembly, she'll drop it in the waste basket.

She's glad her class goes to Assembly today; she likes wearing the same clothes as all the other girls. Everyone is always complimenting her on the dresses her mother makes, but she likes how she looks in her navy blue skirt, white middy, and red neckerchief—she looks more American.

Miss McKeon claps her hands for everyone to sit down. Then she opens her roll book and begins calling out their thirty-eight names. Each of them calls back "Present!" except Tommy Ryan and Charlotte Berger who are absent. Then Miss McKeon wants them to sit up straight and tall with hands clasped on the desk. When she is satisfied that all the heads and hands are how and where they should be, she tells them about filing through the halls to Assembly *quietly*, how they must set an example, how they must remember that they are not the other 6As, they are the 6A1! And anyone who expects not only to be promoted to 6B but to stay in the *one* class should remember that both work *and* conduct count. They are grown up now, she tells them, after 6B comes junior high, and to remember that when selections are made for the Rapid Advance Classes, not only work but *conduct* will count!

Esther is eager to go on to junior high, but she will miss P.S. 19. She will *not* miss Miss McKeon with her lipless mouth and her icy little eyes behind the pince-nez glasses and the curly blond wig that looks silly over her puffy face with all the powder on it. She doesn't imagine Miss McKeon will miss her either, or any of them except maybe some of the boys—of course Tommy Ryan who's her pet and David Stern because he's so good-looking. When Lila was in her class, Miss McKeon must have liked *her*—she still asks, "How is that pretty sister of yours?" When she told Lila what Miss McKeon said, Lila looked pleased at first, but then she said Miss McKeon was stupid, that she used to keep asking, "Are you sure your name is Hirsch, not Hennessey?"

Without its silver tinsel and green wreaths and the sprigs of holly, the auditorium looks bare. The boys and girls (the boys in dark pants, white shirts, and red ties) shuffle in to the tune of "Semper Fidelis" which Mrs. Marx is pounding out on the piano. When all the classes are assembled, she stops pounding. There is a moment or two of wiggling and whispering, then an ear-splitting, thundering chord. All signs of life stop. Mrs. Marx launches into "The Stars and Stripes Forever," and the Color Guards, stiff and solemn and shining with pride, come marching down the aisle, and the American flag is placed in its holder on the side of the stage opposite the school's blue and gold flag. Everyone salutes the flag and the auditorium fills with the rise and fall of more than a thousand voices pledging allegiance. Next Mrs. Marx strikes up "The Star-Spangled Banner." Esther doesn't understand about "the twilight's last gleaming," but "the rockets' red glare" and "the bombs bursting in air" remind her of fireworks on the Fourth of July. She loves this part of Assembly. But now, it becomes different. Mrs. Lowell, the principal, picks up her black Bible with the cross on the cover and reads from the book of Matthew. "Then said Jesus unto his disciples, 'If *any* man will come after me, let him deny himself, and take up his cross, and follow me. For whosoever will save his life shall lose it: and whosoever will lose his life for my sake shall find it. For what is a man profited, if he shall gain the whole world, and lose his own soul? or what shall a man give. . . .' " At the mention of Jesus, Esther feels something shrink inside her. She is there illicitly. They will discover she's a fake. She won't be allowed to come to their school anymore. She'll be kicked out of the Christmas parties. They'll make her give back the Christmas present Miss Kelly gave her in 3A. That was the best of all the Christmas parties. They didn't have just candy canes and cookies; Miss Kelly brought in Dixie cups, and everyone got a present. She got quivery inside while she was untying the green ribbon. Then she opened the box and lifted the tissue paper and saw the little cups and saucers—white with tiny yellow flowers around their edges, and a small fat teapot, and a sugar bowl with its own little cover, and the dainty milk pitcher. Hers was the nicest present in the whole class; she felt a little funny about it. They said it was because she was the smartest girl in the class, but she thought maybe it was because she was the poorest. She walked home from school that day very slowly and carefully, hugging her beautiful dishes. She couldn't believe they were really hers.

Maybe it was a sin to keep that present. She wishes Mrs. Lowell would put down that Bible so she can't see the big silver cross on the cover. She feels her face get hot. It happens every time. It's even worse when they sing "Come All Ye Faithful," and she gets to ". . . Christ the Lord"; she can't sing those words and she has to move her mouth to make it look like she is. She knows she's not the only one; whenever the singing fades and words get slurred, the teacher's eyes start sliding around to see who's responsible.

Finally, Mrs. Lowell sits down. Now Miss Donnelly walks onto the center of the stage and raises her baton. At least they won't sing Christmas songs today, but they could still sing "Onward Christian Soldiers" and come to that part about the cross of Jesus. Miss Donnelly nods to

Mrs. Marx who promptly pounds out the first few bars of "Mine eyes have seen the glory of the coming of the Lord...." It's one of Esther's favorites and she sings loudly through all the Glory Glory Hallelujahs. She isn't sure which Lord the song is about, theirs or hers, but it doesn't matter; there are none of those words in this one. Next they sing "Abide with Me," which is another nice one. Esther feels better now. The last song is "Rally 'Round the Flag."

After they are seated, Mrs. Lowell announces the Elocution Contest which will take place in three weeks. She explains that it would be lovely if all the boys and girls could participate, but since that is not possible, contestants will be selected by their teachers. Everyone in Esther's class looks at David Stern. They *know* Miss McKeon will pick him. Even though Julius Ginsberg has a louder voice and reads with more expression, she still picked David for the biggest part in their Assembly play, Philip Nolan in *Man Without a Country*—probably because Julius is small and skinny and wears glasses. Then Mrs. Lowell talks about the hair examinations for the 6As which is why the Assembly must be short today and how she hopes *her* boys and girls have immaculate heads. She wants P.S. 19 to have a perfect record!

Some classes are going to have their hair examined by their teachers, but Miss McKeon told them she has never examined hair, and she doesn't intend to start with *them*. Esther felt dirty. Then she went on, telling them about not being nervous. When she said she was sure no one in *her* class would dream of coming to school with filthy hair, her eyebrows went up and her eyes settled on Shirley Fogel; she must have heard about last year. Shirley's sallow face shut up tight and her eyes got glassy.

Now all you can hear are their pencils scratching, their

erasers rubbing, and the ticking of the clock on the wall. Many of them have had to "leave the room." Others reach up from time to time and touch their hair. Any minute they will be taken to the nurse's office. Meanwhile, they are doing the arithmetic problems Miss McKeon put on the board. Here and there a seat squeaks when someone squirms. Suddenly, Miss McKeon starts snapping her fingers and telling them to pass their papers forward. At once!

Before they leave the room, Miss McKeon warns them about absolute silence when they pass through the corridors. Other classes will be working and must not be disturbed. "Remember! Absolute silence!" Esther wonders why Miss McKeon is forever warning them about silence. The worst thing anyone does in public school is whisper once in a while. Even the boys never make noise or act wild like in Hebrew school.

Outside the nurse's office, they are divided into dozens and instructed to enter a dozen at a time. The others are to wait, *silently* against the corridor wall. "After you have been seen, you are to come out and stand *silently* against the opposite wall."

So far, there have been no nits. Everyone has come out heaving an ostentatious sigh of relief. Miss McKeon has been pacing up and down between the walls, her wary little eyes shifting from side to side. Esther is in the third dozen, waiting her turn. Shirley Fogel is standing next to her. Suddenly, Esther sees horrified faces across the corridor and feels her shoes being splattered. She springs away. Urine is streaming down between Shirley's legs. Miss McKeon comes rushing over, her pince-nez have fallen off, her face is moving in all directions. She tries to grab Shirley without stepping in the puddle, but her arms are too short. You can tell she wants to scream, but the other classes are working and must not be disturbed.

She hisses at Shirley. "You dirty girl! You filthy thing! Get out of here! Move! Get your things and leave this building! Go home and stay there!"

Shirley sloshes through the puddle. Her legs are apart. Her stockings are soaking wet.

The tongue depressor running along her scalp makes her shiver. Esther feels her hair being parted this way and that way. She is scared. She focuses her eyes on the nurse's pink neck, but she keeps seeing Shirley standing in the hall and peeing on the floor. The nurse is smiling and saying, "Such a nice clean head! I can still smell the good strong soap." Esther smiles back. She's glad she doesn't have nits, and the nurse likes the way her head smells, but she's still seeing Shirley.

When she comes out, everyone is standing against one wall, staring across at the puddle of pee. The boys' mouths are slithering. Some girls are biting their lips. Miss McKeon's glasses are back on, but her powder seems to have blown off; her face is red, and her eyes are rolling around like little marbles.

At last, it's all over. No one in their class has nits. While they wait for David to come back with the janitor, eyes keep returning to Shirley's puddle. The janitor, with David strutting beside him, comes down the hall carrying a pail in one hand and a mop in the other. Miss McKeon thanks God he's come, then leads the way as they file back to the classroom. This time there is whispering in the line. Twice, Miss McKeon stops, turns around, and glares.

Esther and Millie walk home together for lunch. They are quiet until Millie says, "I *despise* Miss McKeon!" Esther says nothing. The whole morning was awful. Miss McKeon kept being in a terrible mood. They were taking turns reading aloud from *Tales of Young Americans*. Peter, the boy in the story, was going fishing when Julius Ginsberg peered up through his glasses and raised his hand. Miss McKeon glanced at him and said, "No, Julius, you may not leave the room." But Julius said he did not want to leave the room, he wanted to know what "tackle" was. Miss McKeon's eyebrows jumped up. "Who would like to tell Julius what tackle is?" No hands went up. Miss McKeon's mouth got crooked. "Come now, any fool knows what tackle is!" But no one seemed to know. Nathan Weiss raised his hand, timidly. "I think it's something you do in football." Miss McKeon looked disgusted. "Football?" she shrieked. "This story is not about football! It's about fishing! Fishing! Think! Think!" She turned to John Coppolla. "John, don't *you* know?" John shook his head. Miss McKeon took one of her deep, despairing breaths. "It's too bad Tommy is absent today," she sighed. "*He'd* know." The lunch bell rang. Miss McKeon said wearily that she'd tell them about tackle in the afternoon.

Esther recalls the time in 2B when no one knew what a rake was for and Miss Kelly was surprised. But she didn't look disgusted with them. Actually, Miss Kelly looked a little sad while she explained it to them. Esther wonders why Miss McKeon thought that John, and certainly Tommy, would know about tackle. It must be something Christian or not kosher.

14

A TO LET sign is pasted in the window of Mr. Lieberman's store, and her father is outside, fluttering about the son who keeps tightening his camel's hair belt and turning his head away. Her father looks like a clown, Esther thinks. He looks like Charlie Chaplin trying to get in good with a big shot. The son has completed the required period of mourning and is going home. As he picks up his valise, her father takes him by the shoulder and speaks up into the smoke of his cigar. "What's your hurry?" he asks. "Another hour and you can daven Mincha Maariv and say Kaddish with the minyan. How can it hurt you? Believe me, for such a handsome young man a wife will wait." The son smiles, but lifts her father's hand from his shoulder. Esther winces. Her father puts his hand in his pocket and moves back a step. His eyes are huge. He has stopped fluttering. "Go," he says. "Go in good health." Esther feels something like a bone sticking in her throat. She squeezes the money her mother gave her for a measure cream and a pound pot cheese and runs to the grocery store.

Melnick is behind the counter with his red beard spread out and his big white apron tied around his fat stomach. He is counting out a dozen rolls for a customer, a man in a lumberjacket—the same man who came looking for his dollar on Mr. Lieberman's counter. Melnick finishes counting the rolls but keeps holding on to the bag. He is talking his head off. His English is terrible, but that doesn't stop him. She can't believe it; he's commiserating with the man about that dollar. Melnick, who Mama says you gotta watch he doesn't put his finger on the scale, you should see the measure is full to the top before he pours the cream. Melnick, of all people, saying how terrible it is there are thieves everywhere. Well, he should know! Maybe people who are dishonest themselves think that everyone else is too—so they don't feel guilty. But Melnick really is mean. When kids come into the store and stand in front of the cookie bins and can't decide if they want to spend their penny on a round marshmallow sandwich one or a long, skinny chocolate-covered one, Melnick always comes rushing over to tell them to hurry up. He's afraid if he takes his eyes off them for one minute, they'll steal a cookie. Some of them do steal sometimes. Once, she almost stole a marshmallow sandwich; it looked so good, but also she wanted to trick Melnick. She wishes she hadn't lost her nerve. When is Melnick going to stop blabbing? And his voice is so loud—up and down, up and down. Another customer comes in, a small pretty woman with a Pekingese dog. Melnick gives her a big hello, gives the man in the lumberjacket his rolls and his change, and asks the woman what he can do for her today. Before the woman can speak, Esther bursts out, "It's *my next!*" She grips the counter, trembling. He's not going to do that to her again! And she lets her dollar bill show so he'll see she's not buying on trust this time. Melnick's mouth drops open, but his eyes slide over the dollar bill. Looking at the small pretty woman, he tosses his head in Esther's direction. "That's some mouth," he says. Esther keeps holding on to the counter. If she lets go, she'll jump up and scratch him.

Melnick looks down at her. His eyes are insulting, while his voice oozes out. "All right, tzatzkele, what would you like to have today?" Esther hesitates. If she tries to talk, she might cry. She mustn't. She mustn't cry! Hoping her

111

eyes are scorching him, she raps out what she wants. As Melnick turns his back to ladle the cream from the vat, Esther suddenly smiles with satisfaction; she has spoken up—for the first time. She didn't let somebody treat her like a dummy—or like a beggar. She didn't hold in her hurt. She opened her mouth and let it come out. Oh, how good it feels! She watches Melnick lower the dipper into the cream. She raises herself on tiptoe to see if it's full before he pours it into the container. If it isn't, she'll tell him. Yes, she will. Melnick seems to be moving awkwardly, as if he knows she's watching and she'll start screaming and hollering if he tries anything funny. When he brings up the dipper, he even turns toward her a little so she can see he's giving her a full measure. Esther keeps her eyes nailed to the measure while Melnick turns it upside down and holds it over the container until the last drop has dripped in. Yes, he knows she's watching. Next he takes up a scoopful of pot cheese and dumps it into another container. Esther stares fixedly at his hands as he places the container on the scale. His fingers seem to jump away immediately as if the scale is hot. Esther watches him rubbing his hands up and down along his apron while he waits for the numbers on the scale to stop jiggling. It's like he's having trouble keeping his hands where they belong, she thinks. The pot cheese is short two ounces. Esther's eyes leap from the scale to Melnick's face. She looks straight into his eyes. He scoops up more pot cheese and dumps it into the container. "All right?" he smirks. "All right," Esther says. She hardly recognizes her voice; it's so sharp and clear. The grocer covers the containers and puts them in a bag. Esther shoves her dollar across the counter and waits for change. The lady with the Pekingese dog must have been watching everything; she smiles approvingly at Esther. "You're some kid," she says. Esther smiles back. Melnick slams her change down on the counter. She looks up at him. His blue eyes have turned black. Esther shudders; she has made an enemy.

Outside, the wind is rumbling. It is only four o'clock in the afternoon, but suddenly dark. The street is empty. The streetlamps are still off and windows are unlit. The buildings look uninhabited, desolate hollow skeletons with gaping eye sockets. Huddling over her paper bag and clenching her fist over her change, Esther hurries past them. A garbage can has been blown over. Averting her eyes from the gutted grapefruit rinds and the mauled meat bones, she runs toward her house.

She is still standing in her coat and shivering after her mother has put the cardboard containers away in the wooden box outside the kitchen window.

"What's the matter?" her mother asks. "Why are you standing there shivering? Is it so cold outside?"

"No, it's not so cold. It's nothing. Nothing's the matter," Esther says, and goes to hang up her coat. She hates Melnick. She hates him like poison.

"I have to eat soon," she snaps at her mother when she comes back in. "I have to be in Talmud Torah by six o'clock. Remember!"

Her mother glares at her. "To whom are you speaking like that? What's the matter with you?"

"Nothing is the matter with me. I'm just *reminding* you."

"Such reminding I can do without!"

"All right, all right," Esther mutters, opening her Chumish. It's not her mother's fault. Why is she taking it out on her? She tries to read that night's assignment, but can't concentrate; by the time she gets to the end of a page, she's forgotten the beginning. Yesterday was her first day back in Hebrew school after her sickness. She expected everyone would act surprised to see her, but it was like nobody even noticed that she was absent for a whole week.

113

Only Thelma Halperin said anything about it. Mr. Podoloff sneaked a look at her when she came in, but acted like nothing had happened either. Not that she can imagine Mr. Podoloff saying something really nice to anybody, like "We missed you" or "How do you feel?" He seems scared of Irving Greenhouse. He didn't call on him once yesterday, or even look at him. And Irving kept his head down all the time, like he didn't want to see Mr. Podoloff either. Thelma told her Irving didn't want to come back after that time, but his father made him. I can understand how come Irving is so fresh. If I were a boy, I'd be fresh a lot. If you're a girl and you act fresh, the other girls think you're terrible. But if you're a boy, the other boys think you're funny and you have guts and they all want to be your friend. Nobody's fresh to Miss McKeon; everybody's afraid of her. Someday I'm not going to worry whether Miss McKeon likes me or not. I'm just going to tell her off! Esther smiles to herself. Wouldn't Miss McKeon be surprised? Her eyes would pop out of her head. Maybe she'd start jumping up and down, and her wig would fall off, and she'd stand there in front of the whole class—bald, with her eyes popping out. Esther laughs out loud.

Her mother stares at her. "What is with you?" she asks.

"Nothing," Esther says, still giggling. "Nothing." She opens her dikdook notebook to a fresh page and, running her pencil slowly down the edge of her ruler, draws straight, evenly spaced lines for her verb conjugations. She can hear the wind outside growing louder. "I think it's going to snow," she says.

Her mother pours broad yellow noodles into a pot of boiling water. Then she goes to the window and looks out. "It's snowing already," she says, "and the wind is strong. It looks like a blizzard. You'll stay home tonight."

"But Ma!"

"What Ma? You'll stay home and that's all."

Esther appreciates her mother's persistent fear of snowstorm (she has often wondered what her brother who died in that blizzard would be like), but she doesn't want to stay home. She doesn't have a new library book, the stories in the Books of Knowledge she knows practically by heart, the poems too; she's not in the mood for the other parts. Lila will probably be doing her homework or something, and Ben will go up to his room and close the door. Even Papa is gloomy lately.

She can hear the men coming in upstairs, stamping the snow off their feet, coughing, and clearing their throats. Her eyes are tired from reading and writing in the kitchen's smoky ochre light. The heat from the coal stove against her sweater is making her back itch. Every time the door opens upstairs, it lets in the clean, bracing smell of the snow. She waits for the door to open again, but it doesn't. She wants to go out. "Maybe, the snow'll stop soon and I can go," she says to her mother.

"This snow is not stopping so soon. Go look," her mother tells her.

Esther stands on tiptoe and wipes the fog from the dining room window. The snow is coming down hard, slashing the air sideways. The wind squeals, sweeps the snow up into the air, and swirls it around. She doesn't want to go out anymore, and she wishes Lila and Ben would come home. The snow is almost blinding. Suddenly, there is someone standing in front of the house. It's her father. For a few moments, he stands erect, casting his great head about, like a bear sniffing the air for quarry. The wind whips at his unbuttoned coat. Then he begins to stalk back and forth, with his head thrust forward, butting like a bull into thick white gusts. "Mama," Esther calls, "come quick! Papa's walking around outside with his coat open!"

Her mother rushes to the window. "God in heaven!" she groans.

"What is he looking for?" Esther asks.

Her mother stands nodding her head knowingly, as

though witnessing the derangement that must inevitably come from stubborn adherence to faith and optimism in the face of impending disaster. When she speaks, the air about her becomes heavy with the portent of new and increasing misery. "He's looking for the Messiah," she says.

Esther feels a stirring of panic. "Please Mama! Tell me!"

"Go upstairs, Esther," her mother tells her. "See how many men are in the shul."

Esther dashes up the steps, flings open the synagogue door, and counts. Eight. She runs down calling, "Eight, Mama! Eight!"

Her mother is still standing by the window, clutching herself and rocking back and forth. "Eight and Papa make nine," she says. "Thank God he needs only one more. After all, how many Messiahs can there be frolicking about in a blizzard?"

Dismayed by the mocking complacency in her mother's voice, Esther says, "But he'll get sick."

"So he'll get sick," her mother says. "What can I do?"

"He'll get sick!" Esther shouts.

Wearily, her mother turns and looks at her. "You're right. He must come in," she sighs. "Go Esther. Dress yourself warmly and go outside. Tell him." And as Esther leaves to get her coat and hat, her mother cries out after her, "Tell him I said to come in! To come in this minute!"

The wind slaps against the window. The cold air cuts through the cracks and creeps over her. Malka covers her chest with her hands. Outside, the same wind is clawing at her husband. Pity and scorn come painfully together inside her. Anguish and bitterness. Madman that he is! Stubborn ox! Tormented creature! Look at him! Scouring the streets like a scavenger! For what? For some miserable wretch who will save the world. God in heaven, what kind of horror have you created that enslaves men's minds to such senselessness? Tell me, what is so sacred about a minyan? Who are your ten righteous men? They are Melnick, the thief! They are a rabbi with a false soul and an overstuffed stomach—a Hungarian pig who pays Melnick to sell aliyahs for him on Shabbes! Who but a pig would promote the sale of blessings over your holy Torah on the Sabbath? And my husband must look on and be silent. Oh, the shame you heap on him. How helpless you have made him. Look at him! With clenched fists, Malka pounds at herself. Master of the Universe, how I detest the absurdities and the delusions! How I detest that mockery of a rabbi with his pious eyes and his rotting house with its rats! Tell me, God, has my life not been plagued enough? Must you now send vermin to defile me with their filthy eyes? Malka shudders with revulsion. If once more she encounters that vile gray beast lurking in the corner of her kitchen, she will scream blasphemies! She will curse God! Trembling with sudden terror, Malka leaves the window and returns to her boiling noodles to stir them so they will not stick.

Esther steps out onto the sidewalk. The snow stings her face. Her father is alone in the empty street, standing firm-footed against the lashing wind, his face upturned as though, the streets having yielded him nothing, he is now searching the sky. His lashes and brows have grown white; his coat is furling and flying out behind him. He reminds her of the picture of Moses in the Manischewitz Haggada. She runs to him. "Papa, Papa, come inside! Close your coat. Mama said you should come inside!"

Her father stares down at her. His eyes are watering, but his voice is strong. "What is the matter?" he asks. "Why are you here? Go back inside!"

"Mama sent me," Esther tells him. "She said you should come in this minute."

"This minute? She sent you? Tell her I'll come when I'll come."

"Papa, please!" Esther begs.

But her father is squinting into the distance. Suddenly, he lurches away from her. She runs after him. Something is hurtling toward them. It is a man, hunched up and bent over like an animal carrying a huge, invisible burden. Her father rushes up to him and seizes his arm. The man recoils; his eyes leap with fear. Her father pulls the man under the lamplight, peers into his face, and asks in English, "You Jew?" The man does not speak. He keeps shivering. Her father asks again, "Jewish? You Jewish?" The man's eyes bulge, and his jaw begins to quiver, but he does not speak. He keeps clutching his coat, trying to keep it closed. Esther stares in disbelief at the ugliness before her. A huge elongated head is perched on a narrow neck that is so long she can see the sharp bump of his Adam's apple above the top of his upturned coat collar which he is holding together with a bony fist. His coat is too big for him, and the top and middle buttons are missing. His shoes have no laces. He has no hat on, and the snow is splattering on his hair and dribbling down his forehead onto his nose which droops like a broken limb down to his mouth. Thick black hairs hang from his nostrils. His cheeks are pitted and pustuled and dark with stubble. He is like something patched together from what others have despised and discarded. Her father, as if to reassure him, jabs at his own chest and says, "I Jew." Then he pokes at the man's chest and asks again, "You Jew?"

The man opens his mouth as if to speak, but remains soundless as he points a finger into his open mouth and shakes his head back and forth.

"No Jewish?" her father asks, his voice faltering.

The man nods his head vigorously up and down. Then he points into his mouth again and shakes his head back and forth again. Her father stares bewildered until the man, as if in enormous pain and desperation, throws back his head and with his mouth wide open grimaces in a ghastly way, as if he were howling. Yet no sound emerges. But the man has made his meaning plain. He is a mute. Now her father begins vigorously nodding up and down and pointing to his own head to indicate he understands. And as the man does not appear deaf, her father asks again, "You Jewish?" And the man's head moves up and down—frantically.

Her father brings forth his warmest, most engaging smile. "You come with me daven. You come pray. Shul! There!" he says, pointing to their house. Esther wonders why her father assumes he must speak English to the Jewish mute? Looking pleadingly into the mute's eyes, her father repeats, "Pray. Shul."

The mute looks confused.

Her father tries again. He tilts an invisible glass into his mouth. "Whiskey," he says. "Cake," and he rubs his hand over his belly.

The mute breaks into a gummy grin. His teeth are large and yellow. His head is moving up and down. Yes, yes, he understands. He will come.

Her father is overjoyed. Wrapping an arm around the strange man's shoulder, he leads him to their house and up the steps. Esther scurries behind them. Then she stands in the hall watching while her father places a yarmulka on the man's head and takes him into the synagogue past the gaping faces of the other congregants. Mr. Shleeman cringes quietly. Melnick gasps. Her father turns and glowers at him. And he seats the mute on a bench. The sudden warmth after the cold has painted comical pink spots on the mute's cheeks and drawn mucus from his nose. With a swift sweep of his coat sleeve, he wipes his nose. Her father flinches, but resolutely places an open Siddur in the speechless man's hands and points to the place. The mute smiles idiotically up into her father's face, shrugging his shoulders and shaking his head from side to side. He cannot read. Her father's face darkens but he pats the mute reassuringly on the back and walks away to his own seat. The service begins.

Esther cannot tear herself away from the synagogue door. She is both repelled and fascinated. There is something horribly warped in what she is seeing. It is not only the disgusting appearance of the man himself. Something more complicated keeps struggling to come to the front of her mind. Suddenly, her heart contracts. This tenth man, this voiceless creature, so vile-looking as to seem barely human, is sitting in Mr. Lieberman's seat! She remains standing at the open door, looking from the small black yarmulka incongruously stuck on the huge wet head to the snot-stained sleeve to the Siddur lying limply beneath the black fingernails. Her father motions to her to close the door; she is letting in the cold air.

Downstairs, Lila has come home and is hungrily plunging her fork into a plate heaped with broad yellow noodles smothered in pot cheese and sour cream. She looks up and smiles when Esther enters; her face is flushed, and her lips are shiny and smeared with cream. She looks funny and lovely and exudes a glorious sense of well-being. As Esther looks at Lila's friendly, welcoming face, the gloom that has been gripping her becomes lighter. She tells her mother only that her father has come in with a man for the minyan. Then she sits down and waits for her supper. She does not want to tell about the mute. She does not want to think about what has happened, lest she find herself again in that abyss of confusion and frightening conjectures. As she eats her supper, the golden buttery smell of the noodles and the good taste of the melting cheese and the rich cream soothe and comfort her. And she feels a strange sense of wonder at how the growing warmth and fullness inside her is softening the edges of her bewilderment.

They have both finished eating by the time Ben comes home. The cold air has brought color to his face, and his eyes sparkle with a rare animation. There is a buoyancy in his step as he enters the kitchen and hands each of his sisters a package. Both of them look at him, puzzled and expectant, but he says only, "Open them."

Lila quickly unties the string and unfolds the brown paper. "Oh, how beautiful!" she exclaims, holding up a long flowered cotton housecoat. "How gorgeous! Thank you! Thank you, Ben," and she gives her brother a hug.

Esther fumbles with her package. She is both anxious and reluctant to find out what is inside. If she's disappointed, Ben will notice and feel bad. Please be something I'll love, she prays. She unties the string and bends back the paper. There is a flash of brilliant blue and then a glimmer of white. It's a raincape! A beautiful rubber raincape! Just like Millie's! Only nicer. The blue is deeper and it has a hood with a scalloped white border. She can't believe it! "Ben," she squeals, "Ben, is this really for me?"

"No," Ben laughs, "it's for your Aunt Tillie."

"But why?" Esther asks.

"Yes, how come?" Lila joins in. "Why are we getting presents?"

"Because I was promoted to the stockroom and I saw these and I figured I'd better buy them before the spring orders start coming in. That's why."

"I hope it fits!" Lila calls out as she dashes out of the room and runs upstairs.

Carefully, Esther places the raincape over her shoulders and the hood over her head. "How do I look?" she asks Ben.

"Like a bunny rabbit," he says.

Esther laughs and turns to her mother. "How do I look?" she asks. Her mother smiles. Kisses seem to spring from her eyes, but she remains standing where she is. "Nice. Very nice," she says.

"Go upstairs and see for yourself," Ben says.

Esther reaches up and flings her arms around Ben's neck. She kisses him on the cheek and whispers into his ear, "Thank you, Ben. I love you so much." And she runs from the room.

In response to his mother's questioning look, Ben explains in Yiddish about the presents and his promotion, adding, "I'll be making two dollars more a week."

Malka smiles and says, "Dahnk Gott," and tells her son to sit down, his supper is ready.

Upstairs, Lila is pirouetting before the mirror. Her new long housecoat is turquoise with pink and yellow roses. It hugs her waist and then fans out, sweeping the floor as she swirls about. "Isn't it gorgeous?" she asks as Esther enters. "It fits perfectly."

"It's beautiful," Esther agrees. "But isn't it a little too long?"

Lila climbs up on the bed so she can see herself full length in the mirror. "No, I love it this way," she says.

"But you might trip," Esther says.

"Oh, for God's sake, I'm not gonna trip," Lila says, stepping off the bed and seeing Esther for the first time standing there in her new raincape. For a moment, Lila looks surprised. Then she comes over and closes the snap of the hood under Esther's chin. "You're supposed to close it, dummy," she says. "Now, go look at yourself."

Esther stands before the mirror. Her eyes look bluer, and the white border hugging her face makes it look rosy.

"You look pretty," Lila says softly. "You really look pretty."

Esther slides between the icy bed sheet and the freezing cold comforter. She lies shivering until gradually the bedding takes on the warmth of her body and gives it back. She is both exhausted and excited, her senses still throbbing from the alternating assaults and caresses they have received. Her mind keeps retracing its way back and forth over the extraordinary, turbulent day. How at each point when the intensity of an emotion threatened to become unbearable, the poignancy was suddenly diminished—because unpredictable things happened, like Lila's welcoming smile and Ben's presents and his cheerfulness. She suspects that a new dimension has been added to her awareness, that somehow her perception has been altered. But when she tries to sort out pieces and threads and to decipher particular meanings, everything becomes tangled, and she finds herself becoming afraid again. Sitting up in the dark, she reaches forward until her fingers feel the smooth rubber of her new raincape. She has laid it out across the footrail of the bed so she will see it the minute she wakes up in the morning.

15

The mute comes again the next day at dusk and the next, and sits dumb and dirty through the service, waiting for his whiskey and cake. And Zalman gives it to him and watches while he chews, licks the crumbs from his fingers, and gulps down two shot glasses of whiskey. When he holds out his hand a third time, Zalman says, "No! Enough!" And the mute smiles agreeably and goes away. Zalman goes downstairs and sits with his head in his hands, trying to encompass what has befallen him. God has sent him a golem. What does it mean? Is it a sign of grace or of mockery? Zalman does not know. He dare not tell his wife about the dumb creature with the hairy running nostrils who sits stupidly through the service waiting for whiskey and for her honey cake which he munches like a horse with his huge yellow teeth. She would be filled with revulsion, and, even if she were to remain silent, her eyes would be debasing.

Zalman presses his hands to his temples. He does not understand, and his ignorance frightens him. What will come of this? Will the mute continue to come when the air is warm again and he can find sustenance elsewhere? And what of the others? How long will they put up with the abomination that sits among them like an equal? Shleeman is afraid of him, and Melnick has already expressed his anger. "Better no one," he blustered, "than a filthy animal! I will not have it!" Oh God in heaven, Zalman beseeches, is it wrong to bring a Jew from the cold into the warmth of a place of worship? But as the words form in his head, Zalman's heart knows their falseness. It was not out of the goodness of his heart that he brought in the mute from the cold, but out of his own need. But who else do I have? Lieberman lies buried in the ground and has left no replacement—only a son whose eyes spit contempt. And when I am buried in the ground, will you grant that my son replace me? Zalman sighs deeply and lifts his eyes heavenward. Forgive me, God! Who am I to ask? Sinful man that I am. You have sent me a man to preserve the mitzva of the minyan, and I am grateful.

But why God, why a golem? Why have you even wrought such a creature? Tell me. To save me? To torment me? Why?

Malka serves supper to her husband and sees that he sits troubled and eats with no appetite. "What is with you? Are you not well?" she asks.

"What should be with me? Why am I not well? See how I eat and drink like a healthy ox. I am well!" Zalman declares.

Malka shrugs her shoulders. "All right. As long as you say so, it is so," she says sarcastically and returns to her chores.

Zalman looks at her broad back, set like a wall between them. "As though you care!" he bursts out. "You care if I am well? You care about me like one cares for a dead dog! What do you care about, wretched woman? If you had it your way, you would not even be here. And your precious son could grow up fatherless as well as Godless."

Malka's face is fierce as she turns toward her husband. "What are you ranting about now, madman?" she rasps.

"Look! Look at her innocence. She doesn't know. How should she know about a wife who would desert her husband?"

"Oh God," Malka moans, "how long must I endure this? How many more times must this be thrown up to me? What have I done to provoke this?"

"Nothing! You have done nothing!" Zalman shouts. "You are an angel to endure me! Look, people! Behold an angel! A mother who turns her son from the path of the Torah. Is she not virtuous?"

"Why?" Malka's voice is hoarse with apprehension. "Why do you speak suddenly of my son? What has happened to him?"

"Nothing! Nothing has happened to your son! I am mad! I am out of my senses!" Zalman roars. And he falls suddenly silent, trembling with the terrifying awareness of where his desolation and his confusion have taken him.

Malka grips the back of a chair and asks again, "What is the matter? Benjamin has not come home yet from work? Has something happened?"

"No, no, foolish woman," Zalman says wearily, "your treasure will soon arrive. I am tired. I am going up to bed. Don't worry. All will be well."

Malka watches, mystified, as her husband leaves the room. She hears him mutter as he ascends the steps, "God will help. All will be well."

16

The snow has turned to ice and all week, late each afternoon, the mute has appeared, shivering and blue with cold, and Zalman has taken him in.

It is Friday morning, a warm sun blooms in the sky, and the snow is beginning to melt. Zalman sits in the kitchen, lingering over his glass of tea. The girls have gone off to school, and Ben has gone to work. He watches his wife make preparations for the Sabbath. She has already set the chicken to simmer on the range and placed the challah to bake in the oven. He looks at her strong, reddened hands as they gently form and pat the fish mixture into smooth ovals. Carefully, she places each one on a large wooden spoon and slides it into the kettle of boiling broth. He knows how delicious her fish will taste—so sweet, they melt in the mouth. The light falls on the whiteness of her forearms below her rolled-up sweater sleeves. How he loves the immaculate softness of her body! If only he could reach her heart. He aches with longing for her love, for her tender respect. If only he could reveal to her the heaviness in his heart. He has still told her nothing of the golem, the ugly mute who gobbles her cake with his great teeth. And now the holy Sabbath is approaching. What does such a creature know of the sanctity of the Sabbath? His very presence, unkempt and smelling like a dunghill, will be a desecration. And who knows what vile impropriety he will perform? The sun has grown warm; perhaps he will not seek the shelter of the synagogue. Perhaps he will find nourishment elsewhere. An awesome thought surfaces in Zalman's mind. Perhaps what he took for a man was not a man, but indeed a golem, and whatever power created it will destroy it. He recalls the stories of how in times of oppression, Talmudic saints had created such robots to be protectors of the Jews and how, with wonder-working words, endowed them with all signs of life, except the power of speech. Mutes! And the robot carried out the orders of his creator—but without will or reason.

No, it cannot be! Who? Who could have created his golem? Certainly not he. He was unworthy. He was nothing! Those to whom the power had been given were saints! Reb Dovidl of Dorbiczen. The holy Baal Shem Tov himself! And shuddering, Zalman remembers the famous story of Rabbi Judah Lowe of Prague, Der Hohe Lowe. It was a time of great peril for the Jews, and the divine voice ordered the rabbi to create a golem and revealed to him, in a dream, the life-giving formula. And the golem served the rabbi and protected the Jews from their enemies. And every Friday, for fear the golem would profane the Sabbath, Rabbi Lowe would remove from him the life-giving formula, leaving him a harmless hulk of clay. But one Friday the rabbi forgot to remove the magic formula and evening was approaching, and the rabbi, alarmed lest the golem desecrate the Sabbath, pursued him throughout the town and caught up with him outside the synagogue, and so terrified was he of the golem's potential sinfulness that he smashed him to pieces.

Zalman sits trembling. Dare he even think such a thing? On the Sabbath there can be a minyan without a golem— his son will worship with the congregation. Zalman prays for the dissolution of the golem. Then horrified by the audacity of what he has been thinking, he asks God to for-

he may have become, or how he had roared and thundered, on the Sabbath he was transformed and sang with jubilation. But tonight, instead of euphoria, there is a desperation in the way his eyes are shut so tight, as though determined not to see, and the veins in his neck seem to be straining with all their strength to express exultation appropriate to the Sabbath.

Throughout the remainder of the night and all of the Sabbath day, during the morning and afternoon and evening prayers, Zalman cannot tear his thoughts away from the strangeness of what has transpired. And what has *become* of the mute? Where *is* he? Are his needs being satisfied elsewhere? Will he come again? With trepidation, Zalman recalls his prayers for the destruction of a golem. Is such a thing possible? Could he have vanished from the face of the earth? And at each service of the Sabbath, Zalman sees his son walk to the last bench in the synagogue and take his place.

17

The Sabbath departs. The following morning there is no minyan. The Barchu and the Kdusha must be omitted from the service. Zalman's face is ashen as he thanks God that there are no mourners among them, for the Kaddish also may not be recited without a minyan. Drawing his tallis over his head, Zalman buries his face in its folds and praises God. He beseeches acceptance, deliverance from the power of sin, from scorn, from evil inclination. He asks the Lord "to remember to us the covenant of our fathers, as Abraham our father suppressed his compassion to his only son, and he wanted to slaughter him, in order to perform Thy will, so may Thy compassion suppress Thy anger against us." He acknowledges to the sovereign of all the worlds that the preeminence of man over beast is nought, for all is vanity before the Lord. And admitting his unworthiness, he pleads for mercy and for strength.

But after the prescribed prayers have been mumbled in the holy language, Zalman's heart remains heavy with unexpressed anguish, and he continues to stand and sway in silent supplication. He asks for understanding of all that has befallen him. He prays for parnussah—some kind of livelihood so he will not be shamed before people. He entreats God to still the anger rising in him against his son who sleeps upstairs disdainful of the Divine Presence. Painfully mindful of signs of sickness in his son, he asks for guidance. Keep me from casting him further away. Restrain my rage. Stay my hand. Help me to reconcile my love for my son with my obligation to you.

Zalman removes the phylacteries from his forehead and folds his prayer shawl. He is alone. The other congregants have all gone. He did not even hear them leave.

Downstairs, the house is silent. Malka must have gone out to market. Esther must already be in Talmud Torah. Such a wonder, his Esther, thin and gray like a sparrow, yet with eyes that take in the whole world. But without parnussah, what will he be able to do for her? Leah does not have Esther's mind, but she is a beauty. Only if what he suspects turns out to be true, let her beware. Zalman Hirsch's daughter will not disgrace him!

Zalman pours himself a glass of coffee from the pot on the range and butters himself a roll. How much longer can the shul provide him with a roof over his head? From where will a minyan come? Lieberman lies in the ground, Koopitz has one foot already in the other world; since his wife died, the Galitzianer's children are urging him to go to an old age home. Who will replace them? Their sons? As likely as yesterday becoming today. The Relief investigator told him that if he goes to work for the government, they will give him more money. But what kind of work? To dig with a shovel in the streets. He cannot bring himself to it. Perhaps he should dare to consider the Litvak's offer. What housewife would not buy fresh eggs straight from the farm and for cheaper than she pays that thief, Melnick? The Litvak will go himself with a truck to the country in the morning, and they will deliver the eggs the same day. The small overhead and the large volume of sales will compensate for the lower price. The Litvak needs a partner to invest; a truck costs. And who will give them credit right away? But Zalman has misgivings. Has he the nerve to go once again to his cousin, Sam Gittleson, for a loan? True, Sam is a wealthy man with a good heart. But he owes him yet from the other times. However, if with God's help this business succeeds, he'll be able to pay back everything. Zalman's face brightens. One must have hope. God will help.

Ben enters the kitchen carrying a rolled towel under his arm. He's going to the YMCA to wash himself among the goyim, Zalman thinks. How would it have hurt him to come down a little earlier and make a minyan, he wants to ask. But instead, he asks only "Have you prayed already?"

"Yes," Ben answers.

"Come sit down then," Zalman says. "I will make you a boiled egg."

"I've eaten," Ben says. "I'm going out."

Zalman stares in disbelief. When? When did he eat? Is it possible he was up early and stole past the synagogue door, quietly and deliberately to avoid coming in? Could Malka have served him his breakfast, knowing? It is too much to bear. He is afraid to let himself think. He is afraid of what he is feeling. He says nothing. The morning is unseasonably warm. Ben is in his shirtsleeves. Zalman finds his eyes trying to pierce the cloth of his son's shirt to see if he is wearing the fringed garment underneath. His heart pounds. He cannot be sure. He follows his son out to the hall and watches him put on his hat and coat. His suspicions are choking him, but he does not speak.

After Ben leaves, Zalman sits with his palms pressed to his temples, trying to still the turmoil in his head. Then, as though driven by the devil against his will, he rises and runs from the room and up the stairs. He throws open the door of Ben's room, hesitates, and then crosses the threshold. His eyes rest for a moment on the narrow, neatly made bed, then race across the rows of books, some arranged in a fruit crate on the floor, others held together by two bricks across the top of the bureau. One of the bureau drawers is not entirely closed. He moves toward it.

He pulls it open and rummages among its contents—folders with old school papers, pencils, a bottle of ink, a chessboard, and a box of chessmen. In the next drawer, there are shirts and two sweaters, nothing else. Zalman opens the bottom drawer. He looks through the socks, he lifts the underclothes. The frenzied movement stops. Wearily, he removes the tallis koton from beneath the undershorts.

Sitting down on his son's bed, he fingers the fringes that the Torah decrees should be worn all day to remind one of the commandments of the Lord. His emotions waver between fury and melancholy as he confronts his son's sinfulness and considers himself. How low he has fallen, stealing like a thief into his son's room to search for what he dare not ask. And most upsetting of all is the possibility that the fear of estranging his son comes not entirely from paternal love, but from practical necessity. He needs him. The income his son contributes saves him from the shame of shoveling in the streets. He can feign a bad heart, a weak back, and the Relief does not press him. His family is not hungry, his daughters do not go ragged, and the Sabbath can be provided for. Without his son, where would they be? Even the roof over their heads might be taken away. On weekday mornings and all of Shabbes his son still comes to the service and there is a minyan. Would anyone bother to come if they were never a minyan? God forbid it should come to that! Zalman pushes from his mind the events of the past week, the whereabouts of the mute, that morning's bleak, meager service. God will not forsake him. God will help.

But as he sits like a stranger in his son's room, like a cowardly intruder before the opened, ransacked bureau drawer, and looks at the disarray he has wrought, he sees that his dependency is a disease, eroding his dignity and his self-esteem. No, he cannot let this be. He will do whatever it is possible to do.

Resolutely, Zalman rises from the bed, still clutching

Ben's fringed garment in his hand. He will not sit like a dolt. Parnussah will not fall from the sky. He must go once again and seek a livelihood. He will go to Sam and speak to him. But he must present himself properly. He will shave and put on a clean shirt, and he will go.

Zalman walks with a firm step down the stairs and into the dining room. He enters the kitchen and puts the tallis koton on the table. The house seems strangely desolate. Why isn't Malka home yet? Where is Leah? Is she still asleep? What time did she come home last night? What does she do until so late? He must speak to her. He must be a father. But where is everyone? Then he remembers that Malka was to go with Leah this morning to pick out material for a new skirt for school. He can already hear the wrangling that will ensue when Malka starts making the skirt. Whatever Malka suggests, Leah will want the contrary. And whatever Malka does, it will not be good enough. He suspects that Leah's carrying on comes from a deeper unhappiness than has to do with a skirt—she is generally disagreeable—but what vexes her so much, he cannot figure out.

Zalman mixes the depilatory powder with water until it becomes gray mud. He lowers his suspenders and removes his shirt. He looks into the small mirror above the washstand in the downstairs toilet. With the same smooth bone implement he will later use to remove it, he applies the foul-smelling stuff to his face, carefully avoiding his mustache and his small beard. Then he leans back in a kitchen chair, to keep the depilatory from dripping onto his underwear and tallis koton, and waits for it to take effect. Ben's tallis koton is lying on the table beside him. Zalman hears the front door open. "Esther?" he calls. No answer. "Malka?" A moment later, Ben is standing in the doorway, looking at his tallis koton on the table; he says nothing. With his head still hanging over the back of the kitchen chair, Zalman shouts to him, "Why are you standing there like a golem? Have you nothing to say? Or are you mute?" And as Ben turns swiftly away and starts to leave, Zalman thinks he sees a small smile flicker across his face. He leaps from the chair and flies at Ben, waving the fringed garment in the air like a banner of battle.

When she opens the door, Esther hears the clamor. Oh no! Not again! She doesn't want to listen! She doesn't want to look! She wants to run upstairs. But she stops at the doorway to the dining room. She sees her father, the gray mud dripping from his face, his fringes flying, his yarmulka askew on his head, his suspenders dangling, his left hand holding up his pants, and his right hand raised in a fist clutching a tallis koton, lunging at Ben, screaming, "Meshumed! Apikoris!" Ben is running ahead of him around the dining room table, pulling out the chairs behind him to block her father's path. Her father sweeps the chairs out of his way, and they crash to the floor. She can see the bones in Ben's back, like tiny wings through his shirt, and his neck, narrow and vulnerable, is like a doomed chicken's just before the slaughterer bends it in his bloody hands and slits it with his sharp knife. She begins to move aside to let Ben run from the room when her father lets go of his pants with his left hand and grabs Ben. His fist crashes down on Ben's back. Her father keeps standing there, his pants drooping around his hips, the gray mud dribbling and splattering, while he pounds on Ben's back and on his neck and his head, thundering, "Apostate! Renegade! Momzer! Bastard!"

The front door swings open. Her mother is standing there, holding a full shopping bag, with Lila beside her. Both of them remain frozen for a moment. Then Lila dashes up the stairs, and her mother drops the shopping bag and rushes into the dining room. She pushes her way between her husband and her son and stands facing her husband. She looks suddenly tall and powerful and imperious. "Enough!" she commands. "Enough, I say!" Her face is ferocious. "Whom do you dare to call 'bastard'?" she snarls. "You vile person! You piece of excrement!"

Her father's eyes blaze. "You dare to vilify me before my children?" he shouts. "Out of my way, evil woman! Devil! Heartless whore!"

Her mother does not budge. "I will *not* move out of your way! I will *not* let you destroy my son!" She sees the fringes hanging from her husband's fingers and knows what happened. "I spit on your tallis koton!" she hisses. "I spit on your stinking Hassidim! I spit on you!"

Ben runs from the room. The outside door bangs loudly. Her father grows pale and quiet. He lowers his raised fist. Her mother runs to the door and out into the street. Esther sees tears rise in her father's eyes. A few minutes later, her mother returns and falls into a chair, and sits rocking back and forth, and moaning.

18

Her mother keeps swaying from side to side like a broken branch, her soft moaning like the endless echo of the storm that damaged her. Esther feels sorry for her, but wishes she'd stop. The agony in the eerie sound is penetrating her, entering into her most protected places. And she hates the way her mother looks—her face contorted, her body visibly tormented; she looks ungrounded, distant. She wants her mother to come back, to reassemble herself into a familiar person. She wants her mother to make lunch, to tell her she should sit down and eat before whatever it is gets cold or warm or dried out.

On the other side of the room, her father sits, suddenly dwarfed by the tall, brocaded back of the dining room chair, his huge head hanging, his shoulders narrowed, his chest sunken. Esther is appalled; she does not pity him. He looks malformed. She finds him sickening.

Neither parent looks at the other. Each appears desolate. And neither seems to be aware of her. She feels herself dwindling in the enormity of their grief. Huddled on a chair in a corner of the room, feeling frighteningly alone, she becomes angry with Ben. *He* made it all happen. And what for? He knew what would happen if Papa found out. What's so hard about wearing a tallis koton? Even Papa doesn't care about letting the fringes show, so nobody even knows you're wearing it. Ben is so peculiar. It's like he does things on purpose just to get himself punished.

Suddenly her mother stops moaning, goes into the kitchen, and begins to prepare lunch. Her movements are distraught, violent. Esther winces when her mother stabs the can of tomato herring and again as she watches her slice the onion and cucumber, holding them in the palm of her hand and cutting into them quickly and fiercely. It's like she wants to cut through and slash her own skin. But she doesn't. And she puts rye bread and butter on the table and goes into the dining room to tell her husband that his meal is ready. She sends Esther to call Lila.

Their eating together, she and Lila and Papa on an ordinary Sunday, has for Esther, unexpectedly, a feeling of drama which is not completely unpleasant. It is promptly dispelled and replaced by an oppressive wretchedness when she sees her father eating absently, with wide terror-filled eyes. She turns away and stares at her plate while she eats, trying to make sense of her disparate emotions. When she looks up, she sees her mother standing by the sink, filling the kettle with water for tea. She can tell from the set of her jaw that the turmoil inside her mother is subsiding, and taking its place is a determination once again to endure. Lila is reassuring too, with her feelings hidden behind her perennial pout, as she separates the tomato herring with her fork and fastidiously removes its backbone. Esther butters her bread and bites into it. She is sure she is still miserable, only she is hungry and the food tastes good and it becomes hard to be as miserable as she wants to be.

Zalman's face mirrors his horror at what he has done. His food sticks in his throat. Why is he eating? He still feels his son's bones under his fist and he sits, like an animal, stuffing his mouth with food. And who is he to denigrate the animals? Does even the wild beast attack its own young? No, only man is capable of such perversion.

But where does it come from—the unbridled fury, the terrible violence? Surely God is not guiding his hand. Yet the desecration of God's commandments is what incites him. But who is he, sinful ordinary man that he is, to assume the role of the Almighty? Even Moses our Teacher did not presume to avenge the faithlessness of Israel. Moses was God's servant, but he—he is a slave, not to God, but to himself, to his own treacherous pride. But is pride so evil? Is it any more than a person's good opinion of himself? How is one to live without it? And how is a father to respect himself if his son affronts him? Dear God, how am I to respect myself when my wife's love for her son demeans me? No, he cannot have to come to this. Not to vanity. A mother is obligated to love her son and protect him. But what of a son? Must not a son honor both his mother *and* his father? And the Torah admonishes a son not only to love them but to fear them. How is one to instill fear? And why? The Torah does not tell us why.

From somewhere deep in the recesses of his being, the teachings of his youth return to Zalman. "He that smiteth a man so that he die shall surely be put to death." No, the Almighty will not permit it! His hand will be stayed. The guidance he seeks will yet come. "And if a man strike a servant so that a tooth or eye is destroyed, he must lose the servant." He has struck, again and again, not merely a man, not a servant, but his only son, and with force not only to destroy an eye or a tooth, but his entire body, his senses, his spirit. And his son is sick—the strangeness has been apparent for years. But not from birth. No, he was beautiful, perfect. They wrote letters from Russia telling him that his second son was exquisitely beautiful, remarkably bright and winsome. From where did his affliction come? Zalman shudders; he dare not think of what—of who the source might have been.

But why? He loved his son with all his heart, only the boy never seemed to understand. Even when he was little.

Can he ever forget when he saw his Benjamin for the first time, how his heart leaped when he saw them descend the gangplank from the ship together, and his terrible anxiety as he waited for them behind the wired wall? Would she find him changed? Did he look better with the mustache he had grown? Would he be more pleasing in her eyes now that he was rich and well-dressed? Would she harbor bitterness toward him, blaming him for the death of their first son? The agonies he endured while he waited! When finally they came face to face, he dared not touch her. And she did not touch him. His son stared up at him with huge brown eyes, clutching his mother's hand and pressing against her. How was he to understand that I was his father? How was he to even know what a father was? I bent to embrace him and he drew away. For months afterwards, he would not let me near him. What they went through before the child became accustomed to sleeping in a room by himself. How he pounded on their bedroom door, pleading to be let in. And when they let him in, he would crawl into bed beside his mother and stare across at me with what I can only call hatred in his eyes. It happened any time—at night, in the morning, even when he and Malka were lying together. That's when he first struck his son, and the boy stopped pounding on the door. And his mother no longer had to keep explaining that it was not the child's fault, that she and the boy had become as one, especially after his brother died—traveling across Europe together, always just the two of them, and on the ship how he slept nestled against her. But he must learn, he told her. The child was bright; he learned. The boy stopped clamoring for his mother. He became quiet. And when sisters came, he was gentle with them. It seemed that all would be well. But shortly after his Bar Mitzva the strangeness began, and later on the stubbornness, the resistance. And what did I, a father, do? I struck him—over and over again. And not like a father—but with the fury of a fiend!

Zalman digs his nails into his temples and draws them down over his cheeks. Oh how thin and frail are the false faces we wear for the world! He is false! False! But he does not will to be. He wants to crush the monster in him. But again and again it eludes him, breaking through all his restraints, baring its fangs, becoming something bigger and stronger than itself, sprouting murderous arms, crushing fists! And why? Against what did he rail and pound? Against not wearing the fringes. Foolish, foolish, foolish! It cannot *be* that the essence of Torah lies in a contraption of knotted strings! It is only his own limited mind that fixes so relentlessly on superficial symbols. And what is it that drives him? No, it is not concern for the symbol, but the gnawing awareness of his insufficiency, the meagerness of his claim to koved. Why? Why is he plagued with this hunger for honor? The Shulchan Aruch itself prohibits placing a heavy yoke upon one's children; it warns us that if we are overly exacting with them in matters pertaining to our honor, we may cause them to stumble. And the beating of a grown-up son is absolutely forbidden; so heinous is this act that punishment is the severest of all. Excommunication!

The sight of the food left uneaten on his plate sickens him. Zalman covers his face with his hands. He is a desecrator; he has desecrated the entire idea of righteousness. How often and how carefully the Rebbe has explained the significance of the *inner* person, of the righteous motive in the observance of outward law. How beautifully he has spoken of the kindliness, the humaneness of the Baal Shem. How gentle is the Rebbe himself. How it must hurt him that neither of his sons chooses to succeed him. Yet does he force his will upon them? Does criticism by his Hassidim affect him? No. Calmly, he explains that if his sons are keepers of the Commandments, he rejoices. God, he says, will send a successor—a son-in-law, a grandson; someone worthy will take his place. The Rebbe does not presume to inflict his desires upon his children. But *he*, ignorant and coarse, has inflicted himself on his son with such force that he has not only caused him to stumble, he has driven him away from the Commandments. Even when Benjamin observed the precepts, when he bound the phylacteries around his arm and placed the name of the Almighty upon his forehead, the blankness in his eyes, the emptiness—like a golem. I made of my son a golem! And then, even then, was the beast in me satiated? No!

A painful groan wrenches itself from Zalman's throat. If only he could unravel what he has wrought! It is all a maze, a massive tapestried maze. But is he its creator? Or merely another thread inexorably stitched into place.

The tea set before him has grown cold. Zalman looks up toward his wife and sees her back set firmly against him. How he envies her straightforward sorrow! Yet how he pities her. If only he could reach out and touch her. But what right has he got? Even with her, he has been a violator. For it is written that a man may not cohabit with his wife when she hates him—even though she consent. And oh, how often that precept must have been violated. But how helpless he has been and—even when their limbs were locked together, their most intimate parts pressed into each other, when he pours into her the sap of his body—how isolated.

Malka hears her husband's groan, but she does not turn to him. She cannot bring herself to. She does not hate him; she simply has not the strength. She does not love him either. He is a human being, and he is suffering. But she cannot help him.

As soon as she has finished eating, Esther mumbles the Grace after Meals, dresses quickly, goes outside, and sits down on the steps. The sky is blue with wisps of white clouds. The winter sunshine feels warm and soothing to the disquiet fluttering about inside her like a lost bird. It

144

was awful watching Papa at the table. She kept trying not to look, but sometimes she couldn't help it. She hopes Angie'll come out soon and they'll play and little by little, she'll forget.

When Angie comes out, she asks if Esther wants to go to the movies. After a moment of confusion because, under the circumstances, going to the movies seems indecent, even sinful, and yet not sure exactly why because, after all, this isn't the first time her father has screamed and hollered and hit Ben, Esther realizes that she can't go anyway because Ben isn't there to give her money. And after what happened, she certainly couldn't ask her parents.

"No," she tells Angie. "It's too nice outside."

"But *The Invisible Man* is playing!"

"I saw the coming attractions and it's too scary."

"Oh come on, it's not so scary. It'll be good! And the other picture is with Loretta Young."

"Loretta Young!" Loretta Young is her favorite actress.

"Yeah. Come on."

"No. It's too nice outside."

"Okay," Angie says sadly. "I guess I'll go with my brothers. Are you sure? Are you positive you don't want to go?"

"I'm sure," Esther says in a weak voice. How she wishes Ben were home.

As she watches Angie and her two little brothers go off, Esther sets her face stoically and again that peculiar pleasure begins stirring inside her. Her forbearance in the face of privation feels ennobling. Only this time, when she relates the good feeling about herself to *why* she feels deprived, she experiences a disturbing distaste for herself. But no! She doesn't want Ben to be home only because he could give her money for the movies—and an extra nickel for a Betty Boop bar. No! She wouldn't care if he never gave her money or brought her presents or anything. She's sure of it.

Besides, she thinks (wandering toward Millie's house

and hoping Millie won't ask her about going to the movies too and offer to treat her and she *couldn't* let her because that would show that she really cared about the movies), she doesn't really like scary movies. She remembers the first time a movie frightened her. They were still living on the East Side, so she must have been pretty little. They lived right across the street from the Cannon, where you could see two movies and a comedy and an episode all for a nickel. On Thursdays, it was two for a nickel. And sometimes her mother went with her (probably because she thought it would help her learn English). The movie was called *Murder by the Clock*. She can't remember the whole story, only the part where this man, who had a horrible mean smile and very small eyes and walked hunched over, was hiding behind a tall grandfather clock waiting to jump out and strangle the girl. Her mother had on that black coat that she still has, with the big fur collar, and just when the girl walked into the room and the man started coming out from behind the clock with the rope in his hands, she buried her face in her mother's fur collar and squeezed her mother's arm. When she looked up again, the man was standing and staring down at the girl, and the rope hanging from his fingers was like a snake. She felt sick. All through the rest of the movie, she kept hugging her mother's arm and brushing her face against her mother's fur collar. She still remembers how good it felt.

Nobody answers the doorbell at Millie's house. She walks over to the store. Mr. Brenner is in the office, with the tape measure dangling from his neck, and his face is all red, and he's screaming at the new bookkeeper about something she did wrong. When he finally notices Esther, he calls out gruffly, "Millie's not here," and goes back to screaming at the bookkeeper. Esther leaves without asking if he knows where Millie is.

She spends the rest of the afternoon bent over the dining room table, drawing. She draws people made up in her head, nobody she actually knows, mostly girls and women. She's not good at drawing boys or men. Mr. Epstein next door, who's a real artist, said she should try to draw boys and men too. And not made-up people; she should draw real ones. But she had to look at them real hard first; she'd be surprised how different they were from what she imagined, if she looked at them real hard. And she should draw other things too, everything she saw around her. It was summer and there was no one around—Millie had already gone to camp; Angie had gone to the beach with some relatives; Shirley Goldblatt, who sometimes came over to her block to play, had gone to the mountains with her family—she was sitting on the stoop and drawing when Mr. Epstein came home from work and stopped to see what she was doing. He picked up her pad and looked for a long time at her picture of a little girl with long curls in a fluffy dress. He told her it was a good picture of a made-up little girl, but it would be better if you could tell something about her. He asked her all kinds of questions about the little girl that she couldn't answer. Then Papa came out, and Mr. Epstein showed him the picture and said that there were art classes at the Educational Alliance on the East Side where he taught and that Papa should send her there, that she was talented. Papa looked at the picture, and then he looked at her as if he'd never seen her before. She was sure he was going to get angry, that art classes were something goyish. (Mr. Epstein never came to shul or wore a hat or anything.) But instead, Papa's face became sad. "Such pastimes are for rich men's daughters," he said. Mr. Epstein said you didn't have to pay at the Educational Alliance, it would only cost the three cents each way for the trolley car across the bridge. Her father sighed heavily and said, "I know, I know," and went into the house. Mr. Epstein looked at her mournfully for a moment, then turned to a fresh page in her pad and handed it to her. "See that baby carriage

147

across the street," he said. "Draw it. Just like it is—sagging, a little bent, the hood is torn, see where the paint is coming off. Lots of babies have slept in that carriage. Don't draw it like it just came new from the store. Do you understand?" She said she understood and Mr. Epstein left. It had never occurred to her to draw a beat-up old baby carriage. And when she got through, she kept looking at her picture. It was the realest thing she had ever drawn.

She's trying to do just what Mr. Epstein told her; she's trying to draw the dining room chair just like it looks now—with the cloth ripped a little near the top and the back lumpy, but so you can tell it once belonged in that big dining room she can still remember (even though Lila insists she was too little) that had a soft rug with blue flowers in it on the floor and a crystal chandelier hanging over the table. She wants to show the way the design is faded, but that it used to be beautiful brocaded cloth. It's so hard! How she wishes she could have gone to those art classes, but she didn't bring it up again. She figured they couldn't afford the carfare, and she didn't want to walk all the way to the East Side by herself. She kept remembering the time she had to walk across the bridge all by herself to go to the dentist. She had a terrible toothache, and Papa said that a dentist on the East Side, who was the son of one of his landzmen, would take care of her toothache for nothing. He said there was no money for carfare; she should walk across the bridge, and he told her how to go to Avenue B where the dentist was. She didn't ask anybody to go with her; she went all by herself. She was nine years old, and she was scared and her tooth was hurting, but she didn't get lost, and the dentist pulled her tooth out. When she came home, her father said to her mother, "See how she doesn't need you to go with her." And her mother nodded resignedly, as if she knew she wasn't very useful. She wanted to say to her mother, "But I did need you! Even if you can't read the street signs and ask directions in English, I needed you." But she didn't say anything. She just told them that the dentist pulled out her tooth. They didn't ask to see where and they didn't ask if it had hurt. She can't remember if that made her feel bad at the time, but now she feels bad. Someone should at least have asked her. She looks very hard at the dining room chair. She seems to remember that they seemed preoccupied when she came home from the dentist. Maybe that was another one of the days they didn't know where Ben was.

That night, somehow, the three of them eat together again, as though the family has dwindled and is huddling together against a chill that comes from the gaping absence of Ben. Esther hopes Lila will stay home after supper and maybe talk to her. But as soon as she finishes eating, Lila leaves the house. Without even saying the Grace after Meals. And her father doesn't seem to notice or care.

It is time to go to bed, and Ben has not come home. Both her parents move about the house like spectres, formidable and unfamiliar—disconnected from her. She feels cast out, discarded. She blames her brother. For God's sake, Ben, what's the *matter* with you? Why don't you come home? Still furious, Esther climbs into bed and crawls under the covers and lies shivering. It pains and confuses her to feel such anger against her brother, who has always been so good to her.

The next morning, she throws off the covers and rushes out of bed. He *must* have! He *must* have come home! Ben's door is wide open. Her heart contracts. His bed has not been slept in. She keeps standing in the cold hall and staring at the empty bed, beginning to sense that she must not be angry with her brother, that there are secrets which have not been revealed to her because she is too young. And that of all of them, Ben is the most alone. But

149

please come home today, she pleads to the neat, narrow bed. Please!

Lila comes out of the bathroom and asks what she's standing in the freezing cold hall for, and tells her she'd better hurry up or she'll be late for school. Lila's unexceptional manner reassures her. Until they are eating breakfast and her sister, uncharacteristically, keeps chattering while her mother continues to move about, unseeing and unhearing. The kitchen becomes suffocating. The oatmeal scorches her tongue. She is eating too quickly. She wants to get out. She stumbles over the beat-up door lying across the floor and nearly falls. She wants to get away—from the strangeness, from the murky light, the disintegration, from the turgid air of tragedy relentlessly distending itself in the brittle house. She wants to get to school. She wants to be encased in a strong, solid building with the good clean smells of chalk and paper, with the stimulating, expectant smell of ink, where she gives the right answers and feels good because they think she's smart. Even if Miss McKeon doesn't like her, she still gives her high marks. And not only the girls are friendly to her; the boys act like they like her too—even though she isn't pretty and her clothes aren't so nice. If only she doesn't have to wear those special shoes the Home Relief gives you for free, that are ugly and everyone knows how you got them. She heard Lila arguing with her mother about them. Lila said she'd go barefoot or stay home rather than wear those shoes. Her mother didn't answer Lila and so far they haven't had to get them.

Walking to school in the crisp, buoyant air, Esther begins to feel better. Millie catches up to her. Esther asks where she was yesterday. Millie says she wasn't home because her aunt and uncle came from Flatbush and took her and her mother uptown for "chinks" and later they went to the Roxy. The Roxy! Esther is impressed. They call it a movie palace. Imagine going to a *palace*! They say the lobby is enormous and gorgeous—all marble, and the seats are covered with velvet, and the stage show is so beautiful you can faint! Millie is lucky. But *chinks*—how disgusting! Of course she doesn't believe her father (probably, just because it's not kosher, he says that what they serve in Chinese restaurants is chopped mice). Still the thought of eating chinks makes her nauseous. But she wishes she could eat in a restaurant. Millie is lucky.

She forgets about Ben all morning in school. She remembers about him when her mother doesn't talk to her all through lunch. Her mother doesn't talk much lots of times, but at least she says *something*. She forgets about Ben again when she returns to school and, on the way home, she arranges to play with Millie until suppertime.

Malka scoops up the potato peelings and dumps them into the garbage pail. She sits down to wait for her husband. He has gone to telephone, to find out if Ben is at work. She is exhausted. When she finally fell asleep, it was worse than being awake. Such dreams! Horrible! Benjamin, two years old, drowning in the river by their house. Dragging him out, blue and bloated and smeared with mud. God, I beseech you, wipe away my memory. Let me not recall such dreams. And the other one. God, why do you paint such monstrous pictures? My Benjamin at his Bar Mitzva, tearing off his new silken tallis, jumping on it up and down like a crazyman, his face ugly with big teeth and popping eyes, stamping and kicking until the beautiful tallis was torn and filthy. People pointing at him and laughing. Insane such dreams! Malka's eyes fill with tears. How beautiful he was! And when he chanted his haftorah, his voice was so clear, so golden. Everyone remarked. No one had ever heard such a performance. But tell me, where is he now? Where is my golden son? With a frightful moan, as if to expel her torturing demons, Malka rises and begins grating the potatoes. She hears her husband enter the house; she stands frozen, her hand pressed down hard on the grater.

Zalman comes into the kitchen. Malka turns to him. "Well?" she asks.

"No. He's not there," Zalman says.

"You didn't tell them who you were?"

"No," Zalman says.

"You didn't say why you were calling?"

"No," Zalman says. "No. I gave them no idea anything was wrong. Don't worry."

"Don't worry, he says. *Of course*, don't worry! What is there to *worry* about?"

Zalman's face is haggard. His voice is heavy with fatigue. "What do you want from me?" he asks.

"What I want? As though it matters what I want," Malka says wearily and goes back to grating the potatoes.

Esther puts her books down on the hall radiator and comes into the kitchen. Her parents hardly look at her. "I'm going to Millie's house," she says.

"Go," her mother says.

Her father says nothing.

19

Four nights have passed. Ben has not come home. It is longer than he has ever stayed away. On the morning of the fifth day, Esther lies awake for a while before she gets up and goes to look in Ben's room. Early rays of sunlight fall across his bed, illuminating the undisturbed emptiness. There is a frightening finality in the bedspread's chiseled, unstirring folds. Seeing his rows of books standing tidy and straight and patient like good children awaiting inspection, Esther feels a painful surge of love for her brother. How could she have been annoyed with him? Poor, poor Ben. Where *is* he? What has happened to him? Suddenly, she is filled with dread of something unimaginable and incomprehensible to her.

She comes down to breakfast. Lila has stopped trying, and her mother moves like a sleepwalker. She wonders where her father is. The shul was empty when she went by. Somebody else's father might be out working. But not hers. Oh no! Zalman Hirsch wouldn't think of taking a job! He's too special! Esther realizes she is thinking what Lila expressed when she was having that argument with her mother about the Home Relief shoes. Her mother told Lila to shut her mouth, what did *she* know! But it's true—Papa does think he's special. She has to admit that sometimes she's liked the difference between them and other families, like being the only ones on the block with a succah, and she and Lila decorating it—hanging fruits from the ceiling, making Jewish stars out of crepe paper and pinning them to the white sheets on the walls. All their friends coming to see it and saying how beautiful it is. And she's liked it when anyone asked her what her father was and she didn't have to say he's a cutter or a furrier or a milkman. She could say he was a business-man. Of course, sometimes she felt funny because he didn't have a business, but she didn't think she was lying because probably he would have one again soon. She never tells anyone about being on Relief. Nobody told her not to, but she's sure she's supposed to be ashamed. They talk about the depression in school and about people being on Relief, so she knows she's not the only one, but still. . . .

Lila said that Papa doesn't even *try* to get a job and that's what makes her so mad. It's all right for him to do what-ever he likes, Lila said, even though other people have to suffer for it. And not only that, but he expects everybody to do what *he* wants them to. No one can even *say* anything to him! We all have to go around like we don't even have *tongues*! What Lila said made her remember the horrible mute, and she wondered if he couldn't speak because his tongue was missing. Lila was terribly upset, but Mama just kept on chopping onions, so you couldn't tell if the tears rolling down her cheeks came from them or because she was upset too. I wonder what Mama really thinks. She didn't actually disagree with Lila; she just kept telling her to shut her mouth. But Lila's right. Everything she says about Papa is true. Look at the way he treats Ben who isn't even a child anymore but he treats him like one. It's not so wrong about the minyan, because sometimes there aren't enough men and he *needs* him for that. But why should it matter to him if Ben wears a tallis koton? Nobody can even *tell*. Except of course God. That's probably what bothers Papa. He's afraid God will know and blame him.

He'll do anything he thinks God wants him to. He reminds me of Abraham.

Esther puts on her hat and coat, takes her books, and leaves the house. The sun is bright and warm, but she feels cold. Abraham was going to kill Isaac just to please God. A hollowness spreads inside her. No, Papa couldn't care more about God than about us. No, it's not always God making him act the way he does. Sometimes it has nothing to do with God. For instance, God doesn't care if you swim in the ocean or not; the ocean isn't anything religious. She remembers that the first time she was afraid of her father, the first time she hated him, was that day they went to Coney Island.

Esther was five years old when Zalman Hirsch awoke that summer morning imbued with what seemed like a heavenly commission to initiate his daughters into the glories of the sea. Immediately after breakfast, with Lila clutching a shopping bag containing their towels, their lettuce and tomato sandwiches and hard-boiled eggs, he marched them over to Havemeyer Street where, reassembled single file, the three of them set about funneling their way through bottlenecks of marketing women in blooming housedresses. Fruits and vegetables sunned themselves on the pushcarts. Teacups, stew pots, cutlery, yard goods, and bloomers shimmered on the stands. People watched impassively as carp and whitefish thrashed out their last moments in rectangular tanks of water while overhead, men's pants and ladies' slips floated shamelessly together in air pungent with the smell of pickles souring in briny barrels. Esther loved the colors and the smells. She loved the sounds of the vendors hawking their wares in booming voices. It all heightened her anticipation of Coney Island which, from what she had heard, was the most magical experience there was. In Beryl Miller's dry goods store, she and Lila were outfitted in blue woolen bathing suits and, wearing them hot and itchy under their dresses, were swept into the subway.

When they got off the train at Coney Island, the air was salty and exhilarating. They walked along Surf Avenue for a while, and she could smell popcorn and hot dogs; and when they passed frozen custard stands, she saw chocolate and vanilla custard castles twirling on top of golden toasted cones. She knew she couldn't have any of it, but her father said that on the way home they could go on the big merry-go-round.

Lila loved the sea at sight. Esther was terrified. Undaunted by her howls, her father carried her over the rushing foam and dipped her over and over again into the thick, green, undulating ocean. When a wave loomed, large and dark like an open mouth, he jumped up, raising her high above his head, laughing lustily up into her face and shouting above the clamor she was making that she was not to be afraid. She kept screaming and screaming until finally she scratched him. He stopped laughing and looked startled and carried her back to shore past Lila who was squealing in ecstasy because she was sinking in the sand while the water ran out from between her toes. He didn't scold her for scratching him; he just looked disappointed. Then he wrapped her in a towel and sat her down, whimpering and shivering, and told her not to move while he went back in. She sat where he put her, the tears still trickling, her nose running, and watched her father go back in. He didn't swim because he did not know how. She could hear the noisy sounds of relish he made as he dunked himself up and down. He had on nothing but his black bathing suit with the round cut-outs in the sides and his yarmulka. She hated the way he looked. She hated the noise he was making. She hated him for scaring her. She hated him for making her think there was something wrong with her. She wanted to go home. She didn't even care if she went on the merry-go-round.

Yes, that's what he does, Esther decides. He makes you believe you have to be a certain way or else there's something wrong with you. He makes you afraid to make up your own mind about anything. *He's* the one who decides what matters and what doesn't and what's nice and what's not nice. There are a lot of things about him that I don't think are nice. Like sitting around in his undershirt and tzitzis, and slurping his tea. He doesn't even care if my friend is in the house. He doesn't care about anybody but himself!

Approaching her school, Esther sees no one outside. She must be late. Miss McKeon will be mad. It's all *his* fault for making me walk slow. She runs into the red brick building and races along the empty corridors. She enters her classroom with her heart pounding. Miss McKeon's eyebrows go up in the air and her mouth gets squeezed together. Esther hurries to hang up her clothes. She hears Miss McKeon say behind her, "Good *afternoon*, Esther!" She has to say something back but she doesn't know what. When she turns around, Miss McKeon is looking at her with her mouth twisted to one side. She's waiting. "I'm sorry," Esther says, and sits down in her seat. She wonders what Miss McKeon would say if she knew. What if she told Miss McKeon that her brother had disappeared and no one knew where he was. Would she apologize for being sarcastic to her? What if she told Miss McKeon that something terrible might have happened to her brother? Would she feel sorry for her? But Miss McKeon doesn't know about anything that happened and is nasty to her all morning.

When she comes home for lunch, her mother is not downstairs. "She's lying down," her father says. "She's not feeling well." He runs his hand gently over her hair and tells her he'll make her a fried egg and that he went out specially to buy bananas so she could have bananas with cream. Esther doesn't know what to say—all morning she has been hating him.

Her father puts the bottle of ketchup and the buttered slice of pumpernickel on the table before he breaks the egg, stirs it, and slides it onto the sizzling butter in the frying pan. Esther watches him bustle about the kitchen and hover over her omelette. He turns it very carefully, waits a few moments, and lifts it gingerly onto a plate. Then, with a sweeping flourish—as though she were a princess—he presents it to her and waits, with an expectant smile on his face, for her to taste it. His eyes beseech her approval and bathe her with love. The omelette is delicious, but she has difficulty swallowing; there is a lump in her throat.

He wants me to like him. No matter what he does, he wants people to like him. Why should I feel bad? He's *still* just thinking about himself. But the way he's looking at her—it's like when she was in the hospital because she had double pneumonia, and he told her to eat whatever they gave her, not to worry. It was even Passover and still he told her to eat anything she wanted to. He looked at her the same way then. And when they came to visit her, he looked so happy and excited, carrying that big cardboard rabbit dressed in little green pants and a pink jacket and it was holding a straw basket full of chocolate Easter eggs wrapped in shiny colored paper. He probably didn't even know it was something goyish, that it was an Easter bunny. And then when they brought her home from the hospital, there was the piano, a little toy piano, and how when he handed it to her, he said, laughing, "It's just like the one that used to stand in our parlor, only smaller. But with God's help, it will grow." And she laughed too.

Esther tells her father that the fried egg is delicious,

and when he presents her with the dish of sliced bananas covered with sour cream and sprinkled with sugar, she exclaims how good it looks. Before she leaves, she hugs her father and kisses his cheek. And walking back to school, she feels like skipping. Then she remembers that she forgot all about her mother, lying down upstairs because she didn't feel well. And she forgot about Ben. She didn't *mean* to. It just happened.

As soon as Esther leaves the house, Zalman puts water up to boil and pours tea leaves into the teapot. Then from the wooden box outside the kitchen window, he takes a large black radish and a tomato. He peels the radish, cuts it into thick white slices and puts them on a plate. He quarters the tomato and arranges it beside the radish. He studies the plate for a moment, returns to the wooden box, removes half a cucumber which he slices and adds to the plate along with a buttered piece of pumpernickel. Carefully, he salts everything. When the tea has brewed, he pours it into a glass, assesses the color, adds more water, and stirs in a sugar cube. Then he ascends the steps, carrying the tea in one hand and the plate of food in the other.

Malka is lying on the bed with her back to him. He approaches softly and leans over to see if she is asleep. Her eyes are open.

"I have brought you something to eat," he says to her back. She does not move or speak. "Malka, please," he begs, "you must eat something." He waits. "At least take some tea." No movement, not a sound. "Malka, I am putting the food down beside you and I will leave you alone. Only after I go, take something."

Zalman places the food and drink on the chair beside their bed and stands staring down at his wife's back. He reaches out his hand, hesitates, then gently touches her shoulder. Her back stiffens, but otherwise she doesn't move, and she says nothing. Zalman stands silently, his empty hands hanging at his sides, before he turns and leaves the room.

As she listens to her husband's footsteps descending the stairs, Malka shuts her eyes tightly, but tears press their way through and stream down her face onto her pillow.

Lying in bed that night, Esther hears it again through the wall. The steady creaking of the bed in her parents' room. The first night she heard it, Lila heard it too. She could tell because Lila began tossing around and finally put the pillow over her head. She asked Lila, "What's that noise? What's happening in there?" Lila muttered from under the pillow, "They're doing it." "What?" she asked. "What are they doing?" "It!" Lila hissed. "But Lila—" she began. Then Lila got angry and said, "Stop bothering me, you dumbbell!"

She's not such a dumbbell anymore. She listens to her father's heavy, rhythmic breathing. Suddenly the bed stops creaking and her father lets out a strange moan. Then it becomes quiet. All the time she hasn't heard her mother make a sound. Until a few minutes later when she gets up to go to the bathroom and passes her parents' door, she hears her father ask in a trembly voice, "Malka—Malka, did you feel anything?" And her mother answers, not unkindly, "I felt. Don't worry. Go to sleep."

20

The next morning, Esther is in school on time. Miss McKeon said the geography test on South America would begin "immediately after I take the attendance. Immediately!"

Books are put out of sight and paper is passed up the rows. Miss McKeon is going to call out the questions and wait two minutes for them to write down the answers. "I will be watching every one of you," she tells them. "If your eyes are looking in the wrong direction, if your head turns to either side, and you all *know* what I *mean*, your paper will be *destroyed!*" Backs grow rigid, eyes widen with alarm, some children nibble their nails. All this seems to please Miss McKeon. Esther thinks she looks like Krazy Kat watching a mouse come out of a hole.

The test has been pretty easy so far—capitals of countries, principal products. She might even get a hundred. "The jungles of Brazil contain many *blank* people." Esther hesitates; she knows the answer is "uncivilized," but she wishes she didn't have to write it. She wants to write "Indian" and it would be right because the book called them Indians, but she has a feeling she'll be marked wrong; Miss McKeon is always talking about them being uncivilized. She calls them "uncivilized savages." In history, when they were learning about the discovery of America and how the white man wanted to civilize the

Indians, somebody asked Miss McKeon what "civilize" meant, she said "to make them Christians." Lots of kids stared down at their desks, looking embarrassed. Miss McKeon must have noticed that something was wrong because her face got red and she said, "Well, not necessarily Christians—but just civilized people, people who behave properly, who can read and write." Esther remembers how awful that made her feel. Since then, she's been ashamed to admit to anyone that her mother can't read or write. Not that she can see what acting properly has to do with reading or writing. Mama acts *very* properly; she doesn't even make noise when she drinks tea. Esther's heart leaps; she writes "Indian" on her paper— not "uncivilized."

Miss McKeon goes on. "The highest mountains in South America are the *blank*. The longest river in South America is the *blank*." Who *cares* if she gets a hundred? "When it's winter in New York, it's *blank* in Buenos Aires." As she writes "summer," Esther again finds it difficult to imagine. And it's hard to believe that the earth moves around the sun. But if they write about it in school books, it must all be true. Still, she thinks, passing her paper forward, they probably used to write in school books that the earth was flat, and *that* was wrong. She wishes there was someone she could ask about all these things. Certainly not Miss McKeon! If she had wondered about all this in 3A, she would have asked Miss Kelly. She *loved* geography in 3A. You didn't have to learn capitals and it didn't matter if a place was in the temperate zone or the torrid zone and all the other boring things; they read stories about children who lived in different countries. In Brazil there was an Indian boy named Pimwe and his sister, Kima. Miss Kelly never called them savages, and she never said they were uncivilized even though they lived in a forest and probably couldn't read or write. She said, "They were children just like you," and that was hard to imagine because they lived with twenty-four other families in one house that had a grass roof (probably like a big succah) and other things too, like not going to school. The best part of the story was when the children climbed to the top of a tree to see what the rest of the world was like, figuring that if they climbed high enough they could see beyond the forest. But the higher they climbed, the more forest they saw, until Pimwe said to his sister, "It's no use. There is nothing in the world but forest." It still makes her sad to think about Pimwe and Kima.

On the way home from school, Esther is quiet. She doesn't feel like talking to Millie. She wonders if Miss McKeon will mark her wrong for writing "Indian," instead of "uncivilized." I'm glad I wrote it, she assures herself. So what if I get a lower mark? Who cares about Miss McKeon and her stupid test anyway? Miss McKeon really doesn't seem very smart, even if she *is* a teacher— and it's not because she doesn't like me. She used to think all her teachers were intelligent, even if she didn't like them. Now she wonders. It's strange and scary thinking teachers aren't intelligent. When she was little, she thought that when she got older, she wouldn't be afraid anymore. But now there are things she's afraid of that she didn't even think about when she was little. Like not knowing who's right and who's wrong. And what if she's almost certain she's right and nobody agrees with her. Esther digs her hands into her pockets and determines not to care; she is tired of being encumbered by other people's thoughts. Just because Miss McKeon thinks something is so doesn't make it true. Miss McKeon would probably think Mr. Brenner is civilized just because he speaks English and can read and write. But what if she knew he bit the bookkeeper on the neck?

Millie asks her why she's so quiet.

"I was just thinking," Esther says.

"What about?"

"Oh, nothing."

"You can't be thinking about *nothing*."

"Well, nothing *important*."

She's glad when Millie leaves her. She likes Millie, but she doesn't want to have to tell her everything. Is it possible Millie suspected what she was thinking about Mr. Brenner? That's crazy. How could she? Still, it was odd that Millie kept asking. And sometimes she imagines *she* can tell what other people are thinking, even if they don't say anything. Most of the time, she hopes she's wrong because usually she imagines a person is thinking something bad about her, or things that aren't nice to say. Maybe that's what being civilized means—acting like you're supposed to act no matter how you feel or what you're thinking. Maybe she's not the only one who sometimes thinks mean things, disgusting things—things she'd die if anyone ever found out about. Maybe everyone has terrible feelings that nobody knows about, and everybody thinks about certain things they wouldn't dare tell anyone. Esther is awed by a sudden awareness of what appears to her as a wonderful revelation, both disturbing and exquisite—like a sparrow soaring into the sky and spreading its wings and catching fire in the sunlight, becoming suddenly, marvelously, an extraordinary creature of many colors. Too excited to walk, Esther runs home.

Out of breath, her heart pounding, she enters the house. She hears her father's voice, animated, joyous. "Thank God!" he is saying. "God has helped." Her heart turns over. Ben! Ben must be back! She rushes into the kitchen, tears gushing from her eyes. "Where is he, Papa? Where is he?" she cries. "Is he upstairs?"

Her father stares at her, confused. "What are you talking about?" he asks. "What's wrong with you?"

"Benjamin! Where is he?"

Her father's eyes become huge, and his voice wavers. "I don't know. Do you know?" he asks.

Her mother has turned away from the range and is standing rigid, squeezing a wooden spoon, her mouth quivering.

Esther looks from one to the other. "I thought—I heard Papa say 'God has helped,' so I imagined. . . ."

Malka's shoulders drop. The spoon falls from her hand. Esther picks it up and gives it to her. "I'm sorry, Mama. I just thought. . . ." Malka's eyes fill as she caresses Esther's cheek. She opens her mouth to speak, but cannot. She turns back to the range and continues to stir the soup.

When Esther returns from hanging up her hat and coat, her father is sitting down and his animation is gone. But he goes on, speaking still of God's goodness. "Who would have thought it?" he says. "A pious young man—like a messenger from the Almighty. No, God has not forsaken me."

Esther is bewildered and impatient. "Who?" she cries. "Who are you talking about?"

Her father tells her that Mr. Lieberman's store has been rented.

"Who rented it?" she asks.

"A tailor."

Esther is still baffled.

Her father cannot contain himself. He explains that this tailor has just come from Europe, that he is a fine devout young man with a wife and two children, who fled from Germany, from that momzer, Hitler.

Esther wants to cover her ears. She understands! She understands now why he sounded so happy, why he was thanking God. His minyan! His minyan is saved! He has a substitute for Mr. Lieberman. And for Ben! That's all he cares about. He doesn't even really care about Ben. She can't look at him!

"One must have faith," he goes on. "One must not give up hope."

But what about *Ben*, she wants to shout. Have you forgotten about *Ben*?

Her father goes on, his face rapturous. Her mother places a bowl of potato soup on the table and tells her to sit down. Esther looks up into her mother's face, her eyes pleading. Why doesn't she stop him? Her mother's face is expressionless—as though she has stopped feeling anything.

Malka hears the door bang shut behind Esther. The child is upset, angry. Why not? She is young. She still thinks her anger will matter. If I thought it would matter, I'd be angry too—not empty, exhausted. She puts a glass of tea before her husband. Look at him, sitting there with his eager eyes as though nothing has happened. Poor, miserable fool, what else can he do? But she cannot bear it. Abruptly, without a word, Malka leaves the kitchen and goes upstairs.

She stands in her bedroom, her eyes searching, until they fall on the bureau. She opens the center drawer and from under the slips and nightgowns—presents from her son—she takes out his torn shirt. She cannot even remember what it was that time that brought it about, but he stood once again facing his father's fury, silent, not striking back—until suddenly he began tearing at himself. She did not find the shirt until months later when she went to turn over his mattress.

A cry fills the room before Malka presses her lips into her son's shirt, and weeps quietly.

21

A green express truck is parked across the street. The new family has arrived. The woman outside directing the moving men is small and wiry. Her black hair is pulled back from a white face into a tight bun. There is a proud tilt to her head and from a distance she appears striking. But she is not a pretty woman. Her nose is beaked, and premature pouches under her darting eyes give her both a haggard and predatory look. When she smiles up at the thick-necked men, admonishing them as gently as she can to "take care," "please not to scratch," the pull at the corners of her mouth seems painful, and the bulging cords in her neck convey a stifled scream.

A tall man is standing silently beside the door of the tailor store. He is slender and pale, with a delicate nose, a soft, supplicating mouth, and azure eyes retreating into a profusion of blond lashes. He appears disengaged from what is going on, except for the sporadic, furtive shifting of his eyes in the direction of the men moving the furniture past him. The woman, following protectively behind each piece of furniture, seems unmindful of him. But Malka, watching from her window, sees a fierce little person trying to shield her fragile husband from the indignity that has befallen him. As if it wasn't enough that he had to become a tailor—to have to live yet behind his dingy store in two small dark rooms. Zalman told her the man had been a teacher of mathematics at the *gymnasium* in Berlin. She is still not certain about mathematics, but a *gymnasium*, he told her, is like a high school where Lila will go next year. When Hitler came and Jews were forbidden to teach in the schools, the young man went back to Frankfurt to help out in his father's tailor store and became a tailor too, and a cleaner and presser. But then it became so bad he decided to leave altogether. His father refused to go with him; his home, he said, was in Frankfurt, and he was too old to go looking for a new one. So both parents stayed behind, and who knows what has happened to them by now. Malka sighs. It's the same story. True, her parents were already lying in the ground, but whomever she had, she left behind. Terrible things have been going on in Russia too. Who knows what has happened to her sister? It's a year already since the last letter. And whom does she have here? No one. He? He has. Brothers, sisters, cousins—family. She has no one— only her children. And now her son has vanished. Where is he, God? Where is he?

Grudgingly, Esther eyes the newcomers from the top of her stoop. They are intruders. The desolate store, with its fixtures still and silent, seemed a fittingly solemn memorial to Mr. Lieberman. These strangers, who didn't even know him or care about him, are messing it up. And sometimes, she imagines the yellow light bulb is burning, and she can hear the soft hissing sound of the pressing machine, and she's sure Mr. Lieberman is still there, raising and lowering it, and sweating. She's imagined him leaning back with the long pole in his hand, reaching for a garment on the high rack, while she waits in suspense to see whether or not his yarmulka will fall off his head. Often, she can't believe he is dead, and she'll never see him again. Inside her, he's alive. But if the store becomes somebody else's, new images will wipe out the old ones, and little by little, there will be nothing left of **Mr.** Lieberman. She walks down a few steps, hesitates, then descends to the bottom step and sits down. The tall man across the street seems to sense she is scrutinizing him and goes into the store. He stands behind the pressing machine, running his hands over its surfaces. He begins raising and lowering it. Esther moves to the curb so she can see better. He doesn't look right, standing there behind the machine; he doesn't look like a presser. And it's not because he has his hat and coat on; it's his face. He looks afraid.

She crosses the street and surreptitiously glances into the back of the moving van. It's almost empty. The small stringy-looking woman sprints out of the store to stand beside the moving men while they lift out a huge chifforobe. Esther can't help staring. It's different from any furniture she's seen before—much bigger and more decorated, with flowers and leaves carved into the heavy dark wood, and animal heads for handles. As the splendid-looking chifforobe approaches, the store seems to become smaller and shabbier. Esther senses that something especially sad is happening. The men have trouble fitting it through the door, and the woman keeps pleading, "Please be careful. Try not to scratch." The man in front, a beady-eyed giant with hairy hands, growls over his shoulder, "One of them pain-in-the-ass mockeys!" The man in back snickers. Esther wants to leap up and claw them. Luckily, the woman doesn't hear or doesn't understand. When the woman comes out again, Esther smiles at her. The woman smiles back. Maybe it won't be so bad. She's heard they have children. She wonders whether they're boys or girls and how old they are. The woman is even more nervous when the men lift the next piece of furniture out of the van. It's a desk! Not even the principal's desk in school is so big! And this one has designs on the drawers, and the top is beautiful, glossy leather with a gold border. She's never known anyone who had a *desk* in the *house*! She wonders where the children are.

Finally, a girl and a boy come running out of the store. They stop abruptly when they see Esther looking at them. Their eyes quiver. She smiles at them. Their mouths move uncertainly. They seem to want to smile back, but don't. The girl looks like her father, only sturdier, and her coloring is more vivid, with rosy cheeks and thick reddish-blond braids that hang down over her chest almost to her waist. After a moment, her eyes stop quivering and become bold, almost defiant; they are green with amber flecks and straight lashes. Her mouth is full and curved and red, and the light freckles all over her face give her an iridescent gleam. She looks more like a picture than a person. She reminds Esther of Johanna in her old geography book who lived in a village in Bavaria. The boy is a startling contrast, black-haired like his mother, with a large head and a thin truncated body. His eyes are blue like his father's, but livelier; they race over Esther's face and come to rest at her mouth.

Esther says, "Hello."

The brother and sister keep staring at her. The girl looks as if she is about to speak. Esther remembers that Johanna who lived in Bavaria spoke German. Papa said they came from Germany. Maybe they can't speak English.

At last the girl speaks. "Wie geht's," she says.

She *does* speak a different language. It sounds like Yiddish but not exactly. Esther wonders if she should say something in Yiddish. While she is deciding, the girl, flushing self-consciously, speaks again. "Hallo," she says.

The accent seems different from any she's heard before. "What's your name?" Esther asks.

The girl's face closes up in confusion. The boy's eyes are still fixed on her mouth, and he looks bewildered. Esther points to herself and says, "Esther." Then she points to

the girl and looks inquiringly at her. The girl's face opens
up and her eyes brighten. "Liesl," she says eagerly, pointing to herself. Esther is delighted. She points to the boy
and looks questioningly at him. He blushes violently and
says nothing. Finally, his sister says, "Rudi. Er heisst
Rudi." Now Esther is confused. She understands what the
girl is saying, but isn't sure it's Yiddish. "Do you speak
English?" she asks.

Liesl shakes her head sadly. "Nein," she says. "Nein."
But when she sees Esther's shoulders fall, she adds
quickly, "Ein bisschen," and then hesitantly, "A little."

Esther decides to take a chance. "Do you speak Yiddish?" she asks in Yiddish.

"Ja! Ja!" Liesl exclaims, nodding her head vigorously.
And the boy Rudi smiles for the first time, shivering with
excitement.

The three children stand together, all speechless with
inexpressible wonder and their sudden sense of relatedness. Liesl is the first to speak. She is like a bottle of
bubbly beverage coming uncorked. The words spurt and
gush and stream out, her eyes sparkling. She is so happy
she has found a friend she can speak to! And so soon! So
quickly! She never believed! Her mother and father told
her not to worry, but she did. All the way over on the ship
she couldn't sleep. She was afraid everyone would make
fun of her if she tried to speak English like she learned
in school. She had just started learning when they wouldn't
let her come to the school anymore. Her parents told her
that children would understand Yiddish, but she couldn't
imagine it. None of her friends in Berlin spoke Yiddish.
If her grandmother had not come to live with them when
she was little, she would not know Yiddish either. How
lucky that Grandma came! When they had to leave Berlin
and go to Frankfurt, her other Grandma and Grandpa
spoke Yiddish too. "No one here speaks German. Do they?"
she asks suddenly.

Esther shakes her head quickly, hoping Liesl will go on with her narrative. She is enchanted and awed by the volubility, the drama, the names of places she's never heard about—Berlin, Frankfurt. Coming across the ocean in a ship! (Just like Mama!) Not being allowed to come to school anymore! Why?

"Why?" she asks. "Why wouldn't they let you come to school?"

"Because we're Jews," Liesl tells her, clearly surprised that the reason was not obvious. "Before they made us stop coming," she goes on, "the other kids were mean to us. The girls would pinch me so hard, they'd leave marks on my arm. Some scratched me—girls who used to be my friends. The boys were worse. They made Rudi deaf."

"Rudi is *deaf*?"

"Yes. That's why he keeps looking at your mouth. If he doesn't watch your lips, he can't tell what you're saying."

Staring at Rudi, whose pale face has turned crimson again, Esther asks, "Can he speak?"

"Yes, he can speak. But he's very bashful since it happened."

"How did they make him deaf?" Esther asks.

"They beat him up. Boys bigger than he was. They left him outside in the snow, bleeding. He didn't come home from school, so my mother and I went looking for him. When we found him, the blood was frozen on his face and all over his neck. People had walked by and had seen him lying by the school fence, but no one helped him. It made me so angry! My mother told me I must not hate them, that they were not bad people. They were only afraid."

"What were they afraid of?"

"Of the Brown Shirts, the Hitler Youth, of the other people."

Esther is reluctant to ask who the Brown Shirts were. Liesl acts as if everyone naturally knows what she's talking about. The Hitler Youth were probably children who believed in Hitler, like believing in President Roosevelt. No, it can't be the same thing. President Roosevelt is important and you can admire him, but you don't *believe* in him, like in God—or like Angie believes in Jesus. It could be something you got elected to if you did something Hitler thought was good. Maybe you had to pass a test. "Were the boys who beat Rudi up Hitler Youth?" she asks.

"Probably. They're the worst ones. Some of them even squeal on their parents."

"To whom?"

"To the Gestapo."

"The what?"

"The Secret Police. They're horrible."

Esther is baffled. How can the police be horrible? "What do they squeal on their parents about?" she asks.

"Mostly if they say something bad about Hitler, or if they break the Nuremberg laws."

"Break what?"

"Laws," Liesl says again in German. "I don't know the word in Yiddish. Laws are what you must do or else the government punishes you."

Liesl uses a German word for government but punishment is spoken in Yiddish, and Esther thinks she understands. "Like the Aserehs Hadibros," she says.

"The what?" Liesl asks.

"Don't you know what the Aserehs Hadibros are?" Esther asks, feigning more astonishment than she feels.

"No, I don't!" Liesl says, resentfully. Her green eyes suddenly smoulder and her chin pushes out pugnaciously.

Abruptly, Esther senses that Liesl is not at all what she seems, that she is painfully vulnerable, that she is afraid of being found wanting; her impressive manner is her protection. She must be careful not to hurt Liesl's feelings. Liesl could get really mad at her. It's true she kind of wanted to get even with Liesl for making her feel ignorant, but she really is surprised that someone who speaks Yiddish doesn't know what the Aserehs Hadibros are. She tries to explain to Liesl in Yiddish about The Ten Commandments, but has difficulty because she knows only the Hebrew word for commandment. And she doesn't know other Yiddish words she needs to explain about them. Finally she asks, "Didn't you go to Hebrew school?"

"No," Liesl says. "Grandma wanted me to, but my father said they would teach me only fairy tales and foolishness. Now he wants me to go, and I don't want to. They'll put me in a class with little children."

"He doesn't think it's foolishness anymore?"

"I don't know. He just says I should go. He even wants Rudi to have a Bar Mitzva. I heard him tell my mother. She became annoyed. She doesn't want me to go to Hebrew school."

Esther is puzzled. Why should anyone be annoyed about a Bar Mitzva? You had to have one or else you weren't Jewish. But she has a feeling that if she says so to this girl, she will evoke either derision or hostility. Instead she asks her, "How old are you?"

"Ten," Liesl tells her.

"*Ten*?" Esther is amazed. "You seem much older."

"I know," Liesl says, somewhat smugly. Esther isn't sure whether or not she's going to like this girl. "How old is *he*?" she asks, looking at Rudi. She is afraid to ask him directly—to break into his silence. It seems precious to him. But Liesl, speaking suddenly in a stern, pedagogical manner, says, "You must ask *him*, not me! You must not treat him as if he is dumb just because he is deaf. He is not a fool! He was first in his class before everything happened."

Esther is embarrassed. She is also put out with Liesl. Who does she think she is anyway, scolding like that? But

174

enunciating slowly and carefully, she asks Rudi (whose cheeks are burning), "How old are you?"

"Nine," Rudi answers softly.

Liesl scolds her again. "You must not speak to him in that silly way! He can read lips very quickly. You only have to be sure to face him when you speak. But you must speak to him the same as you do to other people!"

Esther's shoulders stiffen and rise. How is she supposed to know how to speak to a deaf person? She's never done it before. What nerve this girl has—bossing her around and calling her silly!

Liesl seems to know immediately that the new friendship is in jeopardy. Her eyes tremble. "I didn't mean to offend you," she says anxiously. "I can't help myself sometimes. I become upset and I talk too harshly. I'm sorry. I want you to be my friend. Don't be angry with me."

Esther is moved and ashamed of herself. Liesl reminds her of Millie. "I'm not angry with you," she says. And turning to Rudi, she asks him briskly, "What is your last name?"

"Tauber," he says, a little more confidently.

Liesl smiles approvingly at both of them.

Everything has been carried in and the emptied moving van is clattering down the street. Mrs. Tauber, wearing a blue smock over her black dress, appears in the doorway and summons her children. "There is work to be done," she tells them, glancing warily at Esther. She speaks German, but Esther understands. Liesl says, "I must go in now," Rudi smiles apologetically, and the two children follow their mother into the store. Esther calls after them, "I'll see you later." She runs across the street. She is relieved as well as excited. It was a strain. She's never had such a long, complicated conversation in Yiddish. Talking with her parents was different; with them she never had to search for the right word. And something else had made it exhausting. All the time she was talking, she was self-conscious. No, it wasn't just because her Yiddish wasn't so good. It was something else. After a brief pretense of perplexity, Esther confesses to herself. She's always been a little ashamed of speaking Yiddish in front of her friends. It was wrong and stupid of her, she knew, but still.... And hammering unpleasantly in her head is the probability that it has to do with the way she feels about her family—about their poverty and its humiliations, about her parents' uncouth epithets, their ignorance (already she's learned things in school they've never even heard of), her father's ugly rages, her mother's disfiguring grief. And Ben—and his strangeness. Only Lila, even though she's often disagreeable, acted like most other people.

But her parents' language holds the seed of friendship with the new girl. She must think more about it. There is so much to think about. What if Papa knew that the pious man he's so happy about wouldn't let his daughter go to Hebrew school, that he said it was foolishness and fairy tales? And how come he changed his mind? Is he really religious now? Imagine being pinched and scratched and beat up just because you're Jewish! It's like when Mama was a little girl in Russia. But that was in the olden days. How can such things happen *now*? But maybe in Europe they can. Not in America. No, not in America. But why? There is so much to figure out. She runs up the steps and tiptoes to her bedroom. She wants to be alone for a while. She wants to sit quietly and think. Just thinking can be more exciting than almost anything else.

22

The next day on the way home from school, Esther tells Millie about the new girl and her little brother and everything that happened to them. Millie is fascinated; she can't wait to meet them.

"But you won't be able to talk to them or understand them," Esther says.

"Yes, I will. You said the girl could speak a little English."

"Only a tiny bit."

"Then you'll be our translator, and little by little I'll teach her English." Millie's doleful brown eyes brighten. Her sallow cheeks take on color.

"What do you mean *you'll* teach her?" Esther says, suddenly annoyed with Millie. "I can teach her too, you know."

"Who said you couldn't?"

"Nobody did," Esther says sullenly. Something in Millie's manner is making her apprehensive.

"She'll need lots of help from both of us," Millie says earnestly. "After all, she'll have to go to school. And her little brother too. Is he really and truly *deaf*?"

"What do you mean, 'really and truly'? I told you he was."

"But people can be just a little hard of hearing."

"No, he's not just a little hard of hearing," Esther says,

still irritated with Millie. "He's deaf. He has to figure out what you're saying from the way your mouth moves."

"You mean lip-reading," Millie says, in what seems to Esther a superior tone.

"Of course, I mean lip-reading," Esther says, wishing she hadn't just heard the expression for the first time.

She has barely put down her books and had her milk and cookies when Millie arrives, breathless. She must have run all the way. She wants them to go over and call for Liesl and Rudi. She seems just as interested in the younger boy as in the girl. Esther finds it odd. "Hold your horses, Millie," she says. "I'm not finished. Want one?" she asks, proffering her mother's cinnamon cookies.

"No, thank you," Millie says. "Hurry up."

It's the first time Millie has refused a cinnamon cookie.

As they start across the street, Liesl and Rudi come out of the store, looking as if they'd been waiting. Esther introduces Millie, adding promptly, "She doesn't speak Yiddish."

"Is she Jewish?" Liesl asks immediately.

"What did she say?" Millie asks.

"She wants to know if you're Jewish."

"Tell her of course I am! Tell her!" Millie demands.

Esther says that Millie is Jewish. Both Liesl and Rudi look relieved. "My mother told me there are Christians next door, a girl my own age," Liesl says.

"She means the Riccios," Esther says. "The girl's name is Angie."

"Is she your friend?" Liesl asks.

"Yes, she's my friend."

"What is she saying?" Millie asks Esther. "What are you talking about?"

"She wanted to know about Angie. I think she's worried because Angie's a Christian," Esther says. And in an undertone of solemn significance she adds, "You can imagine why."

Millie, visibly agitated—her eyes jumping back and forth from the sister to the brother—asks Esther, "How do you say I would like to be your friend?"

Esther is finding Millie's zealous wooing of the newcomers eccentric and tiresome. "For goodness' sakes, Millie, that sounds silly," she says.

"Tell me anyway," Millie insists.

Reluctantly, Esther translates. Millie repeats after her, looking soulfully into Liesl's eyes and then into Rudi's. Her pronunciation is awkward. Rudi blushes. Liesl's eyes twinkle with amusement, but Esther can tell she is finding Millie appealing. She asks Esther, "How do you say in English, I also hope we will be friends?" Esther tells her, and Liesl, looking fervently at Millie, carefully repeats the words. Millie's eyes do not twinkle at Liesl's foreign accent; they fill with sympathetic concern. Esther is finding the interchange between the two girls annoying. She is the link between them, but she's beginning to feel left out.

23

Weeks pass. Esther feels more and more left out. Liesl's and Rudi's English improves. Their parents studied English in Germany and help them and, using Esther as an intermediary, Millie has been diligent and relentless. Liesl is enrolled in school; they put her in 5A. Esther still finds it hard to believe that Liesl is younger than she is; she seems old—like Millie. Rudi will have to be sent to a special school for the deaf. Meanwhile, his mother takes books out of the library and teaches him at home. She used to be a teacher in Germany, Liesl tells Esther, and so was her father. Esther is awed; she's never had friends whose parents were teachers. No wonder Mr. Tauber looks peculiar behind the pressing machine. And maybe that explains her mixed-up feelings about Liesl and Rudi. She feels sorry about the dreadful things that happened to them and the trouble they are having now, but not the way Millie seems to. Esther can't help feeling that in some ways, they're luckier than she is—except, of course, for Rudi's being deaf. The more she has to do with her, the more she perceives a certain pride and resiliency and strength overcoming Liesl's insecurity and, in a strange way, Rudi's too. Like when Liesl refused to let Millie help with her homework, saying she never needed help with schoolwork before and she didn't want any now. Millie was so disappointed; but it didn't stop her from being intensely concerned with Liesl, and with Rudi as well. Both of them like Millie too—the way Liesl kept apologizing afterward for refusing the help with her homework. She can't explain exactly why—no one is unpleasant to her—but Esther feels forsaken. She spends more time with Angie, who is delighted. She's always liked Angie just as much as she did Millie, but Millie generally managed to exclude Angie. They even had a fight about it once, with Millie furiously insisting that she was *not* jealous of Angie, that it was the stupidest thing she ever heard. But Esther is sure she was. Now Millie doesn't seem the least bit jealous. And no matter how nice Angie acts, Liesl is still a little afraid of her. That seems to please Millie too.

Lying in bed beside her sister, Esther wishes Lila wouldn't fall asleep just when they were talking. Lila can be so exasperating! But she's probably right about Millie, that she needs someone to feel sorry for so she can feel important. "You told me yourself how her parents make her feel like dirt," Lila said. "She thinks those kids across the street are in worse shape than you are, so she switched to them." Lila has an awful way of saying things, but she's right. Millie probably loves it when I don't have money for the movies, so she can treat me. She looked so happy when she brought us rolls of toilet paper so we wouldn't have to use torn-up newspapers. And how excited she got when she sneaked the cardboards out of her father's shirts and cut them out to stick in my shoes. I was grateful because I didn't want Mama to know about the holes in my shoes; I was afraid she'd make me get the Home Relief ones. Millie was probably glad I had holes in my shoes. I didn't understand, but now I do. And she understands about Rudi too, why Millie is always hovering over him, even when Liesl doesn't want her to. Rudi, small, frail and damaged, is like that sparrow they found with the broken wing.

The following evening, walking to Hebrew school in a driving rain, Esther is filled with shame and guilt. In a desperate effort to reclaim Millie for herself, she told her about Ben—not only how long he's been missing this time, but about the other times, even about finding him all tied up under the steps. She didn't come right out and say it, but she tried to give Millie the impression that there was something wrong with Ben, that in a way she couldn't explain, he was damaged too. Millie's face grew rapt as she listened.

The rain is coming down in sheets and the wind is strong. Her mother wanted her to stay home, but she couldn't. Right after she finished telling Millie, she began to feel bad. All through supper she felt so sick, she could hardly eat. When it began to rain, she wanted to get out. She wanted to feel the wind slapping her and rain spitting in her face. She told her mother she had an important test, that she *had* to go. Her mother said she should at least put on her raincape over her coat and tie the hood tight around her head. Wearing it for the first time, the new raincape Ben gave her just before he disappeared, she is miserable. She walks with her head bent, mumbling to herself. "Please forgive me, Ben. I shouldn't have talked about you, not for such a stinking reason. I'm sorry, Ben, and I hope Millie doesn't like me better now. I hope she *hates* me. I really and truly do. And I don't think you're crazy. I just don't understand a lot of things about you. But please, please come home." When she raises her head, rivulets of rain mingle with the tears running down her cheeks. "Please God, forgive me," she says softly. "Don't punish me by making Ben stay away. Please God, I miss him."

Arriving at the Talmud Torah, she wipes her face with her coat sleeve and pushes open the heavy door. The primary grades are still in class. The early arrivals for the second session are gathered in the auditorium waiting for the six o'clock bell. Her entrance creates a stir among the girls. Exclamations of "How *pretty*!" "I *love* it!" "When did you *get* it?" It's the raincape; she almost forgot she had it on. The girls cluster around her. She feels the distaste for herself dissolving and her misery diminishing. She begins to feel good. But she notices Gladys Suretsky slumped in a folding chair, with her chin on her chest and her eyes staring sulkily at the raincape. Gladys sitting there and not saying anything is peculiar because generally when they're waiting for the bell, Gladys is surrounded by most of the girls in the class, blabbing away with her big mouth, with her big bust sticking out. (It's probably true that she started wearing a brassiere and getting her monthlies when she was nine years old.) She didn't hang around Gladys; she knew Gladys didn't like her—even before she won the prize for the best composition in the school on "Why I Like to Come to Sabbath Services." When she was up on the stage and Mr. Spiro was fastening her prize, a blue Mogen David on a gold chain, around her neck, she saw Gladys looking at it like any minute she was going to run up and yank it off. Gladys is looking at her the same way now. She's so silly—just because everybody likes my new raincape.

Suddenly, Gladys gets up and smiles and comes over to Esther. "Let's see your fancy new cape," she says, taking it in her hand. Esther watches the big fingers with their long nails run up and down the surface of her cape. She sees one of the fingers stick out. No! She can't believe it! No! Not her new raincape! It's torn! Gladys pushed her finger right through it! She can hear Gladys saying, "I didn't know it was such cheap junk. I would have been more careful." Esther is trembling. Tears are rushing to her eyes, but she chokes them back. That's just what Gladys wants—for her to act like a cry-baby. The bell rings. Thelma Halperin and Beatie Kravitz walk with Esther as she leaves the auditorium. Beatie, who is small and quiet, seems almost as upset as Esther. "She did it on purpose. I saw," Beatie murmurs. Thelma says, "Don't worry, Esther, maybe your mother can paste it together."

Esther hangs up her coat in the back of the room and carefully drapes her raincape over it, soothing its bruise with her fingertips, tenderly, trying terribly hard not to cry, and slowly, as though reluctant to leave her wounded cape untended and alone, walks to her seat and sits down. She sits with her head bent low over her desk, battering her mind against the monstrousness of Gladys' assault, against the enigma of irrational malevolence. How is it born? What nourishes it and sustains it and makes it strike out? Why has she provoked it? Where is it lurking to strike again? How does one escape it? But her efforts only bewilder and frighten her. She finds herself peering into an abyss and being sucked into it. Her impotence is infuriating. Miraculously, Mr. Podoloff doesn't call on her even once—as if he knows and doesn't dare.

When class is over, she is still seething. She lingers behind the others, fussing at her desk; she doesn't want to talk to anyone. But she has to go to the bathroom. Finally she puts on her coat and her raincape over it, leaves the room, and runs down the steps. She opens the toilet door. Good. There's nobody inside. She's still afraid she might cry. She sits down on the toilet. A moment later, she is staring, horrified, at the door in front of her. Scrawled there in huge letters is "LILA HIRSCH IS A WHOOER." Her head falls into her lap. Ugly and mean! It's all ugliness and meanness! She keeps sobbing and sobbing. Her chest is cracking, the jagged pieces are sticking into her, but she can't stop. Suddenly, she's afraid she'll be locked in. She rises quickly and pulls up her panties. Once again, she confronts the scrawl on the door. Hurrying, she opens her pencil box, takes out a pencil, and with its eraser rubs and rubs at the LILA HIRSCH. When her sister's name has been obliterated, she stops rubbing. Her heart thumping, she reverses the pencil and writes GLADYS

184

SURETSKY in the smeared space. She looks at "GLADYS SURETSKY IS A WHOOER." Her head is pounding. Clenching the pencil to keep it from shaking, she adds underneath, "THE BOYS SQUEEZE HER TITS." Then she grabs her books, throws open the toilet door, and runs from the building.

Spring
1937

---

with having Mr. Wexler for a teacher. She likes him a lot. And not because he's Jewish. Miss Rosenbaum in 2B was Jewish and she didn't especially like her. And it wasn't because she was cross-eyed and everybody called her "Cock-eyed Rosie." Mr. Wexler wears glasses too, but he's not cross-eyed. His eyes are light brown and soft-looking, and he has a bushy mustache and keeps a pipe in his pocket. He's always cracking jokes. He never gets angry; he makes everything into a joke. And she can tell he likes her too. He even asked her to copy over her poem so he could keep it. Millie isn't so crazy about him. She doesn't think you learn much in his class; she says he fools around too much. If Liesl were in the class, she probably wouldn't like him either; she'd give the same reason as Millie. They're both so *serious*, but Millie is worse. She's still friends with both of them, but not *best* friends with either one. Angie and Liesl are in the same class in school, but not really friends. Angie says Liesl doesn't like her; she'd be friends with her if she did. Esther concludes that nobody especially cares about *her*, but it doesn't matter so much anymore; she honestly doesn't care especially about any of them either. Maybe that's what Lila means about growing up and being independent. Probably, that's what being grown up means. At least until you fall in love.

Next term, she'll be in junior high. She doesn't know if boys and girls fall in love in junior high, but some of them act like it—walking home from school hugging each other. Sometimes, when she passes Meyers' Candy Store, she sees Lila outside and some boy is hugging her. (Does that make her a whooer?) Nobody knows yet who wrote that awful thing about Gladys on the toilet door. Gladys says she'll find out someday and that person will be sorry. If anyone wrote something like that about me, I'd just erase it and not tell anybody. But no one would write anything like that about *her*, and nobody would ever believe she wrote it. Every once in a while the words she wrote on the door flash through her mind, and how she lay in bed that night, mortified, burying her face in her pillow and that tingling taking hold of her, compelling her body into outlandish undulations and becoming suddenly so excruciatingly pleasurable, she had to brace herself against the bed to bear it. And afterwards, the feeling of release. She doesn't know what happened, but when she thinks about what she wrote and what she did afterwards, she feels dirty and ashamed. She's sure she'll never do it again.

If only she could stop wondering why somebody wrote that about Lila? She keeps remembering last Halloween. Lila stayed out real late and came tiptoeing upstairs, but Ben heard her. He came into the bedroom holding a magazine he must have been reading and slapped her across the face with it. I couldn't believe it! Lila cried out, but Ben told her to shut up, he'd brain her if she woke Mama and Papa. Then he called her a tramp. Lila was crying and could hardly talk, but she wanted to know why, what did she do that was so terrible.

"I don't know what you did or what you didn't do in there but I saw you go in. Candy-store corners aren't enough for you," Ben said between his teeth, "now it's cellar clubs! The Lancers S.A.C. Social athletic clubs they call them. There's only one kind of social and athletic activity those guys are interested in. I know!"

"But it was just a Halloween party with—with costumes and prizes and—"

Lila's coat was unbuttoned and Ben could see her costume. "And that's why you're wearing that ridiculous outfit and that stupid bow in your hair!" he said, ripping the big red bow off Lila's head and throwing it on the floor. Lila had gone as Baby Snooks and had on a little kid's dress that just covered her panties—except probably when she bent over—and the big red bow in her hair.

"But Ben, all we did was dance and—" Lila said.

"I don't want to hear what you did. I just don't want to

see you going in there again. Y'hear?" Ben kept talking between his teeth. "Mama and Papa have enough to worry about without you being a tramp." And he turned and left the room. But a minute later, he was back. "Lila, I'm sorry I hit you," he said softly. "I'm very sorry. I just don't want you to get in trouble. I—" And his voice began to crack like any minute he might cry too. Lila was sitting on the bed and crying and didn't say anything. Ben picked up the red bow from the floor and put it on the bureau. Then he came over and kissed Lila quickly on the head before he went out again.

Esther feels herself choking up.

Why doesn't Angie hurry up? What's taking her so long? She just went in to get her ball. What if she changed her mind about playing and doesn't come out? All of a sudden Esther is afraid. No, she's not independent yet. Actually, she's selfish. She wants people to like her a lot, even if she doesn't care that much about them. When she and Millie were best friends, Angie used to be left out lots of times. Esther remembers that she felt bad about it sometimes, but not all the time.

She can see Mr. Tauber in his store. He's stopping again. He's just standing there and staring down at whatever he's pressing, like he can't believe it's really there. He looks so different from Mr. Lieberman. Even though he's younger and much taller, he looks weaker, like he can hardly push down the pressing machine. And he doesn't wear a yarmulka; he just keeps his hat on. Liesl says he never even used to have a *hat*. Could it be that he doesn't have a yarmulka? No, that's silly; he could have bought one by now. But he's such a strange man—so sad-looking all the time. Mrs. Tauber is just as skinny as he is, but she seems strong—and she hardly ever stands still. She gets Rudi up very early in the morning and rides with him on the train to his special school. When she comes home, she helps out with the customers in the store. Then she goes to bring Rudi home. Rudi talks a little more now. He says soon he'll be able to go on the train by himself.

Angie is coming, running across the street. Her hair is flying and her brown eyes are shining. Esther wants to hug her. She *does* like Angie best.

They have finished one game. Angie won. They are starting another when Willie and Clara arrive. Esther hasn't seen either of them for a long time. The last time she saw Willie was when he was on strike and there was another fight about religion and Willie wouldn't go with her father to make a minyan. She's glad he's come again. She's even sort of glad to see Clara.

Willie kisses her and gives her a big hug and asks if she's still his sweetheart, while Clara stands with her stolid face and square body, waiting for him to finish his foolishness. Then she asks Esther what class she's in now in school and reports that her Ethel got all As on her report card and that they've been shopping already for a graduation dress because before you turn around, June will come and Ethel, only sixteen years old, will graduate high school. Esther can't resist. With an unmistakable smirk in her voice, she says, "Yes, I know. She skipped three times." But Clara's obtuseness is impervious; getting more effusive, she goes on, "You're absolutely right. Three times they skipped her. And who knows how many more times she could've skipped if there wasn't a law."

A law? Esther never heard of such a law. But with Clara you can never tell—maybe she bothered them so much, they had to tell her there was one.

Esther bangs the ball against the stoop. She can hear Clara going down the five slightly broken steps to the basement, gasping and snorting and saying to Willie, "A person could get killed here." Next, she'll go inside and collapse in a chair like God knows what she had to go through to get there, and as soon as she catches her breath she's going to start bragging to Mama about her Ethel and ask about Lila's marks and Mama will say she doesn't know and it'll be true because Mama doesn't pay too much attention to marks.

Esther finishes the game with Angie before she goes in. She wins this time, but she has a feeling Angie let her. Maybe because Angie could tell that Clara made her feel bad. But lots of times she has the feeling Angie lets her win. She's better at jacks than Angie and wins almost all the time. She never lets Angie win. So why should Angie let her? Maybe she's afraid no one will play with her if she keeps winning all the time. It must be hard to be Italian on a block where almost everybody's Jewish.

When she comes in, tea is already on the table, and cinnamon cookies and rugalech, and the cut-glass bowl filled with apples and oranges and bananas. Her mother asks her if she wants a glass of tea. She says she does because she likes sitting with everybody and listening when Willie comes. Clara she can't stand, but sometimes she's very funny. Like now, the way she's looking me up and down trying to figure out what she can find wrong so she can say something about it. It's a good thing Lila's not here—we'd have one of our giggling fits.

Willie, not looking up from the apple he is peeling and with an expression on his face suggesting either mischief or a slightly troubled conscience (Esther can't tell which), asks her father, "What is happening these days with your minyan?"

Esther tenses. Her eyes keep following the dismantling of Willie's apple. She watches the shiny red twirls meander down into his plate. She hears her father say, "The minyan survives, thank God."

Willie cuts his denuded apple into quarters. "Have you found a replacement for Lieberman?" he asks.

"Yes," her father answers. "Lieberman has been replaced."

"By whom?" Willie asks.

Esther looks up into her father's face which grows more and more vibrant as he tells about the fine, pious young man who has joined the minyan: where he came from, what he had been, the suffering he had endured, and how it culminated in his coming to live across the street—concluding his tale with a sigh of thankfulness and "God helps."

Willie, who throughout the long narration has been listening attentively and impassively, erupts.

"God did not help!" he shouts. "Hitler helped!"

Her father's face falls, his eyes darken. "Madman," he breathes. "What are you saying?"

"What am *I* saying?" Willie fumes. She has seen Willie excited before but not like this. "What are *you* saying? You are uttering *insanities*! You are saying that God helps his people by heaping horrors upon them! You are saying that Hitler is a blessing whom God in his goodness has bestowed on you! Without the Nuremberg laws and the embellishments the Germans have added to them, would your fine, pious young man be here today? So it only stands to reason," Willie sneers, "that Hitler is your helper, your saviour. Who knows what wonders he still has in store? He may yet turn out to be the Messiah."

Her father is on his feet. "Azzes Ponim! Apikoris! Meshumed!" he roars. Esther clutches her chair. To call Willie insolent, a heretic, an apostate—to his face! She feels suddenly cold. "Who are you? What are you?" her father thunders. "*You* dare to mock the coming of the Messiah? Amorets! Ignoramus! Boor! You know nothing. Do you know what Yiddishkeit had come to in Germany? It was trampled on, despised. And not by the gentiles! By the Jews themselves! Is this to go unpunished? God does what must be done! He brought the flood! He destroyed Sodom and Gomorrah! He sends Hamans! Reminders! Reminders of our sinfulness!"

As Zalman's fury mounts, Willie's face softens; his eyes grow warm with compassion. "Forgive me, Zalman, for causing you pain," he says. "The truth is painful. For a skeptic like me, it has become a familiar ache. But for a believer, it can be unendurable."

Zalman falls back into his chair, his palms pressed to his forehead. "What is unendurable to me is your chutzpah! Have you no humility? Do you think your simple mind can comprehend the ways of the Almighty?"

"You are right," Willie says. "My mind is simple, ordinary. But even the simplest mind, the cloudiest eye can see that over and over again the pious are punished along with the profane, the saintly along with the sinful."

"There are no saints!" Zalman cries out. "We are all sinners!"

Esther is appalled. Her eyes widen, and her chest contracts. She feels exposed—her subterfuges stripped away. But no! Not everyone! Everyone mustn't be a sinner! Everyone mustn't be hiding terrible things! What if she doesn't know what anyone—even Mama—is really like? And the way her father looks—like he's ripping himself open. Willie has become peculiarly calm, looking down at his plate and munching on a piece of apple, as if he hasn't even heard what her father said. But after a few moments, not looking up, and with the smallest suggestion of a smile flickering across his face, he says, "Your Rebbe? The Balover? He too is a sinner?"

Zalman seems to stop breathing. He does not answer Willie's question. His eyes writhe, like a man struck blind and still struggling to see. Suddenly, as though his efforts have been rewarded and his prayers answered, his eyes light up. His voice is steady. "The Rebbe himself has explained that it is with the blood of pious men that the Almighty redeems Israel. Theirs are the noblest of deaths. For what is more noble than to sacrifice one's body for the soul of one's people? In the world to come they will reap their reward and God's justice will be vindicated."

Willie sighs resignedly and sips his tea. Zalman watches him expectantly. Finally, Willie says, "Go argue about the world to come. Even a scoundrel like me lacks the chutzpah for such an undertaking. Perhaps a learned man like you is up to it, but not I."

Zalman leaps from his chair, his arm raised. Esther stiffens. The women's hands fly to their chests. Zalman's raised arm stops in midair, shuddering. Willie stares up at it and grows pale; his voice is hushed when he speaks. "Zalman, what is the matter? I apologize for my poor jest and my impudent mouth, but what is new about them? And when have we not disagreed? But to raise your arm against me!"

Zalman lowers his arm and sits down and says nothing. Esther is sure she knows why her father is so upset. It's Ben. He's afraid of what he might have done to Ben. He has to believe it was for an important reason, for a religious purpose—that it was what God wanted. And he has to believe that God is good. She looks at her father's misery and at her mother's stricken face. But is he? Is God good?

For a long while, the only sounds are the cracking of sugar cubes, the tinkling of teaspoons, sipping, and slurping. No one speaks. Until Clara, pushing away her plate of banana peel and cookie crumbs, declares, "My Ethel is getting a scholarship to college."

Malka, heaving a deep sigh, asks wearily, "What means a scholarship?"

Willie interposes impatiently. "A scholarship is a prize for a good student to go free to college. And it is also what her Ethel, in all likelihood, will *not* get."

"What are you talking about?" Clara bellows. "Who told you she is not going to get it?"

197

"Nobody told me. Who told you she *is*? In your eyes your daughter is a princess among peasants. But only in your eyes. There are plenty of other princesses, smarter ones too."

Clara presses her mouth together, breathing noisily through her nose. Her eyes burn when she speaks. "As if you could ever have a good word for either of your children!"

"I have plenty of good words for my children," Willie says. "They are good children—like all children."

Clara's huge bosom heaves. Esther can tell she is cranking herself up to give evidence of her children's exceptional quality by reciting their remarkable accomplishments. But before Clara can speak, Willie turns to Malka and asks, "Where is Leah? I hoped this time I would see *both* your beautiful daughters."

Esther blushes.

"Look how her face is getting red," Willie goes on, grinning at Esther. "A pretty girl must not let her face get red."

Malka smiles weakly. "Leah has gone out. Where? I should know? In America does one know where a daughter goes? One is even forbidden to inquire."

"*My* daughter tells me where she is going," Clara announces, "or else she does not go!"

"Yes, yes," Willie says. "We know about your daughter."

Clara's nostrils spread out. Esther tries not to smile—the two of them together are even funnier. Usually, her father finds them funny too and kids around with them when they quarrel. But this time, he's not paying attention. He doesn't even look at them, or at anyone.

Willie turns back to Malka. "And how is Benjamin?" he asks. "What is happening with him? I can't even remember when I last saw him."

Malka's face recedes into itself.

Willie, his eyes darkening, repeats, "Malka, tell me, how is Benjamin?"

Malka's lips begin to tremble. Willie sees she is struggling to speak but is unable. Her body is veering as if about to fall. He grasps her. "What's wrong? What happened? Tell me," he pleads. Malka cannot speak. Still holding on to her, Willie swings about toward Zalman whose face has turned white. "Tell me, Zalman!" he calls across the table. "What *is* it?"

The silence pulls at Esther. She wants to scream out what has happened. Instead, she says quietly, "Benjamin is gone."

Willie's eyes dart back and forth from Malka to Zalman. "What does she mean 'gone'?" Where? For how long? Speak, one of you!"

At last Zalman speaks. "He has disappeared again. We do not know where he is. It is not like the other times. It has been months."

"Months?" Clara shrieks. "I'm fainting away. Months?"

"Be quiet!" Willie tells her. Then looking into Malka's eyes, he begs, "Speak to me, Malka. Tell me. How many months have passed?"

"Two months," Malka says.

"What happened? Did something happen to make him go away?" Willie asks.

Malka looks across the table at her husband who sits with his head bent, his face hidden from her. "What happened has happened," she says. "That does not matter now. What matters is that I do not know where my son is."

Willie turns to Zalman. "Have you searched for him? Have you told the police?"

Zalman looks up. "The police?"

"Yes, the police. Who else can help you?"

"The *police*?" Zalman says again. "To have him *arrested*?"

"Don't look at me that way! You explain to the police that your son is not well, that sometimes he is not himself. They will be good to him."

"The police will be good to my son?" Zalman's voice has grown frail.

"Yes, if you tell them about his trouble. They will be gentle with him."

Clara bangs her glass down on the table. "What is going on here?" she demands. "What is *wrong* with Benjamin? What is his *trouble*? Why have I never been told?"

"Be quiet!" Willie tells her. "It does not concern you."

"Listen to him! It does not concern me. But *him* it concerns!"

"Please Clara, I beg you," Willie says soothingly. "Not now. I will speak with you at home. But now, make an effort—be quiet."

Clara clamps her jaws together and sits with her face huddled up and her heavy breathing resounding through the room.

Willie takes Malka's hands in his own. "You must not be afraid of the police. In America, they will help you," he tells her.

"It's not only the police," Malka says.

"Who? What else are you afraid of?"

"The Relief."

"The Relief?"

"Yes, the Relief," Malka says, staring past Willie at her husband who seems to wither as she speaks. "We have been telling them that our son does not live at home, that we get nothing from him, that we don't know where he is. Now our lie has become true. Who knows what they will do if our lie is uncovered? We must eat. The children. . . . We are helpless."

Willie cannot contain the words; they hiss their way through his clenched teeth. Glowering at Zalman, he says, "How can you be helpless? God. God helps!"

Zalman rises, his face trembling. "I am leaving," he says. "I will go to the police station and I will tell them. What will be will be. God will help."

"Wait! Wait! I'm coming with you!" Willie calls, springing to his feet and running after Zalman, who is already at the door.

25

Ben has not been found, but God helps. The Relief checks continue to come, there is potato soup for supper more often, but they continue to eat. Passover is approaching and neither of the girls gets new clothes for the holiday, but to make sure that the fish for the Seders will be delicious, there is a big black carp swimming in the bathtub. Esther watches it move back and forth, back and forth, over and over. Each time it appears to know where it's going, but almost as soon as it starts moving, it confronts the bathtub's hard blank wall. It turns around and tries again, only to be confronted again by the same wall. And what for? she wonders. Tomorrow, its head will be chopped off, its skin stripped away, its belly slit open; it will be mixed and shaped with other ingredients until it is unrecognizable. Then it will be boiled in burning-hot water and eaten. A strange sadness streams through her. She sees that the carp is not black at all, but covered with an infinity of iridescent scales gleaming golden through the water as its fins, wonders of grace and delicacy, flash past her. Why, she asks herself, did God lavish such skill and intricacy on creatures no one ever really looks at, who exist only to be chopped up and eaten?

She sees the carp's round eyes protruding from either side of its head and, unexpectedly, is reminded of her father. Even the way the carp keeps swimming, coming up against a solid blank wall over and over again but, retaining the same pop-eyed expression, doesn't stop, is like her father, who has charged into preparations for the holiday as though nothing were amiss. Not her mother, whose suffering is manifest in each efficient movement and in the muscles of her face which threaten to collapse at any moment. From the instant he stood up to the challenge of Willie's skepticism and called the police, her father has seemed renewed, as though his manhood has been restored. Willie, running after him, seemed disheveled inside as well as out. They're different, Esther decides. Her father cares mostly about God. Willie doesn't care much about God; he cares about people. But she doesn't know if her father's resolve to call the police, at the risk of losing the Relief checks, bespoke his faith in God or his overriding concern for Ben. Still, he really does believe that God is good, even if it doesn't always look like it. She hopes he's right. Even if it's annoying sometimes when he acts like a king, like whatever he thinks is positively right, it still makes her less afraid. She hates it when he looks scared and hollers and hits Ben, and especially afterwards, when he sits all scrunched up and gaping. Why does he let himself do things he's so sorry for afterwards? Mama is mysterious; sometimes she frightens me. There is something unyielding about her mother. Esther suspects a fearful conflict inside, something unspeakable, deeply hidden and carefully guarded. As far as she can remember, her mother has never laughed real hard; it's as if she couldn't let herself. But her father could laugh.

How she longs for the days when her father laughed a lot and made jokes, though he sometimes embarrassed her. She isn't sure why she was embarrassed—except that he didn't act like other fathers, like she thought a father was supposed to act. Maybe if Ben comes home.... But he might get just as angry with Ben all over again, and it'll never stop. No, this time, he's probably learned a lesson, and he'll be different. He doesn't talk about him, but I can tell he's thinking about Ben all the time. And he must feel terrible because Mama hardly ever speaks to him. Mama never acted like she liked him very much, but now it's worse. Suddenly, watching the carp bump against the sides of the bathtub, Esther feels sorry for her father. She recalls the fervent way he's looked at her mother time and again, even though she never looked at him the same way.

The carp is still swimming back and forth, but not as swiftly, as if he's getting tired. He's moving unsteadily, struggling. What's wrong? Of course! He's hungry. There's no food in the water. Nobody thought of feeding him. What should she give him? But then she remembers that he's going to be killed soon anyway, so what's the point. But at least he shouldn't suffer until it happens. Hurrying out of the bathroom, Esther runs down the stairs to find out how much longer they're going to leave the fish thrashing about in the bathtub.

Her parents are in the kitchen, making the house ready for the holiday. Her mother is burning out the oven so it will be kosher for Passover, and her father is packing away the chumetzdikeh dishes that were used all year for unleavened food. Every year her mother insists that she doesn't need him to help her and every year he helps her anyway. Probably if he had a regular job like other fathers, he wouldn't always be helping. Maybe that's what bothers her mother—she doesn't like her husband acting like a housewife. Esther thinks he also helps because he wants to make sure everything is done right, like he suspects her mother isn't as fussy as he is about religious things. He has that way of coming up behind her, kind of jumpy like he knows he shouldn't but he can't help himself, and telling her how to do whatever it is she's doing. Her mother gets mad. "Twenty-five years I've been making Pesach. I don't need you to instruct me," she scowls at him. Every erev Shabbes it's the same thing too, with his carrying on about how it's almost candle-lighting time and her telling him, "I don't need you to pave my way to Paradise. Don't worry, when the time comes I will light the candles." Today she doesn't seem annoyed, like she doesn't care whether he helps her or not.

"The carp!" Esther blurts out. "He's not swimming right. Like he's straining himself to keep living." Her father looks distressed and stops what he's doing. "An animal must not be allowed to suffer," he says. "I will go take it right now and do what I have to." She doesn't know how he's going to do it. Is he going to hit it over the head or stab it or what?

Her father comes downstairs, carrying the carp, limp and dopey-looking, in a large towel. He must have hit him over the head. Esther leaves the kitchen; she doesn't want to see what's going to happen next. Moments later, she hears a thud. He must have done it. He must have chopped off the carp's head. Blood probably squirted out. When she hears him scraping the scales, she goes outside. The only people she's known who've died are Mr. Lieberman and the fish. That's crazy; the fish isn't a person. But he almost seemed like one. Of course lots of other people died, like her own grandparents, but they're different; she didn't *know* them. She remembers all the different expressions on Mr. Lieberman's face, how serious and sad he looked when he worked the pressing machine, how he'd throw back his head and smile at her when she passed, the way his hand felt when he would pinch her cheek or pat her head, and how he smelled—warm and steamy.

She sits down on the stoop. What is she doing outside anyway? It's the day before Passover when she always liked to stay in the house and do her special jobs. Every year since she was little she's gotten to polish the silver goblet for Elijah the Prophet, with the leaves and branches and little doves that you can feel with your fingers while you're rubbing them with a soft cloth so they'll glisten. How she's loved

Passover with all the preparations that began days and days before! Turning the house upside down and inside out, cleaning out all the drawers and closets. Sometimes you'd find things you'd forgotten all about. One year she found her little celluloid doll that she used to put in an empty cigar box, pretending it was a baby carriage, and pull around the street by a string. The doll was lying in a corner of the closet, her face was crushed, and she had no clothes on. (She used to wrap her in scraps of cloth her mother gave her.) It was so sad finding her. She'd forgotten all about her; she couldn't even remember losing her. And she always liked the way the house started smelling before Passover—the strong soapy smell of newly scoured woodwork and scrubbed linoleum, the vinegary pungency of the clean, shiny windows, and then all the good cooking smells. But this year it's not the same. Esther misses the fresh, buoyant air of happy expectancy. Even with the windows wide open and spring breezes blowing in, the house has been stifling, the air thick and sour with seething emotions. And it probably won't get any better tomorrow. Unless, like a miracle, Ben walks in just in time, it will be the first Seder without him, and you can tell everyone is wondering what it will be like. And it's been so quiet. None of the back and forth, the wrangling, the fussing, the lively commotion that went with the overwhelming amount of work to be done, that seemed somehow obligatory to a proper show of concern for a duly honored and unblemished Passover. This year the sounds of scrubbing and scraping, of wrapping and unwrapping, the clatter of dishes and pots resound in a stillness of mute anguish. It's like all of them are holding their breath.

Outside, she breathes more easily. The air feels soft and new, yet full-flavored and ready for Passover. She's sure she'll be able to wear her royal blue spring coat that she loves and not have to wear her frayed winter coat. She knows she shouldn't feel bad about not getting anything new for the holiday because her parents can't help it, but she does—maybe because it's the first time. But at least the pink dress with the gathers that her mother made her last year still fits, only the hem had to be let down. And her shoes are only a tiny bit tight. She hopes she doesn't grow too fast so she won't get too big for her clothes before she can get new ones or before Lila's old things get to fit her. Lila's lucky; she gets all the good stuff from the New Jersey cousins. Last time their aunt came, she brought a big box full of her daughters' clothes that didn't fit them anymore but still looked brand new. Everything Lila tried on looked wonderful on her. On me, they were too big and old-looking. When they stop fitting Lila, I'll get them. I hope they'll still look nice.

Millie is coming down the block, looking surprised, like she didn't expect to find her outside.

"Hi!" Esther calls to her.

"Hello!" Millie calls, hurrying toward her. "I didn't expect you to be outside today."

"Why not?" Esther asks, a little nastily.

"I thought you'd be inside helping your parents get the house ready for Passover. Tomorrow night's the first Seder, isn't it?"

"I know it is," Esther says, her voice still surly for some reason she hasn't quite figured out. It's a certain eagerness about Millie. "I just don't feel like helping today."

"Don't your parents make you?"

"No. Whatever gave you that idea?"

"I don't know. I just thought you were supposed to."

"No, they don't make me. It's not anything religious, if that's what you mean."

"I didn't think it was exactly religious. But if I were you, I'd do it anyway. I imagine it'd be fun."

"Sometimes it is and sometimes it isn't," Esther says.

"What do you mean?" Millie asks.

"Oh, nothing," Esther says, knowing exactly what she

means but not wanting to tell Millie about it. Not because Millie wouldn't sympathize, but because she couldn't really understand. Ever since she told Millie about Ben, she made up her mind never to talk about certain things to anybody, especially outside the family. Even though people act like they understand, they really don't and later you feel stupid and self-conscious.

Millie always wants people to share things with her, not because she's greedy—not those kinds of things. She wants you to share your experiences, your feelings. It's like she wants to be part of something because she's not part of anything—not even her family. But I don't want to share my family with Millie. And Esther knows it's not just selfishness; her family isn't the way Millie thinks they are and there's no reason why she has to find out.

"Has Ben come home yet?" Millie asks.

"No, he hasn't," Esther answers as matter-of-factly as she can. How she wishes she hadn't told Millie! Now she keeps pestering her with that look on her face like she's trying to prove that she's even sadder than you are about it.

"Gee, I'm sorry," Millie says. "And tomorrow night's the Seder. The house'll seem empty, won't it?"

Suddenly Esther knows what Millie wants. It was the same last year. But now she thinks Ben not being home will make a difference. She wants to be invited to the Seder; she's never been to one. But I don't want Millie at our Seder. I suppose it's mean of me, but Millie would be out of place. She wouldn't understand what was going on and it would all seem queer to her, and I'd keep wondering what Millie was thinking, and I wouldn't be able to enjoy myself. Esther remembers how this all went through her head last year, and it'll be worse this year because with Ben missing, who knows how anyone will act and what the Seder will be like.

"You can't tell, Millie," she says, "by tomorrow my brother might be home—especially because of the Seder."

"I hope so," Millie says, "for your sake and your whole family's."

"Thanks," Esther responds, feeling worse and worse about not asking Millie to come to the Seder. Of course, for all she knows, her parents might not let her ask Millie. This year especially, they might not be able to afford to have an extra person. Something occurs to her. "Liesl is probably inside helping her parents get ready for Passover," she says.

"No, she isn't," Millie tells her.

"How do you know?"

"I asked her about it and she said her mother didn't believe in it, turning the house inside out and changing the dishes and everything. Her father wanted them to do it, but her mother refused."

"So they're not having a Seder?"

"No. But they're going to one, at a relative's house."

"That's nice," Esther says, weakly.

"It sure is," Millie agrees. "I guess I'm the only one who has no Seder to go to."

Esther sets her face sorrowfully. "It's too bad, Millie. I'd ask you to mine, but ours is strictly for the family," she says, disliking herself for lying. Their Seder was hardly ever strictly for the family. Every year her father managed to dig up an orech, some stranger who didn't have a Seder to go to; it was a mitzva. One year they had this skinny lady all in black, even her stockings, who never said a word and hardly ate anything; she just kept sitting there looking like a very sad witch with tears in her eyes all the time. Last year there was the man who was having trouble waiting for the Haggadah reading to be over so he could eat. The way his eyes kept shifting to the Seder plate you thought any minute he was going to lunge for it. Afterwards, he ate and ate and kept drinking wine and fell fast asleep before the Hallel. But those people didn't count. They didn't matter to her; she didn't *know* them.

Millie's different. If only she'd stop drooping. Esther is tempted to say that she'll find out first if it's okay and maybe Millie can come to their Seder, but she doesn't. Instead she says, "I'm *really* sorry, Millie," but adds quickly, "I'll tell you what. Would you like to come over a little later and help my father search the house for chumetz? That's really fun."

"Search the house? For chumetz? What's that?" Millie asks.

"You'll like it. My father puts little pieces of bread or crumbs in different corners around the house. Then he pretends he doesn't know where they are and goes searching the house for chumetz, which is the bread crumbs. When he finds them, he sweeps them with a feather into a wooden spoon."

"What does he do all that for?" Millie asks.

"To make sure there's no chumetz left in the house for Passover."

"But then why does he put those pieces of bread all over the house? It doesn't make sense."

Esther stiffens. That's just what she was afraid of! Millie thinks she wants to do religious things. She doesn't understand that a lot of them don't exactly make sense. You do them because you're supposed to. You do religious things for different reasons than you do most everything else. "When I was little, I asked my father the same thing," she says.

Millie looks hurt. "I don't see what it has to do with being little. You can tell me or not tell me, but you don't have to insult me."

"For God's sake, Millie, I wasn't insulting you. It's natural that you shouldn't know."

"Are you going to tell me or not? Or don't you know?"

"Of course I'll tell you. You don't have to be so touchy. My father says a prayer first, before he goes searching, about God commanding him to clean away the chumetz, and since the house has already been thoroughly cleaned, there wouldn't be any chumetz around and he'd be saying the prayer for nothing."

There is a pause before Millie says, "I see," and Esther can tell she doesn't, and she herself realizes that the explanation isn't particularly impressive. But that's what it is, and that's all there is to it. "So do you want to come over?" she asks, hoping now that Millie will refuse.

"Sure I do," Millie says. "What time is it?"

"It's not an exact time. It's just right after it gets dark. But why don't you come over about a quarter to seven? Okay?"

"Okay," Millie says, much happier, "I'll come over after supper."

"Swell," Esther says. "I better go in now and help. I'll see you tonight."

Breathing hard, as though she'd been running, Millie arrives early. Esther notices that her parents act only vaguely aware of her friend's presence, and she sees a cloud pass over Millie's face like she thinks she's not wanted. It's too mean to let her think that. Taking Millie aside, she whispers that they've been acting a little funny since Ben's been missing and not to mind them. Millie's face grows solemnly confidential as she nods her head to indicate she understands.

It's hard to tell if Lila is going to accompany them or not; she seems sort of twitchy. She probably would if Millie weren't there, but now she thinks she'll look childish. When her father is holding the Siddur, preparing to recite the benediction, Esther calls "C'mon" to Lila, who gets up slowly and casually but comes with them. As the benediction is recited, Esther sees Millie's face fill with awe, and she feels suddenly richer and more fortunate than her friend. Impulsively, she hands Millie the candle she is holding, and when Millie looks bewildered, she gestures reassuringly to her. Millie begins to glow and Esther is gratified.

With her father holding a feather in one hand and a large wooden spoon in the other, the four of them go from one darkened room to another, all over the house, into the shul, and upstairs too—never directly to where the bread crumbs were placed; they act as if they're truly searching. Esther imagines that Millie is wondering why they don't put on the lights, but she can see that Millie is getting into the spirit of the search. When they come across a bunch of crumbs on a windowsill or in a corner of the floor, Millie catches her breath and watches fervidly while the feather sweeps them onto the spoon. Lila looks awkward; she doesn't know how she's supposed to act now that she's older.

The search is over. Her father puts the crumbs, the spoon he used, and the feather into a piece of cloth and ties them up tight.

"What's he going to do with them now?" Millie whispers.

"He's going to take them to a special place where somebody will burn them."

Millie doesn't ask why. She just looks impressed. Esther feels bad; she wishes she'd invited Millie to the Seder. But she can't now. It might look like she was lying before.

26

It's come again. Tonight is the first Seder. Esther hurries out of bed, washes and dresses quickly, and runs downstairs.

All the surfaces in the kitchen are covered with fresh cardboard, so the Passover food won't get contaminated, and she can feel the cardboard under the tablecloth. This is the day she gets to have for breakfast what she waits for all year, a soft-boiled egg with farfel in it. They don't have it the rest of the year, her mother says, so it should be special on Passover. Maybe it's a good idea; but they have matzoh meal pancakes all year round and plain matzoh, so she doesn't understand.

The egg with farfel is delicious. It *isn't* her imagination; everything *does* taste different and better on Passover.

As she walks to school, the air is light and clear. Esther feels her heart rising in her chest. How she loves this holiday! And maybe—maybe it will bring Ben home. She imagines herself opening the door that night for Elijah the Prophet, and Ben walking in. He wouldn't be sad or peculiar or anything. He'd be beautiful like—like in a miracle.

The morning drags. She wants to get home for lunch. When the bell rings, she's the first one out of the room. Millie runs after her, and they walk together.

"I'll bet you're excited about tonight," Millie says.

"Yes, I am," Esther answers, wishing Millie would stop hinting.

When their paths separate, Esther runs all the way home.

The matzoh meal pancakes she has for lunch do taste different from the all-year-round ones. Everything is so good today; the whole house smells wonderful—chicken soup bubbling on the stove, potato kugel getting brown and crunchy in the oven, sponge cake and honey cake cooling on the windowsill, smelling sweet and golden. She knew she shouldn't have worried that they wouldn't be able to make Yontev this year. It's always like a miracle. No matter how bad everything was on ordinary days, no matter how poor they seemed, on Yontev—like on Shabbes —they suddenly seemed rich. Reluctantly, she leaves her house to return to school.

When the afternoon session is over, Esther hurries home again. She wants to be sure nobody else makes the charoses. She and Lila used to fight over it, but now Lila doesn't care anymore. Still, she'd better hurry.

Good. The charoses haven't been made yet. Esther wraps one of her mother's aprons around herself and ties it, stands over the table and starts shelling walnuts into a wooden bowl. When she thinks she has enough, she starts chopping and chopping. Her wrist gets tired but she doesn't stop until the walnuts are all crumbly. Next, very carefully, she peels an apple, cuts it into tiny pieces and adds them to the nuts. Then comes the wine. She tastes. Delicious! She asks her mother if she wants to taste. The cooking vapors have made Malka's face pink and dewy, and she smiles when she tells Esther she's sure it's very good, she doesn't have to taste. Esther is delighted to see her mother smile. It *is* going to be a good Passover.

With a wide graceful sweep of her arms, Lila spreads the white linen cloth—its tiny cream-colored rosettes embroidered around the edges—over the dining room table. The cloth and its matching napkins was her mother's wedding present from the Koskoffs. She lays out the heavy carved silver perfectly straight in a special order that is supposed to be right. Handling them lovingly, she places on the table the translucent china plates with their blue and gold borders, then the long-stemmed crystal wine glasses. Esther comes into the dining room carrying Elijah's silver goblet. She sees her sister standing back, admiring the table. For a change Lila isn't pouting; her face is shining. Lila belongs with beautiful things, she thinks; she loves them so much. Esther says how pretty the table looks. "Doesn't it?" Lila breathes reverently. Esther returns to the kitchen to get the satin matzoh cover that she spent a whole summer embroidering and being sure to wash her hands each time she handled it so it would be kosher for Passover. When she comes back, Lila is gone and Esther notices five settings on the table instead of four. Could Lila have forgotten and set a place for Ben, or done it deliberately—just in case? No, Lila's not that way. Papa probably told her he's bringing an orech. I wonder who it will be this time?

They stand together before the candelabrum. Zalman wears his navy blue suit girdled at the waist with the silken cord to separate the godly part of his body, his heart and mind, from the lower part. His face is freshly shaven, his mustache and beard smooth and black. Only a tremulousness in his eyes belies his grandeur. Each of the girls is dressed up too—Lila in the dress she was so glad to get from her cousins because kelly green is her favorite color and Esther in the pink dress with the gathers that her mother made last year. Malka's dress, black and unadorned, defines the pearliness of her neck and the persistent rosiness of her cheeks, but her weary posture and the glassiness of her eyes expose an inner pallor. She places her

27

Esther edges over to her side of the bed. She doesn't want to touch Lila, even accidentally. Lila is awful. As if the Seder wasn't bad enough—her mother's eyes were swollen, and her father, in his ceremonial white robe and reclining on his pillows spread out on three chairs, instead of looking like a king, looked like a tired old actor dressed up for a part he couldn't play anymore. They kept trying to do everything right, not to profane the holiday, especially in front of the orech her father had brought—a Yeshiva boy from Torah Vedaas across Broadway who at the last minute didn't go home for Pesach because his parents couldn't send him train fare to Springfield, Massachusetts. She kept waiting for him to talk so she could hear if he had the same accent as Mr. Farrell, the school janitor, who also comes from Massachusetts; but he didn't say a word all night, except for the Hebrew in the Haggadah. When he first came in he looked all right, but then Lila came out of the kitchen and when he saw her, his face got red and stayed that way all night. He hardly looked up from his Haggadah, and he gulped his food when he ate. He seemed a little older than Lila and was good-looking with dark brown eyes and curly black hair. Lila didn't get red when she saw *him*; she just took a real deep breath like you do sometimes when you're getting ready to start a game. All through the Seder she kept staring at him; you could tell she was doing it on purpose. Mama didn't notice anything until after the soup. Lila suddenly disappeared, and when she came back, Mama, carrying in the chicken, took one look at her and almost dropped it. I could see why. Lila had on rouge and (real light so it wouldn't be noticeable, only it was) lipstick. What a silly thing to do! Mama looked like she could kill her! Papa didn't see because he was busy trying to talk to the Yeshiva boy who just kept nodding back and didn't answer him. Probably if Lila hadn't kept trying to embarrass him, he would eventually have talked. And why did she have to go and put on all that makeup? I didn't even know she had it. I know why Mama got so mad. I don't blame her. Lila has a bad reputation.

Esther remembers those words about Lila on the toilet door in Hebrew school. And now she knows what a "whooer" is; she didn't even know then, only that it was something dirty. When she couldn't find it in the dictionary, she figured it was so dirty they wouldn't put it in. She knows now because a few weeks after it happened, Millie happened to say, "Poor Shirley Fogel, it's too bad her mother's a whore." It sounded like the same word only Millie said it different. When she said to Millie, "You mean whooer?" Millie said, "No, the right way to say it is whore," and she spelled it, and said that her cousin who goes to Hunter College told her that another word for it is "prostitute." So she looked up both words in the dictionary. She still had to figure out what "sexual intercourse" meant, so she looked up both those words. Now she's sure she knows. But Lila wouldn't do *that*! Boys just like her and hang around her a lot and that's what gives her a bad reputation. Maybe Mama's seen her with those boys from the candy store she says are bums, and she's worried Lila's a bum too (Mama couldn't possibly know those other words!). Lila sure looked different with the makeup on.

The Yeshiva boy looked up for a minute when she came back into the room. He got even redder and for the rest of the night he kept squirming in his seat. He didn't get up to look for the afikomen even though he wasn't really grown-up. And when Lila did it, you could tell she was just trying to calm Mama down by acting like a little kid. I found it, but I don't even care. Everything was terrible. It was like some crazy Seder you dream about that doesn't make sense.

And afterwards, after the Yeshiva boy went home to wherever he stays, her mother took Lila by the arm when her father wasn't looking and pulled her into the kitchen and hissed at her, "Bummerkeh! Kurveh!" Lila pulled her arm away and ran upstairs. Esther wonders what "kurveh" means. Her mother never used that word before. From the way she looked and how she shook Lila, it might be the way you say whore in Yiddish.

Her father stayed downstairs after the Seder, sitting at the table with his head in his hands. Her mother followed Lila upstairs, and you could hear her. I couldn't tell if she was hitting Lila (Mama doesn't hit) but it sure sounded like she might be. Papa heard the commotion and started going up. It's a good thing Mama heard, and stopped him on the stairs. Papa never hits Lila or me, but this time who knows what he would have done? Mama wouldn't tell him what all the screaming upstairs was about; she said it was none of his business. But later on, she scolded him for bringing the boy. She said there was barely enough food for his own family, and yet he had to show off to people like he was a rich man. I was glad when Papa told her not to worry, someone had already invited the boy to the second Seder. But Papa looked so sad. How he'd love to be rich again so he could show off like he used to. The relatives still talk about it. He wasn't stingy like rich men in the movies. Mama isn't stingy either; I don't think she cared about the food for the Yeshiva boy. It was Lila flirting with him and putting on makeup right in the middle of the Seder.

Esther closes her eyes but can't fall asleep. The longer she thinks about it, the less angry she is with Lila. Lila probably can't help herself; it's like she needs to have boys like her—that's what makes her feel special. But I'm positive she doesn't do *that*. Certainly not for money. Still, I wonder how she got the makeup. One of her friends could have given her some rouge and lipstick. Probably that's what happened. I'm sure of it. Unless—unless she stole them. She could've stolen from the five and ten. She even admitted doing it once. The tie for Ben's birthday. She said Ben was always giving us presents and nobody ever gave him anything. And she wanted us to decorate his room too and surprise him. When Ben saw HAPPY BIRTHDAY in different colors hanging on a string all across his room, he really was surprised, and especially when he saw the tie. He probably couldn't figure out where we got the money. I kept praying he wouldn't ask. He didn't. He just hugged us both. I never saw Lila look so happy. Lila's not at all the way people think she is. No, she wouldn't do *that* for money. She's too young anyway. You probably have to be a certain age before you can do it. Lila still looks like a little kid compared to that girl who's always outside the poolroom rocking the baby carriage, the one everybody says used to do it with all the boys in the back of the poolroom and now she doesn't know who her baby's father is. That must be so sad.

Sure that Lila isn't asleep yet, and suddenly feeling a pang of concern and love for her sister, Esther taps her lightly on the shoulder and whispers, "Lila. . . ." Shrugging her off, Lila rasps, "Oh, shut up! Leave me alone!" Esther feels as if she's been punched in the stomach. She turns over, and for a long time she remains awake, listening to her sister crying.

28

The day is sunny and warm just like she hoped it would be so she could wear her spring coat to the Talmud Torah services. But walking home, Esther feels burdened. The air is thick—it's hard to breathe. The subtle smell of spring has turned full and ripe, foreboding summer heat. Throughout the service the words in the Siddur kept getting out of focus, swimming past her. She sang without volition, joining the chorus of voices like a grain of sand swept along with the tide, and as the morning wore on, the chanting and singing became an abrasive din. What was it all for? she wondered. What has it to do with how people actually are? The sun kept streaming in the windows, boys began mopping their faces, dark circles appeared in the armpits of dresses. The new clothes no longer adorned—they were concealments for sweating bodies. And she became aware of a scent that, while not entirely unpleasant, was suffocating—a fleshy, suggestive smell. She wanted to get out. Perhaps she was just tired from hardly sleeping last night—in the fresh air she would feel better. But the smell is still in her nostrils, and she feels a sudden loathing for the sauntering boys with dark fuzz dirtying their upper lips, and the girls carrying their coats as if to show how their buttocks swing under their silken dresses. And her body is no different from theirs, exuding the same strange scent even though she washed very carefully the day before, bringing three kettles of hot water upstairs. The odd smell has nothing to do with washing. It's inside people, inside her too.

She approaches her house prepared for unpleasantness. She wonders if Lila is up yet. She would have woke her to go to shul because Lila still goes on special holidays, but she thought she'd better not bother her—not after last night. Besides, she had a feeling Lila was only pretending to be asleep.

Inside the house, the familiar fragrance of the upcoming meal warming on the stove is comforting, and her depression lifts a little. Determining to be cheerful, she smiles brightly as she greets her mother, who promptly sends her to bring her sister downstairs. "She's been up there all morning," her mother says. "Tell her I've had enough of her craziness."

As she starts going up, Lila appears on the steps. "I was just going to get you," Esther says.

"Well, now you don't have to," Lila barks and, brushing past her, goes straight to the dining room window and stations herself there with her back to everyone.

It's no use trying to talk to Lila, Esther decides, and her mother is in a terrible mood too. They won't eat for a while because the davening is still going on upstairs. What's the point of staying in the house? When she goes out, she bangs the door behind her.

Feeling desolate, she sits down on the stoop. Strains of "Ayn Kaylohaynu," her favorite hymn, come through the open windows. "There is none like our God, none like our Lord, none like our King, none like our Saviour...." She thinks of the many times she's sung the lively melody and how much she's enjoyed it. But the way they're singing, it sounds draggy and off-tune and sad. It occurs to her that most of the people inside have been singing that song so much longer than she has. They might be tired of praising God by now.

The service ends. Esther gets up and out of the way. People come out of the shul and spread out over the sidewalk. This crowd is not at all like the one she prayed with. They move differently—none of the rhythmic sway of silken flesh, the disregarding swaggers. They step carefully. Descending the steps, most of them hold on to each other as well as to the banister. Melnick, his face puffed up above his starched collar, moves heavily, deliberately. Old Mr. Koopitz, all bent over, his hands shaking, comes down with his wife supporting him one one side and his strange daughter on the other. A few younger men, about Ben's age, come down alongside their fathers. In not too many years, Esther thinks, they will look just like their fathers—they already walk alike, with their stomachs stuck out a little. Ben will never look like Papa. No, he will never be anything like him. She can't imagine Ben with a big mustache, sitting around in his undershirt slurping tea through a sugar cube stuck between his teeth, or Ben hollering and screaming. Ben is gentle. Not that he doesn't get angry sometimes. Like that time with Lila. And when he catches me staring into space, it makes him mad. That time when he was reading his newspaper and looked up and saw me, the way he clenched his teeth together and said, "Cut it out! Stop daydreaming!" and lifted the paper like he was going to hit me with it. He didn't, but if he had, he would've been real sorry afterwards. Is it possible—is it possible that deep down, in a certain way, he's a little like Papa? No, he can't be. He looks so different. His face is beautiful. Feeling a sudden urge to draw him, Esther tries to construct his face in her head, but his features keep fading. She is startled. Of course she knows what he looks like! But if she wants to draw him, she needs to look at him real hard, like Mr. Epstein says you should. She's sure she never looked at him hard enough. She's lost track of how long he's been gone. Sometimes she actually forgets about him. But she does want him to come home. Like today, he'd know how she felt even if she didn't tell him, and he'd talk to her. Where *is* he? *Why* doesn't he come home? She's going to draw a picture of him. She must try to remember him exactly. Only it's Pesach—you're not supposed to draw. She'll have to wait. She'll have to wait until tomorrow night.

Esther comes inside and sits down to eat with her family. All through the meal she tries to put Ben's face together in her mind. For a moment she sees it, then details begin to elude her. They have pictures of him when he was little—the big brown photograph Mama sent Papa from Russia where he's wearing an embroidered shirt with a high collar and holding on to Mama's hand. Her other brother, the one who died in the snow, is holding on to her mother's other hand—he looks more like Papa, the same big head. Ben's head is small and narrow. She found that picture one year when she was helping her mother clean out the drawers for Passover. Her mother didn't want to see it; she said to just put it back under the tablecloths in the buffet drawer. Probably it makes her too sad. Esther bites into her piece of potato kugel. Her mother gave her a corner—it's the tastiest part because it has the most crust. "I love the kugel, Mama. It's the best one you ever made," she says. Her mother smiles wanly, her eyes misted over. Nothing does much good, Esther decides, Mama is just plain sad. No one is talking to anybody at the table—like a family of mutes. How she wishes everything was like it used to be. Not that it was so perfect—whenever they were having a good time together, she knew something would happen soon to spoil it. But still it was better than it is now—not so quiet. And certain times were really nice. Lately, she's been remembering things she thought she'd forgotten, like the lullaby her mother used to sing, "Ruzhinkes 'n Mandlen"—about a white baby goat who lived under her cradle and went out selling raisins and almonds. It was a funny song and ended with how some day she'd marry a man who would study Torah and write holy books, and how she'd stay good and be religious. It seems such a long time ago when Mama sang that lullaby.

She's going to draw a picture of Ben. Even though it's Pesach. But where will it be safe? His room? Nobody'll come in there. Yes, she'll do it. She's got to do it now before it gets harder and harder. Lila is helping with the dishes (she's probably trying to make up for last night). Esther comes into the kitchen and asks if she should help too. Before her mother can speak, Lila turns from the sink and says, "No, we don't need you!" Esther goes happily upstairs.

She takes her pad and pencils out of her bureau drawer, hesitates about whether to take her crayons, and decides not to. Mr. Epstein said not to worry about coloring yet —just to draw. Someday, he said, he'd bring her some paints and show her how to use them, but so far he seems to have forgotten all about it.

She enters Ben's room, closes the door softly behind her, takes off her shoes, and settles down on his bed. She places her pad on her lap and poises her pencil. She'll start with his eyes. Very lightly, she draws an upper lid and stops. Leaning back against the headboard, she tries to imagine what was special about Ben's eyes so when she draws them you'll be able to tell they're his.

Footsteps on the stairs. It's her father—she knows his walk—coming up for his nap. She jumps off the bed, slides the pad and pencils under the spread, takes a book from the fruit crate on the floor, sits back down on the bed on top of the pad and pencils, lays the book open on her lap, and bends intently over it. Her heart thumps. What if he comes in and tells her to get off the bed and the pad and pencils make bumps under the spread and he sees and looks under the spread? All they need now is another explosion. The footsteps fade away and she hears her father close his bedroom door. She takes a deep breath and closes the book she's holding. It's called *The Republic,* and it's by somebody named Plato. She can't tell if Plato is a first or second name. It's funny that somebody should have only one name—like in the Bible. She's always wondered about "the republic for which it stands" in the Pledge of Allegiance. She doesn't know what a republic is. She opens the book. It was translated into English by someone else; she wonders what language it was in first. It must be a play because it starts with a list of persons and then tells where "the scene is laid." The names of the people are peculiar; she can hardly pronounce them—except Socrates. She's heard of him but she can't remember where.

Esther turns the pages. It's mostly conversations between Socrates and a bunch of other people. Some sentences are underlined and Ben has written in the margins. It's strange seeing his handwriting—like he's there in the room. In one margin he's written "dangerous." She reads what he's underlined next to it. "... the best of either sex should be united with the best as often, and the inferior with the inferior as seldom as possible." It's a dirty book! She reads on "... and that they should rear the offspring of one kind of union, but not the other...." No, it's not just a plain dirty book—it's something like the Bible; it just has some dirty things in it. On the next page Ben has written in big letters, "HORRIBLE" next to "... the offspring of the inferior, or of the better when they chance to be deformed, will be put away in some mysterious, unknown place, as they should be." Ben is right; that is horrible. Choochie, who's ugly and in the ungraded class, would be hidden away in some awful place—and he's really nice and he's so happy when the little girls let him jump rope with them. Who else does she know that could be called deformed? The mute! That man Papa dragged in for a minyan. He really was disgusting.

She wouldn't like to see *him* again. She keeps turning the pages mostly to read what Ben has written. It's like he's talking to her, telling her what he thinks about the book. She comes to where he's written so much in the margins and so many sentences are underlined that she decides to read the whole page. It's hard to understand; it's about people in a cave with their legs and necks chained so they can't turn their heads, and they've been that way for years—since they were children. There's a fire burning someplace and a wall like in marionette shows, and the chained-up people can only see each other's shadows on the wall of the cave and the shadows of things above the wall that people behind it are carrying. The book becomes strange and more difficult to understand. It tells about a prisoner being released and looking toward the light and suffering sharp pain and how when he sees real things he thinks the shadows of them he saw before are truer—realer. Esther thinks she understands, but it makes her head hurt. She doesn't want to read the rest. She'll just read what Ben wrote in the margins. "Painful and difficult to look at truth, reality." On the next page he's written "One must disdain the rewards of ignorance." On the page after that, "Most difficult aspect of knowledge to attain is idea of good." There is more writing on the next page and the next, but Esther closes the book. Ben's face is suddenly clear to her. She takes her pad and pencils out from under the bedspread and begins to sketch. His eyes are dark but with light golden flecks, and they're wide apart even though his face is narrow; they're medium-sized with long lashes. After she draws the lashes on the eyes they look peculiar and she erases them. How do you make long lashes? She'll just make the upper eyelids a little darker. White space in the brown part of his eyes show the golden flecks. They look like eyes now, but not especially like Ben's. She'll leave them alone and draw the rest of his face; maybe they'll look better then. She draws a thin nose with the nostrils flaring a little. The mouth will be the easiest—she remembers it best—full and curved; it's the only part of him that looks like Papa. Even though his eyes are brown and Mama's are blue, they look like hers. Esther examines her picture. It looks like somebody who looks a little like Ben, but not him. Maybe when she puts in the shape of his face and his skinny neck and his hair. . . . She continues to make light tentative strokes. No, nobody except her could tell it's supposed to be Ben. What did she do wrong? Maybe the picture of him she has in her mind is not really true, so when she puts it down on paper it's not the way he actually is. She sets aside the pad and pencil and picks up the book again. Maybe, if she reads more that he wrote. . . .

It's a real serious book. That's it—she ought to make Ben's face look more serious. He gets those creases between his eyebrows; she ought to put them in. She keeps turning the pages. He doodles in the margins just like she does. (Only she has to erase everything afterwards because the books aren't hers, they belong to the school or the library.) Ben's doodles are drawings of people too, very little and light. She examines one closely. It's a lady in a nightgown with her long hair hanging down. It reminds her of Mama. A few pages later, there's another picture—the same lady in a nightgown. Then he has a picture of a small boy in short pants. Then some she can't see because he tried to erase them. The next pages have more writing in the margins but she skips over them, looking for pictures. She comes to another one he tried to erase but she can tell it's another one of those lady pictures. The next one isn't clear either, but she can tell its a man. It's a man with no clothes on! Naked! Except for his yarmulka. And —and he even drew the man's *thing*! He drew everything! And the man's thing is so big! And it's not hanging down like when I saw Papa coming out of the bathtub. It's sticking out! She shuts the book, squeezing its covers together. She mustn't look at it. She'll put the book right back and never look in it again. It's disgusting! As she bends to return the book to its place in the fruit crate, she opens it to look *just one more time*. Because she just can't believe it. Sitting on the floor, Esther stares fixedly at a smudgy drawing of a naked man with his penis in erection. Such a crazy picture! Who ever heard of a man's thing sticking out like that? Her eyes move to the yarmulka. The man has a mustache too. No, it couldn't be. The man has no beard at all, but still.... She closes the book again. No! Who could believe Ben would draw such a dirty picture? The room is circling about and her stomach turns over. Who would believe *she* wrote those dirty words on the toilet door? Nobody can tell about *anyone*! It's like Mama's always saying, "a falshe velt." But you can't go around thinking everyone's a fake. No, not everyone. Look at Lila—she doesn't pretend; she doesn't try to act like an angel. But with Lila it's the other way around. Lila's really much nicer underneath. But then why should she act like she does—always doing things that she knows will upset Mama and Papa? Everything's so hard to figure out.

Esther keeps sitting on the floor, her eyes shut tight, her arms crossed over her chest, hugging herself protectively. The room drops away. She feels alone and unenclosed in the vastness of her ignorance. Afraid to reach out and try to touch, for whatever may feel familiar to her fingers, when she opens her eyes, will be something monstrous. Or she may reach and reach and touch only nothing. She digs her fingertips into her skin, and the pain she feels assures her of her own concreteness, and tears of self-pity begin to burn behind her closed eyelids and ooze down her cheeks. She feels herself flowing into the dumb surrounding darkness, becoming part of it, and finding it peopled with piteous creatures like herself, she unexpectedly feels a sad tenderness toward all of them.

When, with a great effort of will, she opens her eyes and rises from the floor and looks about, her compassion diminishes. The homely innocence of her surroundings has

29

The next day Esther stays home from services. Her mother asks her if she feels all right; she says Esther hasn't seemed well since last night at the Seder, having to be urged to ask the Four Questions and hardly eating. Esther wants to say that she hated the second Seder even more than the first—it seemed so fake, all of them pretending, forcing themselves to make thoughtless motions and meaningless noises. But she doesn't say anything. Her mother makes her stick out her tongue and asks if she's moved her bowels. "Something hurts you?" she asks.

"I'm all right," Esther says, shrugging her mother off impatiently.

Her mother reddens, looking rebuffed. Immediately, Esther's heart goes out to her. Poor Mama, it's not her fault, and nobody's nice to her. Even Ben, who seemed to like her so much, always bringing her presents—housedresses and nightgowns and pretty slips from the place where he worked—can't really care about her or he'd come home. Even if he's mad at Papa and wants to teach him a lesson, he's still making Mama worry so much. And he certainly can't care about Lila or me. It's hard to believe, but.... Tears rise to her eyes. She sees her mother's soft round back bent over another of her perennial chores and wants to speak to her. But how is she to tell her mother that what hurts is the pain of punctured illusions? Blinking back her tears, Esther says, "I'm just tired, that's all. I've been having bad dreams."

Her mother turns and looks at her anxiously, but doesn't ask what the bad dreams have been about. She just tells her to take a nap after lunch.

But it's a beautiful day and after lunch Esther goes outside. She can't decide whether to call for Millie or not. She has a feeling Millie could tell she was making it up about their Seder being strictly for the family. Maybe that's why she's not coming over. Millie doesn't have school today either because she's Jewish even though her family doesn't do anything about Passover. Angie's still in school. Angie thinks it's not fair for Christians to have to go to school on Jewish holidays; Jews don't go to school on Christmas. It must be fun being in school when hardly anyone else is there. Angie admits the teachers are real nice on those days, and they do hardly any work; they mostly fool around.

The Taubers' store is closed for Passover. Liesl said that if they weren't going to be sleeping over at her aunt's house, her mother would make her father keep the store open. Mrs. Tauber is a strange lady; she's much stricter than most mothers, but she seems nice. Esther wishes she knew her better. But how can you get to know somebody else's mother? You never talk to your friend's mother except to ask if your friend is home or something like that. She begins walking toward Millie's house. The Jewish stores are all closed, and the streets are littered with people. Not all of them are dressed up even though it's a holiday. She doesn't blame her father for getting mad about people who take the day off from work and then stand out in the street all day with their cigars and cigarettes and their bare heads, desecrating the holiday. Elite Cleaners is open, and Mr. Coppola is behind the counter. John takes after him—the soft-looking lips and shiny white smile.

John Coppola is the nicest boy in the class, but you can't play with boys anymore, especially if they're not Jewish. Marty's poolroom is open, of course, and the same men are outside with their filthy eyes and pointy shoes. She hates them. When she comes to Millie's house, she starts going in but changes her mind and keeps walking. At Broadway, she turns the corner. Brenner's is open. Millie's father *never* closes. No wonder Millie is so peculiar.

At the next corner she stops and waits for the light to change, deciding to continue her walk across Broadway. Some of her friends from Hebrew school live on the other side. She can't call for them—she doesn't even know their addresses, besides she's not good enough friends with them. But maybe she'll bump into someone outside. The light changes. She races across.

On either side of her, dapple-barked sycamores with golden green leaves reach as far as she can see, probably, she imagines, all the way to the East River. The austerity of the orderly rows of brownstones with their long, formal windows and solid stone stoops is relieved by filagrees of sunlight spangling their faces and twinkling along the sidewalks. Esther's pace slows. She feels the symmetry, the flowing rhythm of the street. There is a stateliness and serenity about the people too: the women in their solemn wigs and proper dresses, sitting high up on their stoops with their hands folded in their laps; the men in dark suits and white shirts with black homburgs on their heads—looking like her father except for their full beards—promenading proudly, taking long, confident strides, while children dressed for Pesach, the littlest boys with tiny yarmulkas on their heads, run in and out among them. Strolling slowly toward her, an old Rebbe in satin caftan and fur-trimmed shtreimel is flanked by attentive Hassidim, their heads cocked to catch the pearls of wisdom he might drop along the way. Her eyes embrace the scene.

This, she thinks wistfully, is the way Pesach should be. An inexpressible yearning swells inside her. She wants to enclose herself in the surrounding atmosphere, to weave herself into the richness of its fabric. She feels happier here, gladder—safer.

But as she keeps walking, disturbing speculations insinuate themselves into her pleasure and begin gnawing at it. She knows nothing about these people and here she is stuffing them with goodness and getting gushy over them. Just because it's prettier over here and the people are religious doesn't mean it's altogether different. It's true that Mama and Papa don't live on such a nice street and their house is poorer, but they're religious and dressed properly today too. Who would ever imagine what goes on *inside* their house, the way they act sometimes, the awful things they've said?

Esther stops enjoying her walk and turns toward home. She's not in the mood to meet anybody on the street today. They'd wonder what she was doing in their neighborhood anyway. Even if they acted friendly to her, they wouldn't mean it. They probably don't even like her.

The walk back seems much longer. Esther arrives on her block tired and miserable. It's as if she's locked in a glass box. She can see out and people can see her because the glass is invisible, but inside the glass box she's suffocating. When she tries to reach out and touch the people she sees, her hand strikes hard, cold glass. When she calls to them, they cannot hear her.

If only she could talk with somebody. But who is there? Not Lila—not anymore. Millie will just make her feel worse. Angie would look embarrassed if she got too personal. Liesl might understand, but she's so complicated and unpredictable. Rudi. He listens better than anybody; most people seem a lot deafer than he does. Except he's a little boy. Rudi is walled in too. How can he tell anyone how it feels to live in a silent world? Maybe nobody talks to anyone about really personal things. You're probably not supposed to.

Lila is coming down the street, running, her face shining. She hugs Esther and spurts up the stoop steps. Delighted and curious, Esther runs inside after her and follows her up to their bedroom. Lila is sitting on the bed, looking full of a happy secret.

"What happened?" Esther asks.

"Nothing," Lila says cheerfully. "Absolutely nothing."

"Come on, Lila," Esther urges. "Something must have happened. Something good."

Lila hesitates, her eyes glittering. "Even if it did, I can't tell *you*."

"Why not?"

"Because."

"That's a stupid thing to say."

"You'll think you have to tell Mama."

"Why would I?"

"Because you'll think she should know."

"You don't want her to know?"

"You bet I don't."

"Is it something bad?" Esther asks, her heart beginning to pound.

"No, it's not bad. But Mama will think it is. And if she tells Papa, that would be the end."

"Would you tell me if I promise not to say anything?"

"It wouldn't be fair."

"Fair to who?"

"To you."

"I don't know what you're talking about."

"I know you don't. And you're not going to."

"Come on, Lila. Since when do you care about being fair to me?"

Lila's face clouds and her voice sharpens. "Since when do you know *what* I care about?"

Esther is silent. Lila's ebullience has faded. Both sisters

search each other's faces for a moment and turn away. Esther leaves the room. She is in the hall when Lila calls her. Coming back, she stands waiting.

"Do you really promise not to tell?" Lila asks.

"I promise."

"Even if it makes you feel terribly guilty."

Esther is beginning to feel queazy, but doesn't hesitate. "I promise," she repeats.

"Well," Lila says, "I—I got an Easter present."

"A what?"

"A present—for Easter. Some people give presents for Easter, you know."

"You mean Christians?"

"Yes, Christians."

"But you're not a Christian," Esther says, her voice quavering.

"Of course I'm not. But *he* is."

"*He?* You got a present from a Christian boy?" Esther's dismay is apparent.

"I knew I shouldn't have told you," Lila says. Tears began to shimmer in her eyes.

"Yes, you should," Esther says. "You should have told me. After all, I'm—I'm your sister."

"But you won't understand. You're too young."

"I'm not so young. I can understand lots of things."

"Like what?"

"Like a Christian boy gave you a present because—because he likes you. And that you like him too—a lot."

"We don't just *like* each other."

"You mean you're in love?"

"Uh huh."

"That's silly."

"It is not!"

"You're too young."

"I'm almost *fifteen*!"

"Who is it?" Esther asks.

236

"I can't tell you."

"If you told me this much, you might as well tell me the rest."

"Not necessarily."

"Why not?"

"Because he's a *certain* Christian boy."

"What do you mean?"

"Well—most people don't know how nice he really is."

Suffused in sudden heat, Esther asks, "Does he—does he have a bad reputation?"

"I don't care whether he does or not," Lila says. "We're going steady."

"Oh," Esther says weakly, part of her wishing she hadn't persisted and the other thrilled at being taken into her sister's confidence. Should she try to find out who it is? Probably she'd be better off if she didn't know. But she has a feeling Lila is dying to tell her. "*Please* tell me who it is," she asks.

"It's Tommy Flynn."

"Oh, Lila!" Esther cries out.

"I said you'd be sorry," Lila mutters sadly.

"I'm not sorry. I'm—I'm only surprised."

"Are you going to tell?" Lila asks, her eyes huge with fear.

"What do you think I am anyway?" Esther says indignantly. "I promised. Didn't I?"

"I know," Lila says. "But still—now that you know who it is."

"But Lila, everybody talks about him. They say he raped a girl."

"How do *you* know about rape?"

"Never mind how I know. I know."

"He told me all about that. The girl let him and then she got scared he'd tell, so she said he raped her."

"And his language! I've heard him when he plays ball on the block. It's disgusting!"

"Well, he never talks that way when he's with me. He's real nice with me."

"And his father's a drunk 'n' everything."

"I'm not going with his *father*!"

"But still. . . ."

"Still nothing. I shouldn't have told you. I *knew* it."

"No," Esther insists. "You *should* have."

"Why?"

"Because—because you wanted to. And besides, I won't tell."

Lila springs up from the bed and hugs Esther. "I knew," she says. "I knew you wouldn't tell."

Esther chokes up. "Can I see what he gave you?" she manages to ask.

Lila steps back, slides her hand down into the neck of her dress and lifts out a small heart-shaped gold locket. "I wouldn't dare wear it on the outside," she says, displaying it proudly.

"It's pretty," Esther says.

"Isn't it?" Lila breathes. "He has real good taste."

"Maybe he's not as bad as they say," Esther ventures softly.

"They! They! All you talk about is they! Who the hell are they anyway?"

"You know what I mean, Lila. Besides, he's Christian."

"So what if he is?"

Esther is tongue-tied. She can't bring herself to say that it's a sin. "You know," she finally says.

"No, I don't! It's stupid to worry if somebody's Jewish or Christian. As long as he's a nice person."

"But—"

"But nothing!"

Esther is torn between wanting to remain close to Lila and wanting to get away from her. Lila senses it and curls up again against the headboard of the bed. "You know everything now," she says. "You don't have to stay if you don't want to."

Rushing over to her, Esther throws her arms around Lila and finds herself crying. Lila encircles Esther and holding her awkwardly says, "Gee Esther, I'm sorry I upset you."

"It's not just you," Esther blubbers. "It's—it's everything."

"You mean Ben?" Lila murmurs.

"It's not just Ben either," Esther whimpers. "It's—" She *can't* tell Lila. Her throat aches with the desire to cry out, to tear herself away from Lila's confining embrace and utter a loud piercing scream for everyone to hear. Instead she stutters, "I—I mean it's not just his being missing. I'm—I'm getting used to that."

"Yeah," Lila says.

"Oh, I don't mean I'm *really* getting used to it," Esther protests. "I worry about him and I can't understand. . . . Oh, I don't know what I mean!" she cries, breaking away from Lila, and calling, "I have to blow my nose," she runs out of the room.

She stands in the bathroom, blowing her nose into a piece of toilet paper and calming down. When she returns to the bedroom, she announces to her sister, "I'm glad you talked to me. I really and truly am."

Lila is curled up on the bed again, fingering her locket, her eyes downcast, her exuberance gone. She looks up at Esther and says nothing. Esther leaves.

Outside, she sees Liesl and her family arriving home. Liesl comes running over. "Hello!" she sings out. "I'm so happy to see you. I had a good time at my aunt's, but no one was my age. I missed my friends." Liesl speaks English now to most people, but with Esther she still lapses into Yiddish.

"I'm glad you had a good time," Esther says.

"What's the matter?" Liesl asks. "You look like you've been crying."

"I haven't been crying," Esther lies. "I have a cold."

Liesl makes a sympathetic face but Esther suspects she doesn't believe her. Liesl waits a moment and says, "A person shouldn't be ashamed about crying. I cry a lot."

"I said I had a cold!"

"I know what you said. I'm just saying that I cry a lot."

"That's your business!" Esther says angrily. Liesl is always turning things around to herself!

Liesl looks startled; Esther has never spoken to her this way. She waits a while and then asks softly, "How were your Seders?"

"All right. They were all right."

Liesl hesitates again before she asks even more softly, "Did your brother come home?"

Esther is jolted. Her voice rises shrilly. "How do you know about my brother? Did Millie tell you?"

"Even if she did—everyone knows about your brother."

Esther stifles an impulse to slap Liesl's face, and immediately afterwards wonders why she's so angry. Liesl is just being honest. She isn't saying or doing anything wrong. "No, my brother didn't come home," she says.

"I'm sorry," Liesl tells her.

Esther is sure Liesl means it. She thinks she should respond, but doesn't know how.

"I have to go in and unpack my suitcase, but I'll come right out and we'll play," Liesl says cheerfully.

"All right," Esther says. "I'll wait for you."

While she waits for her friend, Esther tries to recapture her former distress because she recalls how much it mattered, but whatever was troubling her has become less significant. Her sister has confided in her and Liesl is hurrying out to play with her. She isn't truly sad anymore. She's glad to feel better, to feel less apart, but she does not abandon herself to joy and optimism as she might once have done. Dimly, in a deep recess of herself, she is coming to assume the evanescence of all states of being and is uncertain whether to be unsettled by this or comforted.

30

The seven weeks of Sefirah are almost over; forty-one of the forty-nine days of the Omer have been counted; hair has gone uncut, marriages not performed—the killing of Jews over the centuries has once more been commemorated. Shevuos is approaching. Another holiday, Malka thinks, lying awake in darkness; as soon as one is over, another approaches. Life is lived either "before the holiday" or "after the holiday." If there were no holidays, the bleakness might be unendurable. With them, at least, some of the emptiness is filled, tension is displaced, there is so much to do—economizing, preparing, observing, doing honor to. But what is one to do with the remaining void, the anxiety that is not exorcised? Lying in bed every night, straining to hear above her husband's snoring the sound of her son's footsteps. And tomorrow, enduring another endless day without a word, a sound. Nothing. As if the earth has swallowed him up. Again, tears rise in her throat and stream from her eyes, rolling down her cheeks onto her neck, crawling beneath her nightgown along her breasts. Oh God, let me drown in my tears rather than learn of harm befalling him!

More and more she remembers him not as he was when he left, a young man; she sees a small boy, smiling, running to her from his play, hugging her knees, burying his face in her skirt. The softness of him, the sweet taste of his skin. How clean she kept him. The blouses she embroidered for him, the beautiful sweaters she knitted. He left with nothing—only the shirt on his back. What has become of him? Where is my child with his radiant face, his eagerness to please? Oh, how he adored his older brother! Clumsily imitating him, beseeching recognition, approval. And how he stared with great, perplexed eyes as the roughly wrought coffin with his brother's body was placed in the ground. When the shovels of earth splattered the coffin, he screamed. Oh, how he screamed! So tiny but he understood. Barely born and already with such a grief. The weeks of comforting him, the months of being to him not only mother and father but brother as well. And he was to me my light in the darkness, my warmth in the cold. Without him, would I have had the strength to go on—to trudge from one strange place to another? Clinging to each other, we both became strong. He began to smile again, to chatter, to make the world glow and sing for me. Who could have foreseen then what he would become?

Sounds. Downstairs. The opening of a door, the click of it closing. Leah? No. It is Saturday night—Leah comes home much later. But it *must* be Leah. Who else? Zalman is there beside her. Esther is in the next room asleep. Malka waits for footsteps on the stairs. Minutes pass. Nothing. Did she imagine again? She must stop imagining. Every night the sudden violent thumping of her heart, the trembling, the tiptoeing out to the hall, peering into the darkness and seeing nothing. No, she will not go. It was the breeze, the air from the open windows. It was no one. Malka turns over on her side. She must sleep or she will go mad with weariness. She cannot let it happen. They need her; she must be a mother and a wife. They must not be shamed before people. She must sleep. Minutes pass.

She cannot sleep. A door *did* open. There *were* sounds downstairs. The night is warm, but Malka shivers as she gets up and leaves her bed.

She steps out into the hall and stands, waiting, listening. She walks down the steps. At the open synagogue door, she stops. The lamppost outside sends shafts of light through the long windows, illuminating the rows of empty benches. The velvet curtain of the Oren Hakodesh burns like a great flame. Malka steps into the synagogue, her eyes searching. No one. She walks along the hall to the basement steps. She hears nothing. Should she go downstairs to see? No. She must stop. She walks back along the hall and begins to ascend the staircase and stops again. Sounds —sounds coming from beneath her feet, from under the steps. Under the staircase is a closet, a big closet—big enough to walk into. Sounds from under the staircase! Oh God, will it be like before? Clutching the banister, she descends slowly—noiselessly. The closet door is open. Only a little, but open! Enough to keep one from suffocating. Her head is pounding. She moves to the closet door and stands frozen. The light from the synagogue reveals lying on the closet floor—legs! Feet! She flings open the door. They spring up—like specters! Lila and a boy! Malka draws back and they fly past her. Out of the house.

Malka sinks to her knees and falls face down across the hallway floor. She wants to die. Now! Let me die! Enough! I've had enough.

She does not know how long she has been lying on the hard floor, stunned and still, praying for numbness. But her heart keeps beating, her mind gallops and jumps and stumbles and hurts itself over and over again. It will not stop. She must rise. She must wrench herself free from the seductive beckoning void. She is a mother. She must get up.

As Malka is struggling to rise, the front door opens and Lila steps cautiously across the threshold. Seeing her mother crumpled on the floor, she cries out and rushes to her, falling to her knees. Throwing her arms about her mother's neck, she weeps and pleads, "Mama, I'm sorry. I didn't mean anything. I'm sorry. Forgive me, Mama. I'm sorry I frightened you. I shouldn't have done it. But, Mama, don't worry. We weren't doing *anything*, only lying together. Please Mama!" Malka's head falls onto Lila's shoulder as great sobs break from her throat. Lila holds her mother close. "Please believe me, Mama. Please!" she begs. Malka embraces her daughter, and for a long time they remain together on the floor, weeping, their arms around each other.

It will soon be daylight and Malka has still not slept. The room shimmers with phantoms. Apparitions out of a time long thrust from her mind weave their way through the darkness. His hair, like corn silk. When they flew past her, Leah and the boy, it caught the lamplight. Oh the wicked pranks our minds will play! One moment, searing pain, horror, and outrage. The very next instant, an immense wave of tenderness that rose and broke and spilled into rivulets inside her. And the slender girl holding his hand as they ran together into the night. Oh God, how capricious can you be? At such a time, to remind me of him. After so many years, after being so long locked away, to emerge without warning—all the memories. The sun-filled day when she first saw him. (She was not much older than Leah.) She was sitting under an oak tree, resting from the chores which earned her keep at the Koskoffs'. He came striding across the field with his sun-tanned face, his eyes reflecting the sky, and his hair—his glorious hair blowing like the wheat in the wind. He stopped when he reached her, rising out of his tall peasant boots like a young cedar. "What is your name?" he asked in Russian. And she heard herself, without hesitating, tell him. "I am Peter," he said. She knew then she should rise and run, but his smile held her. She did not run. "Malka means queen," he said. "How would *you* know?" she asked. "I have lived all my life near Jews," he said. "I have learned much from them." Why had she never seen him before? she wondered. But she dared not ask lest he guess how his nearness was affecting her. "If you are a queen," he went on, "I must ask your leave to sit down." "Do as you like," she replied, as haughtily as she could. He sat down beside her and for a time he was quiet, looking out over the broad field before him with suddenly weary eyes. She tried again to bring herself to rise and leave, but could not. At last he asked, "Do these fields belong to your family?" She wanted to say it was none of his affair, but she hesitated and he turned and looked into her eyes, and she knew he noticed the color coming to her cheeks. Finally, she said, "They belong to the family for whom I work. I am a servant here."

His eyes became puzzled. "You do not seem like a servant."

"I am," she said indignantly, almost proudly.

"Where are your parents?"

"Dead."

"I'm sorry," he said, looking genuinely mournful.

"They were killed," she said. And after a moment of indecision, added fiercely, "By Russians. Cossacks!" And as she spoke the words, he became transformed for her and she hated him and rose to leave.

He sprang up and took her arm gently. She could have pulled away. But she waited. "You hate all of us. Don't you?" he said sadly.

What a strange peasant, she thought. But she snapped at him, "Yes! Let me go!"

"You may go," he said. "Only do not hate me."

She turned without a word and ran toward the house. For days afterwards she found herself surreptitiously searching for him. She offered to run errands to the village for the slightest reason; she took circuitous routes through the streets, prolonging her stay as long as she could; she walked by the tavern, the church. She imagined him seeing her and longing to speak to her but discouraged by her earlier anger. If he should appear and speak to her, she would be prepared this time; she would be haughty from the beginning. But he would be so smitten that he would persist. After that.... She could not think beyond that. But she did not see him anywhere, and if he saw her, she did not know. She took to sitting under the oak tree each day, bringing sewing with her so she would not appear to be waiting. When she had forsaken any hope of seeing him again, he reappeared.

Indescribable joy shot through her, but when he asked if he might sit down, she replied coldly, "You have no business to be here."

"I know that," he said, "but I should like very much to sit down."

"Do as you like," she said once again, and he sat down beside her.

She continued to sew. Her thread kept knotting and her stitches became uneven, and she knew that he noticed. She asked him nothing, but he told her he had come from the outskirts of a town she had never heard of to seek work. He was a carpenter, a cabinet-maker. His village was too poor to sustain him; he hoped to do better here. He had come last time because they told him the Koskoffs might commission him to build something—a fine piece of furniture. They liked good craftsmanship, he was told. But her attitude had upset him, and he had never asked them. When there were no commissions, he worked in the fields. "To work in the fields is also good," he said. She wondered why he was telling her so much about himself. Why should she care? But she listened to every word, and his voice was wonderful, deep and tinged with sadness. With a great effort, she said, "Why don't you go to the house then and ask if they can use you?"

"I've already obtained a commission from a neighbor of yours that will take a long time to complete."

"Then why have you come?" she asked, staring down at the seam of the skirt she was making for herself, and sewing quickly and clumsily.

"To see you again," he said.

She knew her face was flaming, but she could do nothing to stop it. There was a long silence between them until she said, her voice not as steady as she wanted, "If you keep sitting here, you will not get your work done."

"My work will be done. There is more than work in this world," he said, looking past the fields to the horizon.

"What else is there?"

"There is the sun throbbing in the sky above us," he said, speaking slowly and softly. "There is the foliage of this tree to shelter us when its rays are too hot. There is the sweet smell of green grass, the silvery smoothness of a stream, the sound of a bird singing after a winter storm." He turned and looked at her. "There is the terror of the night when one is alone. There is the warm nearness of another person. There is the pleasure of her beauty."

She sprang up. "I must leave. My work will not be done," she said quickly and ran back to the house.

But she could not forget him. Never had she been so stirred.

For a week she stayed away from the tree, but she could not stop thinking of him. And when she returned to the tree, he came. The moment they saw each other, it was as if they knew they shared a secret. They sat for a long time talking, and before he left he touched her cheek with his hand.

The next time they met, they were seen. Anya Koskoff had come out to cut wildflowers and saw them just as they stood up to take leave of each other and for the first time he kissed her—quickly on the forehead before he went away. When she returned to the house, her mistress was waiting. She remembers her words, and the seriousness with which she spoke them. "Malka," she said, "you are young and lonely, and your blood is warm. I am not angry with you. I only want you to remember that you are a girl with neither a family nor a dowry. You have only your good name. You must not lose it."

She said nothing in response, only bent her head in shame and in gratitude. And she vowed to herself never to see him again.

But she did. She waited until no one was at home, and then she led him to the hayloft where they would not be seen. They lay together in the dimness under the eaves. They lay, not touching, fully clothed except for their bare feet. Neither could find words. After a time—she still does not know whether she intended it—her foot found his, and the silkiness of his instep sent a shiver of sudden ecstasy through her body. Fearfully, she drew her foot away from his; but after a few moments she sought it, and gently smoothed his silken instep with her toes. He turned to her and kissed her on the mouth. He kissed her neck and she encircled him with her arms. His back burned beneath her fingers; she felt its tensile strength, its supple curves. He raised his head and searched her eyes before he undid the buttons of her blouse. She stroked his hair as his mouth found her breast. She can still feel the gentleness of his mouth, the loveliness of his tongue. Never had she known such happiness. Then, suddenly, her mind remembered her mistress' words. They burst in her ears, and she was terrified. "No!" she cried. "No! You must not! I must leave!" He held her. "Please," she pleaded. "Let me go." Sadly, reluctantly, he took his arms from her.

When they had descended the ladder, they stood facing each other. "Do not come again," she told him. "I beg you!"

He turned and left and she never saw him again. Until tonight, in the light from the synagogue, holding her daughter's hand, his golden hair flying past her.

The pillow under Malka's head is wet. The room swims and circles about. What they say is true—the apple does not fall far from the tree. Her daughter, her beautiful daughter. How dare she judge her? What right does she have? What has she given her to gird herself against the world? Leah too has only her beauty and her good name. And if her name is besmirched, her beauty will avail her nothing. Leah too has been left to loneliness; even with parents she has been an orphan—orphaned by her father's fanaticism and her mother's immoderate love for her son. What will become of her? Esther is different—thin and frail-looking, but strong inside. I am sure of it. Esther will have sadness, but she will survive. Only Leah, I beg you, God, look after her. She has no one else.

The sun is rising when Malka finally falls asleep.

31

The morning is a brilliant one. Malka opens her eyes to
a merciless sun plunging through the window of her bedroom thrusting sharply into focus the details of its dingi-
ness: the heavy mahogany furniture looking tired and
battered from its many voyages in moving vans, beginning
with the big house it had once adorned to a succession of
places less ample and less prepossessing; the brown cardboard obelisks of her husband's misadventures sagging
with their burden of unconsummated promise. The bureau
with its broken leg tilts to one side. How surprised she was
when it broke. It had seemed so sturdy. But careless handling will break almost anything. Like with people. Only
a piece of furniture you can mend—maybe the crack shows
in a bright light, or like with the bureau, a missing sliver
of wood makes it stand crooked; a crack in a person or a
piece missing is a more serious matter. Yet we handle each
other carelessly; we break each other. How do you mend
a person who was not properly looked after and became
damaged?

Perhaps it is her fault that Leah is the way she is.
She was not all a mother should have been. No, she did
not take care. Her son needed her more—she cannot recall
pondering on it or even troubling herself to decide. Her
feelings flowed naturally toward her son to protect him
with her softness from the harshness of his father. When

she was pregnant with Leah, her constant concern was Benjamin. The care she took—she would stop nursing her daughter, putting her down abruptly if her son entered the room. When she wanted to caress her daughter, to kiss her, she would not if Benjamin was present. Then Esther was born. Benjamin had grown older and seemed to no longer want her near him. Esther was fragile, a small sparrow of a child; she needed tending. And Leah had become a sturdy beautiful little girl, basking in everyone's admiration—so why concern herself? Oh, how stupid she was! Who should have known better than she? The admiration of strangers is like a flimsy veil in a storm.

Malka cannot bring herself to rise, to confront another day. Tears flow relentlessly from her swollen eyes. A terrible possibility intrudes itself. Has she been punishing her daughter for her own sins? Has she seen in her beautiful daughter her own worthlessness and weakness reborn? It is possible. It is possible. Oh, how she longs to speak to her, to tell her, to explain. But how? Such thoughts, such feelings are unutterable. Our voices are only for the trivial, the fatuous, for subterfuge from others as well as ourselves. When our hearts hurt and want to cry out, when we long most for others to hear, we are mute. Malka's sobs break the stillness of the room.

At last she lies dry-eyed and desolate, even the comfort of tears denied her. Staring at the ceiling, she invokes the aid of God. Riboyneh Shel Olem, she pleads, give me faith in you. Let me believe that you exist. I am a simple woman and I cannot understand your ways. Help me to believe without understanding. Guide me. My child is sore inside and seeks solace from strangers. Let her come to me so I may soothe her. Help me to give her strength.

Malka rises from her bed. The futility that has been oppressing her feels lighter. A task lies ahead. How she will perform it, she does not know. But the timidity that is making her hands tremble while she pulls on her stockings will be overcome. When she steps out into the hall, Malka is not fully aware that the determination to give herself to her daughter contains, besides remorse, the hope that an omnipresent God will witness her penance and return her son to her. She knows only that the day feels fresh and full of promise.

Esther is puzzled. She had breakfast with Lila alone. Her mother was still asleep. She asked Lila if she knew whether Mama was sick, and Lila looked at her with swollen eyes, said she didn't know, and gulped down her roll. Before she left for school, she hesitated for a moment at the foot of the stairs, looking up as if she hoped to see Mama coming down. Then her mother came down, also with swollen eyes, and asked immediately if Lila was still home. She told her no and asked if her mother was sick. Her mother said she was not and smiled. It's been a long time since Mama smiled. Something must have happened. But what? All morning in school, Esther is troubled. Could Mama have found out about Tommy Flynn? Did they have a big fight? Usually Lila screams and bangs doors when they fight and it wakes her up if she's sleeping. And Mama looks sad afterwards; she doesn't smile. Yet Mama's eyes were swollen, like she'd been crying. If she asks either of them what happened, probably no one will tell her.

During lunch, her mother's movements are agile and her eyes are bright. She even asks Esther about her morning in school. But still, she seems distracted, strained, not listening for a reply, but only to the sound of her own voice—adjusting its tone for a distinct purpose. Esther becomes uncomfortable. Her mother isn't being herself; she was always so direct—you never had to wonder what was going on in her mind. Her silences spoke too. She didn't have to tell you she was annoyed or pleased or cared about you. You just knew. Now it's like she's worried that she didn't make herself clear before. What's wrong? But how can she ask when her mother is being so cheerful? All the way back to school, Esther is uneasy; suddenly her mother seems more fragile and vulnerable than ever before.

Mr. Wexler announces an outing. The class is to vote whether to go to the Museum of Natural History or the Metropolitan Museum of Art. Mr. Wexler explains to them what each place has in it. Esther knows where she wants to go. When Lila was in 6B, her class went to the Museum of Natural History and Lila hated it. (She *loved* Central Park where they had a picnic afterwards.) Esther is sure she'll hate the skeletons and stuffed animals too. Please, she prays, please let the art museum win.

"You may talk it over among yourselves first, if you don't get too noisy," Mr. Wexler tells them. "Then we'll vote."

Esther's hand shoots up. "How much does it cost to get into them?"

"It won't cost anything to get in to either one," Mr. Wexler says, "but you'll need a dime for the train. And you might want to bring an extra nickel for a drink with your lunch." And, as if sensing Esther's anxiety, he adds, "Of course, if you bring a fruit along, like an orange, you might not need an extra nickel."

Esther is relieved. She's sure Mama will give her a dime. But just in case, she'll hang around the drugstore and answer telephones. People usually give you something for calling them to the phone—some give a nickel.

Most of the boys want to go to the natural history museum because "Who wants a look at a lotta pictures?" But a few are excited about the medieval armor and weapons in the art museum. John Coppola doesn't say anything. Esther has a feeling he wants to see the paintings and sculptures but is afraid the other boys will make fun of him. John draws real well. The girls mostly want to go to the art museum because "Who wants to see a lotta big

254

ugly dinosaurs and disgusting skeletons? Yich!" The medieval armor group tilts the vote and the Metropolitan Museum of Art wins. Esther is ecstatic. She looks across at Millie who, having been the most vociferous spokesman for the art museum, smiles triumphantly back at her.

Arriving home, happy and excited, Esther finds her parents in the kitchen. Her father is dressed up in his dark blue suit and talking about somebody who has a guldeneh neshuma—a golden soul. " 'Sam,' I said, 'let me explain to you why this business is not like the others. Who doesn't need eggs? And with a truck, where won't we find customers? Groyseh glicken we might not make—millionaires we won't become,' I told him. 'But the debts we'll pay back and there will be a living.' Malka, I don't know if he even heard me. While I'm talking, he's already writing the check. Here it is—five hundred dollars."

Esther walks over to the table to see what a check for five hundred dollars looks like. The signature, bold and florid, reads, "Samuel Gittleson."

"A diamond he is!" her father goes on. "When he gives me the check, he puts his hand on my shoulder and says, 'With God's help, you'll pay back. I'm not worrying.' Then a secretary comes into the office and reminds him that his next appointment is waiting. He tells me he's sorry he's so busy, he sends regards to you and to the children, and then he walks with me yet to the elevator."

Esther has never seen Sam Gittleson, but she's told her friends about this rich relative they have. He must really be very rich, she thinks, and so nice too. She'd already forgotten about the egg business that her father kept mentioning months ago. He stopped talking about it after Ben disappeared. Her mother doesn't say anything sarcastic about it now, like she usually does when he talks about a new business. She says like she means it, "Maybe this time God will help."

It seems to Esther that everyone is changed—that

they've forgotten about Ben, like they've gotten used to his not being there. It's as if they don't expect him to come back. How could they be like this? Would they forget about *her* so fast if she ran away? Is it possible they're even *glad* he's not coming back, that maybe there won't be so much fighting and hollering anymore? No, they *can't* be glad. They *couldn't* have forgotten about him. Just a few weeks ago when her mother lit the Pesach candles, the way she cried and cried. No, Mama must still be hurting inside and just getting used to it. Papa too. Look at me— how happy I feel because I'm going to an art museum where Mr. Wexler said they have pictures more beautiful than you can imagine and because I'm going uptown where I've never been and have a picnic in Central Park. But I haven't forgotten about Ben. Though she has to admit she's been feeling mixed up about him since she saw those pictures he drew in his book. It frightens her that he might really be a different person from the one she remembers. He's even reminded her of Dr. Jekyll and Mr. Hyde, and that scares her so much she forces herself to forget about him. Maybe Mama and Papa are forcing themselves too.

She decides not to tell her parents about the class outing just then. Mama won't understand what an art museum is anyway. Papa might because he's lived in lots of places and made a lot of money once and he's talked about palaces he saw in Europe, and because he seemed sad about not sending her to the Educational Alliance for art classes. But this isn't a good time to talk to him; he's so involved now in his plans for another business, he wouldn't pay attention.

Outside, the afternoon is balmy with mild breezes. Esther sits down on a stoop step with her pad and pencils and crayons. She'll draw Mrs. Riccio sitting in front of her fruit store. She can't see her face too well from across the street but she can see the small stubby body in the flowered housedress planted squarely on the empty fruit crate, the shoulders sagging a little. And set like a dark jewel against the heaps of apples and oranges in the window, her jet-black hair lit by the sun with glints of blue, and its one white streak. Esther bends over her pad. Lila, calling, "Hi!" hurries past her into the house. Esther hardly looks up. Her pencil moves lightly, uncertainly. It's beginning to look a little like Mrs. Riccio, but not enough. She sees the shadow along Mrs. Riccio's nose, down one side of her face and under her chin along her neck; her pencil moves rapidly back and forth, darkening those areas. There! That looks better. She'd like to use her crayons for the apples and oranges in the window and the big yellow bunches of bananas hanging above them, and for Mrs. Riccio's hair and her dress, but then she'll have to color the face too and that'll be hard and if she makes a mistake you can't erase crayon. Maybe next time, after she has more practice. She'll leave it the way it is right now. Even if it doesn't look exactly like Mrs. Riccio, at least you can tell what kind of person it is, that she works hard and how good it feels to her to be resting outside in the sun.

Hugging her pad to her chest, Esther goes inside to have supper before it's time for Hebrew school.

Her father isn't there anymore, only her mother and Lila, and she's interrupted them. She could tell the minute she entered the kitchen that they stopped talking when she came in. Now Lila wants to help make supper. She never did *that* before. Her mother gives Lila the onions to grate into the potato pancake batter. Lila puts on an apron, peels the onions, and begins grating them. They make her cry. Her mother sees and says she'll do it. Lila insists on continuing, saying she'll get used to it. Something *definitely* must have happened. *Both* of them are different. Esther's feelings are ambivalent. This is better than the sulkiness

32

The reconciliation between Malka and her older daughter has been implicit rather than expressed, the few words that passed between them spoken haltingly, hardly doing justice to the depth of emotion behind them. Feelings long imprisoned in dark, impenetrable places came out fumbling and apprehensive. Malka feels better, but she cannot dispel what has become for her a perpetual presentiment of something unexpected and shattering. The new relatedness feels tenuous. Perhaps if they had said all that was in their hearts. . . . But they did not. And who knows if it would have mattered? But to imagine that all has been overcome with a few hysterical minutes of weeping and embracing, with her guilt and remorse, with Lila's gratitude and feeble promises, is to believe in fairy tales. How often she has known emotions that could not be tamed, feelings impervious to reason, to the sincerest resolutions. The times when Zalman's misery, after knowing he behaved badly, moved her, and she determined to accept him and his foibles with grace and to love him. (His inability to live up to the image he set for himself was, after all, piteous.) For a few days, sometimes weeks, it would be well between them. He would behave more acceptably and she would accept him. Then gradually he would grow careless, his frustration would surface, his authoritarianism would assert itself, his joviality with others would seem sycophantic, some interaction would set off the spark. Her feelings of distaste would flare up, and she would hate him.

But Leah is not another person, grown in the womb of some other woman. Leah is *hers*, a perpetuation of herself forced naked and screaming into the world. She is entitled to forgiveness for whatever she may be, to unqualified love. Yet seeing herself in Leah is what imperils the love. How strange that Esther should be so different. She is also her child. Perhaps Esther is a part of herself she never came to know.

Malka bends over the scrub board, rubbing the thick bar of brown soap against the soiled linen. She is weary. Perhaps that explains the uneasiness, the fear that she will not be able to cope with whatever may come. But there is something else too. In the past few days Leah has been looking uneasy. When she asked her what was wrong, she said nothing was. But when Leah looked at her, it was as if a timid fawn sprang up in her eyes for a moment and was frightened away, leaving her eyes dark with its shadow.

Esther comes into the kitchen in high spirits. She has this Sunday off from Hebrew school. It is Jewish National Fund Day, a special day to go out collecting money for planting trees in Palestine. The blue and white collection cans were given out last week with the announcement that there would be a prize for whoever collects the most money. Mr. Spiro explained in Assembly that they were not being given a holiday to sleep late or to go to the movies or to play ball. Their daily schedules were crowded and the Sunday off was, he said, "... an opportunity to fulfill your obligation as a part of the Jewish people."

Malka stops scrubbing, wipes her hands on her apron, and sets about preparing breakfast. Esther is in a hurry. She tells her mother about the prize and that she wants to get started early, as soon as the stores open, before they can say they gave already.

"Where will you go collecting?" Malka asks. "Don't go too far away."

"Everybody will probably go on Broadway," Esther says, "so I'm going to go on Grand Street."

"Grand Street? Why Grand Street?"

Esther sees her mother frown, and she knows why. Grand Street is like Broadway; only Broadway divides the different kinds of Jews, and Grand Street divides the South side of Williamsburg which is Jewish from the North side which is Christian—mostly Polish and Irish. Lots of the stores, like the clothing stores and shoe stores, are Jewish, but the groceries sell bacon and the butcher shops have big hams hanging in the window. The street seems goyish. And every time she goes near a Christian neighborhood, her mother gets scared. Probably because of what happened in Russia. "Don't worry, Mama," she reassures her mother. "Nothing will happen to me on Grand Street. I'm not a baby anymore."

Malka nods her head resignedly and says nothing.

Lila enters the kitchen. Malka is surprised. "How come you're up so early?" she asks.

Lila says she couldn't sleep anymore.

Malka puts Esther's oatmeal on the table. Lila sits down, her face constricted and brooding.

"I'm going out collecting for the Jewish National Fund," Esther tells her.

"That's nice," Lila says. "Good luck."

"Thanks," Esther answers, thinking Lila sounds peculiar.

No one says anything after that until Lila blurts out, "All my friends are going to Coney Island today. Not to the beach, to—to Steeplechase. It costs fifty cents."

Malka's heart drops. Fifty cents? Lila is asking her for fifty cents. How can she give her fifty cents? She counted this morning. Six quarters, two dimes, and a nickel. And she counted the days till the next check—at least four more unless, God forbid, it gets lost in the mail. She sees her daughter's face flushed with embarrassed eagerness and a trace of blighted hope already in her eyes. She cannot bring herself to be abrupt. "What is Steeplechase?" she says instead.

"It's a place—what they call an amusement park—on the boardwalk where you get thirty-one rides for fifty cents. *Everybody's* going!"

"Rides?"

"Yes, like—like the Whip that Papa took you on years ago you told us. And lots of other rides. I have money for the train—Mrs. Hollander gave me a dime for setting her hair for a wedding. I'll take along lunch. I only need fifty cents to get in. I wanted to ask you all week but I was afraid you'd say no."

Malka returns to the scrub board. Clutching it with one hand and scrubbing with the other, she says, "I cannot give you fifty cents." Why is her heart pounding? Why? Why should she feel so bad? What is so important about going on crazy rides? It is foolishness, she says to herself, foolishness. But she wants to weep. Is not a child entitled now and then to a little foolishness?

Except for the sounds of scrubbing and splashing, there is silence. When she finally brings herself to look at Lila, Malka sees the blue eyes burning and tears spilling from them. "Please Leah," she says, "don't be a child."

"Don't be a *child*?" Lila screams. "First you tell me I'm only a child, I mustn't go with boys. Now you tell me *not* to be a child! What do you want me to *be*?"

Before Malka can speak, Lila runs from the house, banging the door behind her.

Esther sits stunned for a minute. Her mother's face twists into an ugly grimace. Esther wants to reach out and comfort her mother, but awkwardness overcomes her. She picks up her collection can, says, "I'm going now," and leaves the house.

Malka keeps standing by the sink, and a sardonic smile slides across her face. I should not be sad, she thinks, I should be grateful. So that's all it was—all that Leah's brooding has been about. That is all she was afraid of. My brain should be cut from my head for the thoughts that passed through my mind.

33

The air is heavy. The sun she saw through the window when she woke up has moved behind a cloud. She hopes it doesn't rain before she's finished collecting. But if it rains, they won't be able to go to Steeplechase, and Lila won't feel so bad. Poor Lila, she's been trying so hard to be nice. She probably feels terrible, not only because she can't go with her friends but because she spoiled everything. She seemed like such a little kid this morning.

It's funny that she should think about Lila as a little kid. Unexpectedly, Esther remembers a time her sister seemed really grown up. That time in the movies last summer. Lila was sitting next to her on one side, and the seats on her other side were empty. The man came along past the empty seats, bent over and whispered to her that he was sitting there before and he lost some money. He wanted to look for it under the seat. They kept watching the movie while the man squatted on the floor feeling around for the money. Suddenly she felt him take her bare legs between his thighs and start rubbing himself against her. His pants were open. She could *feel* it! At first she didn't realize what it was, but then she knew. It was his thing—his penis, hot and slippery, sliding in and out between her legs. She wanted to scream out, but she was embarrassed and afraid. She was even too scared to tell Lila. She just sat there, letting him. That's the way she is—always afraid of getting people mad at her. But Lila isn't. All of a sudden Lila saw what was going on, sprang up from her seat, and kicked the man with all her might, shouting, "What the *hell* do you think you're doing? Get out of here before I call the police!" The man fell over, clutching his fly. He crawled on the floor past the empty seats and, still holding his pants together, scuttled up the aisle. The usher came running over, the people around them wanted to know what happened. Lila, still snorting with fury, said quietly, "Nothing. Never mind. It's all right now." The usher went away and gradually everyone settled down and watched the movie. How grateful she was to Lila for not telling—she was so ashamed. How heroic Lila seemed to her. Esther feels tears rising to her eyes. Lila was so sad this morning. It was like she knew she shouldn't ask but couldn't help herself. She wanted to go to Steeplechase with her friends *so badly.*

Grand Street is quiet early on a Sunday morning. Stores are open but people are still asleep. Some might be in church. The opaque gray sky dulls the fronts of the stores and low flat-topped buildings, giving them a dejected look. Esther's buoyancy is deflated. The street looks grim and unfriendly. She no longer expects to win the prize.

Outside Wisotsky's Shoe Store, she stops. Last year, Mrs. Wisotsky gave her a dime, more than anybody else gave. But now she knows that Wisotsky is one of the places you go for Home Relief shoes; she hates the idea of even going in. She sees that Mr. Wisotsky is alone in the store. He's looking out the window like he's hoping a customer will come. He'll be disappointed that it's only me. But she makes herself do it. Mr. Wisotsky approaches her eagerly. (Maybe he thinks my mother sent me for shoes.) But when he sees the blue and white can, his face falls and he sighs deeply. She doesn't even have to ask. He fishes around in his pants pocket, takes out a handful of change, picks out three pennies, and drops them into the slot of her collection can. She says, "Thank you," and tries not to show that she thinks he's stingier than his wife. But as soon as she leaves the store, she's sorry for thinking it; she remembers his eyes when he was watching out the window. Probably they can't afford a dime this year.

Shindler's Linoleum is another place that gave last year, not much but something. The windows are blocked by tall, shiny, upright cylinders in all kinds of colors and designs, but through the glass door she can see that Shindler's has customers, a young couple with a little kid. All three of them have straight yellow hair, short round noses, and little blue button eyes—clearly Christian, probably Polish. She feels funny about going in with a Jewish National Fund can; they might give each other a look or call her a name or something. Maybe they don't realize that Mr. Shindler is Jewish—he doesn't have an accent. But Mr. Shindler is looking at her through the door. She'd better go in or he might imagine she was going to do something wrong and come running out after her. A bell rings when she opens the door. The gay colors all around and the tangy smell of brand new linoleum revive her spirits, but as soon as Mr. Shindler spots the blue and white can, his eyes shift nervously to his customers and his face gets red. The young couple are walking along an aisle between walls of linoleum and don't even turn around. The little kid looks at her for a minute and then retreats into the folds of his mother's skirt. Before Esther can ask, Mr. Shindler, very quickly, opens the cash register, takes out two coins, and thrusts them into her hand. "Here," he says. "Now go. Go already." He practically pushes her out the door. When she gets outside, she looks in the palm of her hand, sees two pennies, and drops them into the slot of her collection can. She can still feel the pressure of Mr. Shindler's hand on her shoulder. She'll never go in there again! Never!

All her enthusiasm has been eroded, but Esther forces

herself to go on. As she trudges along, she is dimly aware of her omnipresent God watching, appreciating her fortitude in the face of ignominious insult for the sake of the Jewish people.

She pauses outside a new store with signs pasted all over the window. It sells dungarees, overalls, denim shirts, fishing boots, and other men's clothes. Somehow it doesn't look Jewish. She doesn't go in.

The door of the Bar and Grill on the corner is open, and the stale stench of tobacco smoke and beer and men's bodies floats out to the street. She wants to hold her nose— the stink is like pee. A scrawny, unshaven, red-eyed man in an undershirt comes out carrying a small bucket and walking carefully to keep its contents from spilling. But the beer dribbles over the top and splatters the sidewalk. Esther runs across the street. The buttonhole factory in the next store is closed. So is the Plumbing Supplies store. The block looks deserted. But up ahead, someone is coming out of Mollie's Kiddie Shoppe. She runs until she comes to it and is cheered by its lively window crammed with adorable tiny dresses and sunsuits and sweater sets. Little girl mannequins are exquisite in organdy ruffles, and little boy mannequins in neat short pants look angelic above their Peter-Pan collars. She opens the door and steps inside. Mollie descends on her, oozing motherly warmth, her chubby face beaming, her eyes glimmering moistly behind silver-rimmed glasses. "What can I do for you today, doll?" she croons.

Esther backs away a little. "Could you please give something for the Jewish National Fund?" she asks, holding out her blue and white can.

"To plant trees in Palestine. Right?" Mollie says, sounding delighted with herself, like she just gave the right answer on a test.

"Yes," Esther says.

"*Of course* I will! For Palestine I shouldn't give?" Mollie trills, taking a nickel from the pocket of her bright, flowered smock and dropping it into the slot.

Esther smiles and says, "Thank you." Mollie calls goodbye after her as she leaves. What a nice lady, Esther thinks, a little comical but nice. Her step is more sprightly now, she feels optimistic. She has nine cents and it's early. There's still hardly anybody outside. In fact, nobody. The street is empty. Suddenly—she doesn't know from where —a skinny arm shoots out in front of her and a hand grabs her collection can. For an instant, she faces a gaunt tight-lipped boy about her own age. His eyes are slivers of blue flint. Then he is gone. Dungarees, a striped tee shirt, and dank yellow hair are running up the street and disappear around the corner with her collection can. She can't move. She keeps standing and shivering in the warm, humid air. He took it! It's gone! With nine cents in it! Tears stream from her eyes. Then terror takes hold of her and thrusts her forward. The sidewalks heave in huge waves as she runs and runs, as fast as she can, with all her might, until breathless and exhausted she is on her own block.

She runs to her house, down the steps, pushes open the door, shuts it behind her, and leans back against it. Panting, trembling, and crying, she waits for someone to come out in the hall and ask her what's the matter. No one comes. Nobody has heard her come in. Could no one be home? She hears someone speaking. The voice stops her tears. It's Mrs. Hollander. What is Florence's mother doing in *their* house? Her mother doesn't even *know* Mrs. Hollander! Esther's panting subsides. She listens. "Please," Mrs. Hollander is saying in her wheedling voice, "let the child go. Why not? She's only young once." For a moment Esther can't figure out what Mrs. Hollander is talking about. (The scene at breakfast seems years ago.) Then she wonders why Mrs. Hollander makes it sound like her mother isn't *letting* Lila go. Doesn't she understand about the money? Unless Lila didn't say *why* she couldn't go, and just said that she couldn't. Esther moves quietly to the kitchen door. No one notices her. Mrs. Hollander is sitting all spread out in her Marlene Dietrich slacks and her tight batiste blouse with her bulges showing; her big patent leather pocketbook is on the table. Her mother is at the sink cutting up carrots with her back to the visitor and not responding. From the way she's standing, with her shoulders high and stiff, Esther can imagine the expression on her mother's face. Lila is in a corner with wide, wide eyes, astonished, hopeful, and frightened. Mrs. Hollander goes on, her voice getting more oily, "If it's a matter of money, I'll tell you what. Let me treat her. After all, what's fifty cents to me?"

Malka swings around, her face flaming.

"All right! All right!" Mrs. Hollander says, putting up a hand as though to ward off a blow. "I won't treat her. I'll *lend* you the money. A loan. What's a loan? It's for the child. Why shouldn't you want the child to be happy?"

Malka does not move. She just stands with her eyes blazing and the knife in her hand and speaks. "Out! Get out!"

Mrs. Hollander grabs her pocketbook and jumps up. "Control yourself, Mrs. Hirsch," she breathes, backing away. "What's so terrible?"

Malka, the knife in her hand thrust out, moves forward, snarling through clenched teeth. "Get out of my house! This minute!"

Mrs. Hollander yelps. Esther springs aside just in time. Mrs. Hollander hurtles past her.

Lila is upstairs, probably in bed crying her head off. Her mother has returned to cutting carrots. Esther waits in the kitchen, wanting to tell her mother what happened to her. But the words stick in her throat; her mother's

34

When she tells them in the office the next day about not having her collection can because somebody robbed her, Sadie Garber, the Hebrew school's secretary, becomes very sad. First her penciled eyebrows go up in astonishment, then they descend right down to her eyelids while she shakes her head in dismay, her great nose wagging back and forth. Esther is distracted from her worry and embarrassment by noticing that one of Sadie's eyebrows is lower than the other, giving her a lopsided look. She imagines how Sadie looks before her eyebrows are penciled on, and becomes slightly sick. Sadie misunderstands Esther's sudden pallor and hastens to assure her not to worry, that she believes her, and she doesn't have to pay back the nine cents—it's just one of those things.

"But I *want* to," Esther says, not knowing immediately afterwards why she said it.

"Well, if it'll make you feel better," Sadie says. "But there's no hurry. Whenever you get around to it is okay."

Esther says, "Thank you," and leaves the office, liking Sadie a lot. (Why does everyone make fun of her and call her Sadie Garbage? Probably she acts different if you get *sent* to the office.) She's glad she didn't have to talk to Mr. Spiro about it. She's never spoken to him, and she doesn't want to.

By the following Sunday, Esther has twenty-six cents. She feels rich. After she pays back the nine cents, she'll have seventeen cents, two cents more than she needs for carfare and ice cream tomorrow. Should she keep answering phones and make more money? If she does it all afternoon until supper, she might get enough to go to the movies next week. But she doesn't like having to beat other kids to the phone. (It really hurt when Sidney Smolowitz shoved her.) Besides. . . . No, she won't even think about it. But Sadie *did* say she didn't *have* to pay back, and it really *wasn't* her fault that the money got stolen. Esther sits on her bed, tossing the coins in her hand and pondering what she ought to do. It's been ages since she went to the movies. (Millie keeps offering to treat her but she feels funny about it now, maybe because she's older.) She spreads the coins out on the bed, counts them again, and can't make up her mind. Until her ubiquitous God looms before her and reminds her about the trees in Eretz Yisroel and her obligation as part of the Jewish people. As she goes back to the drugstore to wait for more phones to ring, he is beaming approval.

Good. She's the only one around. It's fun this way. She likes talking to different people on the phone and finding out who they want and running as fast as she can to all the buildings, going up the steps two at a time, and announcing breathlessly that there's a phone call for so and so. People act different; the young girls get all flushed and fly down the steps, forgetting to give her anything. Some older people get real scared, but most of them give her something, even if it's only a penny. She likes the way the drugstore smells—so clean. And Mr. Drucker seems pleased to see her. He doesn't mind having kids hanging around his store if there aren't too many and they don't fight. If not, he'd have to leave the store alone to call people and if it's a good customer and he doesn't go to get him, he might not buy there again.

An hour has passed. The telephone hasn't rung once. She'll start reading the names of the things on the shelves and if the phone doesn't ring by the time she's finished, she'll leave.

In the middle of the laxatives—she's just passed Ex Lax and is up to Feenamint—the phone rings. She rushes into the phone booth, pulling the door shut behind her.

"Hello."

"I'd like to speak to Mr. Hirsch, Mr. Solomon Hirsch," a deep voice says.

"Mr. Hirsch?" Esther squeals. It doesn't sound like anyone her father knows.

"Yes, Hirsch. Just a minute, I'll give you the address."

"I know his address," Esther says. "I'll go get him. Hold on." She puts down the receiver and runs.

"Where's Papa?" she asks her mother breathlessly.

"He's upstairs davening Mincha. What's the matter?"

Esther hesitates. Something tells her not to tell her mother about the phone call. "Oh, nothing," she says.

"What do you want him for?" her mother asks.

"Nothing," Esther says, "it's nothing," and races out of the house.

She picks up the receiver, puts it to her ear, and speaks into the mouthpiece. "I'm sorry, but Mr. Hirsch can't come to the phone."

"Isn't he home?"

"He's home, but he's—he's praying."

No sound at the other end.

"He's in the synagogue. The afternoon service is going on," Esther explains. Then trying to sound secretarial, she asks, "Is there any message?"

"Who is this?" the voice asks gruffly.

"This is his daughter."

"Oh, I see," the voice says more softly. "Would you tell him to call the police?"

"The police?"

"Yes, as soon as he can. Ninety-second precinct. Okay?"

"Okay, I'll tell him," Esther says and hangs up.

Filled with trepidation, Esther walks slowly back to her house. The police! The police! Ben! The police! She ascends the stoop steps. The sound of praying men comes through the open windows. She steps into the hall. The synagogue door is open. Holding his Siddur in his hands, her father stands swaying back and forth, murmuring, his eyes shut tight—as though to retain an inner vision of inestimable worth. Esther waits at the door. At last the service is over. Her father opens his eyes, turns and sees her. He comes to the door. "What is it?" he asks.

"A telephone call."

He starts moving past her.

"They're not on the phone anymore. They called when you were davening."

Her father looks questioningly at her.

"They said you should call back."

"Who? Who should I call back?"

"The police. Ninety-second precinct."

Her father's face becomes bloodless. He does not move. Finally he asks, "Mama knows?"

"No," Esther says. "I didn't tell her."

Her father breathes a deep, relieved sigh, waits a moment, and walks heavily out the door.

He is rounding the corner when she runs down the steps, reaches the sidewalk, and hurries after him. He is already in the phone booth when she enters the drugstore, his back to her. She stands outside and listens.

"Yes," she hears him say. "Zalman Hirsch."

A few moments later he says, "I am holding on."

"What?" he asks. "What did you find?"

She sees the hand holding the receiver begin to shake. "A body? Identify? I don't understand."

A moment later he says, "A dead person? Drowned?" and she sees him try to clutch the wall.

His voice is faint. She can hardly hear, and her ears are full of pounding waves. "I'm coming. Right away," he is saying. A pause. "Tomorrow? All right, tomorrow morning. Where? Where I should come?"

His forehead is pressed against the coin box. "Please wait one minute. I get a pencil and paper."

Esther steps aside as her father comes out of the phone booth and asks Mr. Drucker for "Please, a pencil and piece paper." Mr. Drucker gives them to him. Her father returns to the telephone, and says, "Please, please spell for me." She sees him write slowly and unsteadily before he hangs up.

He stands in the opened booth, staring blindly at her. "I heard," she says, her lips trembling.

"No," her father says. "You heard nothing. Do you understand? Nothing."

Esther nods her head.

"And there was no phone call," he says. "Do you understand?"

Esther nods her head again. "I will not tell Mama," she says.

"No one," he says. "No one must know."

Her father steps out of the phone booth. Putting his hand on her shoulder to steady himself, he looks hard into her eyes. "We must not give up hope," he says in a quavering voice before he straightens his shoulders and together they walk back to their house.

35

The train hurtles through the underground darkness. When she woke up that morning, her father was already gone. She assumed he went to that address the police gave him. At breakfast her mother seemed the same as she had all week, so he must have made up an excuse about where he was going. Esther clutches the paper bag containing her lunch with one hand and holds on to the white pole with the other. The rocking and lurching are making her sick. Her palms are sweating. She hopes she doesn't throw up. Millie is saying something, but the rumble of the train and the rest of the class shouting to each other above the noise makes it hard to hear. She motions to Millie that she can't hear, and Millie looks annoyed. She wants to tell Millie to go to hell. She wants to tell everybody to go to hell. She feels awful. The train jolts to a stop. Mr. Wexler calls out, "This is it! Everybody out! Hold on to your partner's hand! Monitors, check your groups!" Millie takes Esther's hand. The class leaves the train and walks in double file along the platform, up the steps, and out into the fresh air and sunshine.

They wait on the corner while Mr. Wexler counts heads. Esther is feeling much better. And at last, she's uptown. It's not Times Square, but at least it's uptown. She squints up at the street sign. The street with all the stores is

Lexington Avenue, the other one is East Seventy-seventh Street. Lexington Avenue isn't famous like Broadway or Forty-second Street or Fifth Avenue, but she likes the way it sounds.

"Esther, you're squeezing my hand," Millie says.

"I'm sorry," Esther says. "I'm just so excited about being uptown.

Millie looks at her glumly. Poor Millie, Esther thinks, she's always moping. But I'm glad she's my partner anyway; we're used to each other. When they were choosing partners, she was so nervous. Thirty-seven kids in the class —somebody wouldn't have a partner and whoever it was would feel terrible. She prayed she wouldn't be the one, that Millie wouldn't be in one of her peculiar moods— mad at her for something she couldn't figure out. Whoever got left over would have to hold Mr. Wexler's hand. He's nice, but still. . . . She felt sorry for Julius Ginsburg; nobody picked him. Only Julius doesn't seem sad. He hasn't stopped talking to Mr. Wexler for a minute.

"This isn't anything to get excited about," Millie says. "We're not even on Fifth Avenue yet. This is just an ordinary street with nothing but dinky little stores."

Esther doesn't answer. It's best to keep her feelings to herself. Sometimes *nobody* can understand exactly how you feel.

Walking along Seventy-seventh Street, she recognizes the speckled bark of the sycamore trees and is surprised; they're the same as the ones in Williamsburg on the other side of Broadway. When they come to the next corner, she reads the street sign. Park Avenue! The ritziest street in the world! She can't believe it. "This is Park Avenue!" she exclaims to Millie.

"I know," Millie says. "It sure doesn't look like much. Just a lot of big apartment houses. They're not even pretty."

"But inside," Esther says, "inside, I bet they're gorgeous."

Millie shrugs her shoulders.

When they've crossed Madison Avenue, even Millie agrees that the neighborhood is getting real fancy, and Esther wishes the line would slow down. Behind the elegant facades—pearl gray and mauve and Georgian rose, the filagreed balconies, the classic balustrades—movie sets are arranging themselves. She creates magnificent rooms with shining chandeliers and shimmering furniture, starched butlers bowing at the doors, ruffle-capped maids carrying silver tea sets, and over every mantel of every marble fireplace a huge gilt-framed portrait of a beautiful woman in an evening dress with bare shoulders. And she imagines tall library rooms with heavy leather furniture and books all the way up to the ceiling. People who live here, she thinks, must be less afraid. The children too. In their schools you probably don't have to prove you're clean. And I'll bet storekeepers always act nice—you're never buying on trust.

"Fifth Avenue is next," Millie tells her.

"How do you know?"

"I know!" Millie says.

Probably Millie *does* know. But why does she have to sound so smart-alecky? Suddenly, Esther thinks she's going to cry. She isn't sure why—except that everything is so hard to understand. Why does she get hurt and feel dumb and threatened every time Millie knows something she doesn't know? A minute ago she was happy, now she feels terrible. Her feelings will not stay put. Don't let me start crying, she prays, not now, not today. But a few incorrigible tears are starting to trickle down her cheeks. Furtively, with a swift movement of her free hand, she wipes them away. Then taking deep breaths, she attempts to barricade herself against the waves of emotion that have been buffeting her about. Her tears are checked, but her mind will not let her be. It keeps tearing her in two. Holding on to Millie's hand as tightly as she'll let her, she wants to run away from her, from everybody, to be some place where existence is somehow simple; where she won't be confused anymore, where the dualism in herself and others and in all things will not find her. The bobbing heads of her classmates, preceding her in double-file, move her abruptly to warm affection, and then moments later, inexplicably, to loathing. I don't know *how* I feel about them, she murmurs to herself. I don't *know* them. I don't know *anybody*. Not even my own family! Everyone is so complicated, so closed up. You have to guess, to keep sniffing around. It's all so hard. She can't figure out *anything*. Especially her own feelings. How could she even imagine having a good time today? But she should—it's a beautiful day and she's coming to a beautiful art gallery and Mr. Wexler said she's going to see the most beautiful pictures in the world. Her heart wants to dance. Only this minute, this very very minute, her brother might be lying dead someplace. Dead forever. And she'll never be able to tell him about where she went and what she saw and how it looked. She keeps seeing him fixing up the chairs into a bed for her when she was sick, and making her gargle with salt water, and playing dominoes with her. And how glad he looked when he gave her the raincape, and now it's torn. Through a blur of tears, Esther sees the trees of Central Park. It won't be Ben they found! No, it won't! He'll come home and she'll tell him all about today. She'll forget about what she saw in his book. She'll talk to him and tell him about everything, and he won't say much, but his eyes will get soft and happy.

"One more block!" Mr. Wexler calls behind him.

Millie turns to her and asks her what's the matter. Esther says, "Nothing," and makes herself smile. Millie smiles back. Now Millie is squeezing *her* hand. She squeezes back. Both of them start laughing. Oh, how good it is to have Millie with her! Millie is *so* nice.

The line stops moving. Mr. Wexler calls out, "We're here! Now don't forget what I told you. No noise. No wandering off by yourself. First we'll go to the lavatories. Girls, when you come out, stay right there, so we boys can find you. Okay? Any questions before we go in?"

Esther hears nothing Mr. Wexler is saying. Her eyes travel up the fluted columns, rest for a moment on the intricate Corinthian capitals, and sweep across the Romanesque arches. It looks like a palace. She wants to stay outside a little longer and keep looking, but Mr. Wexler is leading them up the broad stone steps.

She is inside. Everyone's eyes have grown large and voices are hushed. Esther is seized with the idea that it's like a church. She looks anxiously around for a cross with a bleeding Jesus on it, and breathes deeply and gratefully when she doesn't see any.

When they gather again after trips to the toilets, Mr. Wexler explains that they will not see everything in the museum because there is too much and it would take too long and they'd get tired. But they'll see as much as they can and he'll do the best he can, if they're quiet, to tell them what he knows about the pictures and the artists.

"What about the armor?" one of the boys calls out.

"And the weapons?" another whispers timidly.

"And the weapons and the armor," Mr. Wexler adds, smiling.

She has stared at Florentine ladies in fine jewels and brocaded dresses, at naked rosy ones with round breasts and dimpled buttocks, been moved by ascetic men in introspective moods, admired muscular men with handsome faces, felt distaste for funny-looking ones in pretentious poses. Incredible colors, undulating forms, textures beyond her imaginings circle about in her head. She's getting dizzy, but she wants to go on. Coming to Turner's "Grand Canal in Venice," Esther stands awed, reverent. She sees the luminous sky with its great sweep of clouds, graceful gondolas bejewelling water that glimmers iridescently—blue and green and gold. The lushness, the consummate triumphant radiance fills her. Mr. Wexler's voice drifts into her ears, but she cannot pay attention. She can only look. Reluctantly, she leaves the resplendence of Venice to move along with her class, wondering if there are places so beautiful or is it possible that what the artist looked at and what he saw in his head were not the same.

Here's one that isn't beautiful and yet, in a way, it is. The people are poor and shabbily dressed and look tired. But sunlight streaming in through narrow windows spills over them and makes them glow. Mr. Wexler said to try to remember the paintings and artists they liked best so they can discuss them in class tomorrow. She looks to see who painted this picture which stirs something in her different from the others. Daumier.

She utters a small gasp when she sees Monet's "Sun-flowers"—thrusting, quivering, bursting, soaring. It's like they're on fire, like they're. . . . She searches her mind to find words commensurate with what she beholds, but there are none. Maybe, it occurs to her, this is what art is for—to express what you can't say in words. These flowers, she *knows*, are more beautiful than the real ones the artist looked at. They're more alive! But how did he do it? When she bends closer, she sees many many little brush strokes, different shapes and colors and shades. What looks like one color from far away isn't when you get close up. Nothing in the whole picture is one color! She is gripped by a startling revelation. Nothing in the whole world is one color! And colors change depending on where you're standing—shapes too. There are little shapes inside the big ones. That's why Mr. Epstein told her to look very very hard, to try to practically see right through everything. He's right. And then it strikes her with clarity so astounding that she can barely breathe: this is what makes everything, especially people, so complicated—the shapes and colors and shades that change, depending on where you're standing and how hard you're looking.

The class has moved on to another picture. She hurries to catch up with them. Mr. Wexler is pointing out that the picture, by a man named Renoir, is sparkling and yet smooth. It's a picture of a mother with her two little girls, and all of them are beautiful. She bends over to see it better, to understand why the woman's skin looks so warm, the children's so translucent. Again she sees the brushstrokes, the different colors, even patches of green. She looks at her own hands; they're cream-colored, maybe a little pink too, but that's all. She stares at Millie. Millie looks as sallow as ever, sort of tannish. Suddenly she sees them, in Millie's face! Greens, blues, golds, deep scarlets, all kinds of colors—right there in her skin. Probably most people can't see them, because they don't know how to look, only artists. The words beat loudly in her ears. Only artists.

As they leave the museum, Esther vaguely recalls suits of armor, swords and scabbards and crossbows and shields. Actually she tried not to notice any of it. She wanted certain special pictures to remain in her mind, undisturbed, for as long as possible. She doubted that she would ever paint such pictures, but she'd remember them. She'd store them away in her head and whenever harshness or ugliness presented itself, or she started remembering things she wanted to forget, she'd take out a favorite picture from way back in her brain and it would blot out the other.

"On to our picnic!" Mr. Wexler calls out.

"Yay!" the class shouts.

"How do you feel now?" Millie asks her.

"Full," Esther says, smiling broadly.

"Really?" Millie asks, astonished. "Aren't you hungry?"

"Starving!" Esther exclaims.

Millie looks confused. Esther laughs. "Never mind, Millie," she says, hugging her. "Never mind."

Swinging her paper bag in one hand and her friend's arm with the other, Esther walks with her class along Fifth Avenue until her teacher leads them into the park, to a sunlit meadow where they spread out on the grass and have their picnic.

She closes the door softly behind her. Her elation is about to end, she is almost certain. She follows the sound of voices to the kitchen. Her mother greets her, cheerful, animated. Esther throws her arms about her mother. Mama! she wants to cry out, Mama, I'm so glad to see you smiling! But she hugs her silently, saying nothing. Mrs. Lieberman is sitting at the table, which must be why her mother looks happy—her friend has come to see her. It's the first time she's visited since she moved away to live with her son. Esther is glad to see her too, but she looks different—frailer and her hair is almost white now. She must have just arrived; she's still explaining that she was in the neighborhood to see her doctor. Her son told her that she was crazy to shlep all the way to Williamsburg to go to a doctor, that there were plenty of good ones in Flatbush. "But children—what do children understand?" she says. The voice has turned plaintive. The dismal droop of the eyes betokens further expressions of woe, of misery. Her mother is already nodding her head sympathetically.

Esther doesn't want to hear. She begins to leave the kitchen, but stops at the door. In as casual a tone as she can muster, she asks, "Is Papa home?"

"No," her mother says, still nodding at Mrs. Lieberman.

"Has he been gone all day?"

Her mother looks at her. "Yes, he has not been back since the morning. Why? Why do you want to know?"

"I just asked. It doesn't matter," Esther calls breezily over her shoulder as she leaves the room and goes outside to sit on the steps and wait.

36

Zalman has been to the morgue. A policeman led him through a long, dimly-lit corridor. They entered a small room. Lying on a high, narrow slab, covered with a white sheet, was the corpse of a young man found floating in the East River. The policeman drew back the sheet. The corpse's face was discolored, warped, revolting. It was Ben. Dead. Zalman's body shuddered convulsively. He began to howl, like a great beast struck in the groin.

He felt the policeman's hand on his shoulder. "Take it easy, Pop. Take it easy now." His mouth hanging open, as though suddenly dumb, Zalman looked up imploringly into the florid face of the policeman who asked, "You okay, Pop?" Zalman turned back to his dead son.

The policeman's voice was kind. "Sorry, we gotta put him back now. Rules." He felt the policeman tugging at him. "Come on now, Pop, come on outta here." Zalman let himself be led away and seated on a bench in the corridor. A bare light bulb burned above his head. The policeman said, "We think it's suicide."

Zalman stared at the moving mouth.

"We think he killed himself," the policeman explained.

Zalman's head was shaking from side to side in disbelief.

"Dya think maybe no? Dya think somebody else killed him?" the policeman asked.

Zalman's head stopped moving.

"He have any enemies—people who hated him?"

Zalman stared, paralyzed.

"You got anything to tell us?" the policeman prodded.

Zalman's eyes pressed themselves shut. Tears squeezed themselves from the corners as, bent over and clutching his body, he sat with his great head swinging back and forth.

Another man in plain clothes came in. The policeman got up and whispered to the man, "It's the yid's kid. Suicide," and left. The other man came over and sat down beside Zalman and spoke to him about arrangements. Could he get the body out of there by tomorrow? Zalman nodded. The man got up and began to leave but stopped. "You all right, Pop?" he asked. Zalman nodded again, and the man left.

The rain is coming down in torrents, cascading over the rim of his big black hat, splashing in his face, crawling down his neck inside his collar, soaking him. He doesn't know when the downpour began. It had been hot and sunny, his face had been covered with sweat, he could not find strength to wipe it away. He could only keep walking. Where? Where to go? To whom? People hurry by him, their eyes shifting furtively, their faces dark with fear and suspicion. Children jump out of his way. Zalman walks blindly, insensible to the storm, like a crazyman.

He must stop. His legs are folding under him. He cannot keep prowling the streets. He will collapse. His son is dead and must be buried. But he cannot bring him home. Here, he will say to Malka, here is another dead son. Here is our son whom I have killed. No, he cannot. He cannot inflict this horror on her. No. He must lie. With hope, with illusion, one can be sustained. He dare not take them away. He must suffer alone and silently. It is little enough penance. Oh, how little it is! Would he could tear chunks of flesh from his body! Administer thousands upon thousands of lashes to his bare skin! Scourge himself publicly with vile abuse! But he cannot. Though he gag on his grief and anguish, his lips must remain locked. He must make himself mute.

Zalman moves on through the now empty streets. Arrangements. How is he to make them? What is he to do? Abruptly, a monstrous dilemma takes shape. "Riboyneh Shel Olem!" he cries out, "How will I *mourn* him?" Is my son to be relegated to the ranks of the wicked, to those who must go unmourned, to the destroyers of souls? I—I alone am the destroyer! Zalman leans exhausted against a building. He presses his head into the hard wet bricks. He wants to pound his head against them, to beat his brains into blackness. But he cannot. He must bury his son. But to spare his wife an agony she may not survive, he must deceive her. And if he is to deceive his wife, his son must go unmourned. "Master of the Universe, guide me!" he prays while the rain pounds on his bent back. A voice within him speaks. Go to the Rebbe. He will guide you. The Rebbe. But another voice cries No, you cannot! How cowardly, how base to lay the atrocity you have wrought on his head! The Rebbe's kind face appears before him. No, he cannot face it. Suddenly, he knows what he must do. He streaks across the street, flings open the door of a drugstore, and drops onto the seat of a telephone booth. He feels in his pocket for a coin, takes out a nickel, places it in the slot, and dials. Clara's voice answers.

"It is Zalman," he tells her. "Is Willie home yet from work?"

"No. Probably he won't come home for at least an hour. But with him, who can tell? He can stand on a corner and talk until God knows when."

"What is the phone number where he works?"

"What's wrong?" Clara croaks, clearly ready to collapse.

"Nothing. Nothing is wrong. Only I need him."

"Something is wrong," Clara breathes into the phone.

"Please Clara," Zalman pleads. "It is nothing. I need only—only information. But I cannot waste time. The phone number. Please!"

Clara gives him the number. He hangs up quickly before he forgets it, finds another coin in his pocket, and dials.

"Willie Schneider. I need to speak to Willie Schneider."

"Just a moment, please."

"It is emergency. Please hurry up."

The ensuing silence seems endless. Zalman puts his head against the cold metal of the coin box and prays and prays.

"Hello?"

"Willie. Zalman."

"What is it?"

"I must see you."

"What is it, Zalman? What is wrong?"

"I must see you."

"All right, Zalman. All right." Willie says soothingly, his voice laden with apprehension. "When? Where?"

"Right away. Wherever you want."

"All right. Where are you now?"

"Downtown. The East Side."

"Do you want I should come downtown or you should meet me up here near my place? I am finished in half an hour."

"I'll come to you. It will save time."

Willie, very carefully, directs Zalman to a cafeteria on Seventh Avenue.

"I'll find it," Zalman tells him.

"Zalman, are you all right?" Willie asks.

"I'm all right," Zalman says, and hangs up.

Zalman sits in a corner of the brightly lit, half-empty cafeteria, waiting. He does not know how ghastly he looks in his drenched clothes with his big black hat that he keeps on soaking wet, and his face drained of blood. Willie comes rushing in. He sees his cousin sitting dazed, with haunted eyes. He takes him by the shoulders. "Zalman, Zalman, what is it?"

Zalman looks up at him. "Willie," he says, Willie...."
He cannot go on. His face crumples.

Willie sits down beside him, turning to shield him with his body from the view of curious diners. "Zalman," he says softly, "what has happened? Tell me."

The words tear themselves from Zalman's throat. "Benjamin. Benjamin is dead."

Willie draws in his breath. His face becomes white and his voice breaks. "Zalman—" He puts his arm around his cousin and holds him. "Zalman, tell me what happened."

"They found him in the river. He—he drowned himself."

Zalman is shivering. Willie removes his cousin's wet hat. "A yarmulka, Zalman. Where do you have one?" Zalman takes a yarmulka from his pocket and puts it on. "You are soaking wet," Willie tells him. "Let me take you home."

"No," Zalman says, "not yet. I cannot go home yet."

Willie waits, breathing heavily.

Zalman says, "Malka must not know."

Willie's eyes fill with dread. "What are you saying?"

"It will destroy her."

Willie stares at him but says nothing.

"And—and—" Zalman's mouth contorts with pain. "And it will be unbearable for her to live with me when she— when she knows what I have done."

"You? Zalman, you?

"Yes, I. I, his father, have killed him."

"No, Zalman, it is not true!" Willie's voice is frantic.

"You must not believe such a thing! What happened is —is God's will."

Zalman looks dumbfounded at his cousin. "God? *You* speak of God? What do you know about God? I, I know. God does not commit such evil. Only men. Men who blind themselves, men too vain, too cowardly to see His light, to open their hearts to the Holy Spirit—to goodness and compassion. I locked my heart. I shut my eyes to God's light. I saw nothing but my own wretched self!"

Willie clutches both his cousin's arms. "Zalman, please listen to me."

"I will not listen. You are wrong, Willie. God did not do this. I, with my fists, drove my son to his death."

"No, Zalman, no. A father—a father must sometimes chastise a son."

"Chastise? Oh, Willie," Zalman sobs, "I did much more than chastise. I was a brute!"

Willie keeps holding his cousin, but cannot find words.

"You must help me to bury him," Zalman says.

Tears run down Willie's cheeks. "I will do whatever you want. Tell me what you want."

"A Chevra Kadisha. We must find a holy brotherhood where they don't know me. In your neighborhood you know people. You will come with me. I do not have the strength alone. You must help me." Zalman's eyes are pleading.

"I will do whatever you want."

"You know people?"

"I know people."

"They will be charitable?"

"Yes, they will be charitable."

"We will go to them now," Zalman says, getting up.

"You are soaked through," Willie tells him, "and exhausted. I can go by myself. Only tell me where they must go to—to get Benjamin."

"No, I will go with you. I must know where he will lie."

"Zalman, I beg you. There is no need. It will be arranged properly, just as you wish. I give you my word. Tonight, I will telephone you so you will know where to come."

"I must bury him."

"You will bury him."

Zalman takes from his pocket the piece of paper with the address the police gave him on the phone and hands it to Willie. "He must lie among the righteous. He did not destroy himself. It was I who...." Zalman's voice breaks. He sits down again, covers his face with his hands, and weeps quietly.

"Let me first take you home," Willie says.

"No. Malka will suspect. And the children—they too must not know that—that their brother is dead."

"Zalman—"

"No, Willie, to carry such a burden by themselves is too great, without a mother to comfort them, a father who can...." Zalman's mouth trembles.

Willie speaks carefully. "Is it better for them, for all of them to keep hoping, to live with illusions? The truth, Zalman, what about the truth?"

The silence becomes heavy before Zalman says in a strangely calm voice. "The truth, my friend, is an awesome thing, to be handled with wisdom and with courage denied to ordinary people. Most of us must make do with illusions. Or else—or else we could not endure."

Willie looks tenderly at his cousin. "You, Zalman, you still have illusions?"

"Right now, no. But I will have them again. If not the same ones, then others. God in His goodness will permit me to construct them. He will help me to survive."

Willie's face is baffled, incredulous. But is there not an inconsistency? he is about to say. Only he sees the soaked black hat battered by the storm and the strong hands lying helpless on the cafeteria table, and stops himself. Then with sudden briskness, he says, "Wait here. I will bring you a cup of coffee. You must strengthen yourself before you go home."

"No," Zalman says, getting up. "I am strong enough. Let us go."

Straightening their shoulders and setting their faces, like two conspirators, the cousins leave the cafeteria.

37

The rain has driven her indoors. Esther stands by the window, looking out, waiting for her father. Despair, hope, anxiety, pummeling each other inside her, have been making her stomach churn. When finally she sees him, she wants to hide, but she propels herself to the door to let him in. He looks terrible. Her hand flies to her mouth, but a small cry escapes. "No," her father says. "You must not. It was not him. It was not Benjamin."

Esther keeps searching the pale, haggard face, trying to penetrate the reddened eyes.

Her father reaches out and touches her shoulder. "You have not spoken of the telephone call?"

"No, Papa."

"Good. For there is no need. Do you understand?"

Esther nods her head, pressing her lips tightly together. The need to cry out is still inside her.

Malka comes rushing out into the hall. "Where have you been all day?" she asks. "Look at you! You are soaked through and through! Where have you been?"

"Where have I been?" Zalman repeats after her. "Where have I *not* been? Where does one *not* go to search for— to search for parnussah?" He sees his wife's bewildered eyes. What else can he tell her? That he got wet searching for his soul? Who would understand? But to search for a livelihood—*that* can be understood.

"We will talk later," Malka says. "You must change your clothes. Then you must eat something. You look ill."

"There is nothing to talk about," Zalman says firmly, "and I am not ill, only weary. I will take off these clothes and I will lie down. When I have rested, I will—I will pray. Then I will eat. But talking I can do without."

Malka's forehead furrows, but she shrugs and returns to the kitchen.

Esther watches her father's shoulders collapse as, holding on tightly to the banister, he ascends the steps.

The evening service is over, the worshippers gone. Zalman stops by the synagogue to steady himself, leaning both his hands on the door posts, before he proceeds up the second flight of steps. When he passes Ben's door, he averts his eyes. Stumbling through the dim hall to his own bedroom, he sinks onto his bed and rocks back and forth, his fists pressed into his forehead. He wants to rend his clothes, but he cannot. He needs to cry out, but he does not dare; his suffering must remain silent.

Base, corrupt creature that he is, whom did he think he was deceiving all these years? Whom was he deluding with his rites and ceremonies, his scrupulous adherence to only the least difficult admonitions, his blustering insistence on the least significant precepts? Subterfuge! All subterfuge! Braying and bowing and beating his breast while he profaned the most sacred laws. Oh God, I have demeaned your holiness. In your holy name I have committed atrocities. My son is dead. I prayed to you to stay my hand, but you did not. For in your great wisdom, you were not deceived; I was no Abraham. I was not moved by faith in you, but by vanity, by meanness of spirit. And always I justified. Oh, how I justified! I had the right, the obligation to protect my son from his sinfulness, to bend him to the will of God. Sham! Falseness! It was my *own* will that concerned me, the gratification of my *own* needs. I was an onanist! Yes, yes, an onanist, caressing myself over and over again in unmentionable ways to bring pleasure and satisfaction to myself alone. I have been an abomination! I have nurtured no one's needs but my own! Not my children's, not my wife's. No one's.

Zalman pounds at his body and claws at his face. His vileness is grotesque—over and over again abusing his only son until God could no longer bear to look. Tears spill from Zalman's eyes. Oh Lord who has rescued my son from me, soothe him and heal him, restore his beauty and give him peace. Accord him a place among the angels.

Zalman's great head falls to his chest as he pleads to his compassionate God: I have not the power to express the contrition I feel, but I beg forgiveness for the suffering I have inflicted. I believe in your ultimate justice, that in the world to come her suffering will be rewarded, but until then, sustain my wife. Strengthen her. Help me to love her and love my daughters. Annihilate the evil in me so I will not harm them. Let me hear the hearts of others and, though I am unworthy, let them hear mine. Zalman's body is shaken by stifled sobs. Oh, my son, my Benjamin, forgive me. Forgive your father. Forgive me. Forgive me.

Pain and grief are choking him. He cannot contain them. Zalman rises from the bed and faces the east. Outside the storm has spent itself. Stars, seen through his tears as quivering halos, have emerged in a clear sky as in a repeatedly breaking voice, Zalman intones the evening prayers. "Blessed art Thou, O Lord our God, King of the Universe, who at Thy word bringest on the evening twilight.... And thou shalt love the Lord thy God with all thine heart, and with all thy soul, and with all thy might. ... Thou, O Lord, art mighty forever.... Thou sustainest the living with loving kindness, quickenest the dead with great mercy, supportest the falling, healest the sick, loosest the bound and keepest thy faith to them that sleep in the dust.... Forgive us, O our King, for we have transgressed; for Thou dost pardon and forgive. Blessed art Thou, O

38

Esther can't fall asleep. So much happening all at once: finding out she made Rapid Advance, the visit to junior high, graduation next week, and the day after graduation they move. And from then on, she'll be living in a different house, on a new block, in an apartment with hot water. She's sure it won't matter about not knowing anyone on the block; Millie won't be further away, only in another direction, and she's positive Liesl will come over like she says. Liesl is plenty peculiar but she doesn't say anything she doesn't mean. That's what makes people mad at her. Probably Angie will feel funny about coming over, so she'll have to come back here if she wants to keep being friends with Angie, and she'll do it—she really will. They're sending Rudi away to a different school because where he's been going is just for little kids. Liesl says he's been crying a lot, he doesn't want to live someplace without his family, but her parents say it's for his own good and he has to. Liesl saw pictures of the place and says it's real nice, in the country an' everything, but you could tell she felt bad. She'll probably be worrying all the time that someone is being mean to Rudi and she's not there to interfere. All of a sudden everything's changing. In a way it's exciting and she's glad. But deep down, it's like being about to discover things you might not want to know. Esther pulls the blanket up to her chin; already she feels herself the possessor of more knowledge than her small body can comfortably hold.

She looks at the outlines and shadows of the room she'll be leaving forever. For so long she was afraid it would happen—the rabbi would kick them out of the house. Now it's happened, and it's not even terrible. He sold it and said they had to move. Lila says the new owner is going to fix it up and make separate little apartments and charge real high rent. She says he'll probably end up being disappointed. I hope he will be; the way he went snooping around with that look on his face and muttering over and over again to the rabbi, "Whatta mess! This place sure is run down." What did he expect? Rockefeller's mansion? When he picked up the door from the floor and looked under it, he made a face like he was going to vomit. He didn't even care that Mama and Papa were standing right there. He hardly looked at them all the time he was poking his nose into everything, like it wasn't even *their home*. He was horrible! I hate him. I *detest* the rabbi! I'm glad we don't need his stinking house anymore. And there are plenty of other minyans Papa can go to. He can go across Broadway—probably their minyans are better anyway. I really despise that rabbi. He didn't even introduce the man to her parents; just told them he was selling the house and the man was looking it over. The way they stood there not showing how upset they were, not saying a word. She was so proud of them. It was like she was seeing them clearly for the first time—truly knowing them. And the strange mixed-up feeling that happened, that she was the parent and they were being well-behaved children and not embarrassing her. It hurt her to look at them, but in a peculiar way it made her feel strong. All the time those two men, like giant insects, went crawling in and out of every corner all over the house, her parents stayed silently out of the way. But she tagged along; it was *her* house. That was over a week ago, but it still makes her so mad when she thinks about it.

Anyway, everything's going to be better now. Her father found this apartment for eighteen dollars a month. She was a little disappointed when she saw it. Papa had said it didn't have heat, but it had hot water and a big, sunny kitchen and almost new linoleum on all the floors. She never imagined that the bathtub would be in the kitchen and they'd have to share a toilet that was out in the hall with another family. Mama said they could hang a curtain around that funny bathtub on high legs whenever anybody wanted to take a bath—that part won't be too bad—but there's nothing they can do about the toilet. And she wishes it wasn't what they call a railroad flat. You have to walk through both bedrooms to get from the kitchen to the dining room. The landlord was surprised that we were going to make the front room—because it's the only one big enough—into a dining room. He said his other tenants ate in the kitchen all the time and used all the other rooms for bedrooms. Imagine Papa eating in the kitchen on Shabbes and on all the holidays! Both bedrooms don't have windows and of course you have to walk through one to get to the other, and they're so small. Papa'll have to get rid of those boxes of leftovers from his old businesses—they'll never fit in. I hope he's right about his new business, that it'll be a good one and we'll be able to go off Relief. But what if he ends up with dozens and dozens of eggs?

Her mother was shocked when she realized they'd have only two bedrooms. "Where will Benjamin sleep?" she asked, startling her father. It was like he'd never thought of it. But he said he was planning to keep looking for a bigger place; this was just the best he could find in such a short time. And if Benjamin came home meanwhile, he said, they could curtain off a corner of the dining room. "Like gypsies," her mother said sadly. But her father said not to worry, that he'd find a bigger place before Ben came home. Her mother's face became ferocious. "How do *you* know when he'll come home?" she shouted. "He might come tonight or tomorrow." Papa's mouth just hung open. Mama looked at him real hard and said in a very quiet voice, "Or maybe you know, like I do, that he is not coming home." And her father's voice was all tight when he told her mother she was crazy, that Ben came home before and he'll come home again. What gives her such idiotic ideas? he wanted to know. "What gives me such ideas?" her mother said. "My heart. My heart keeps telling me." Before her father could respond, the landlord came in and asked if they were finished looking. Her father said they were and would rent the rooms. And all the way back to the house, for all seven blocks, nobody said a word. She kept imagining Ben coming home and opening the door and it wouldn't be his house anymore. His home would have disappeared. How would he find them? she wanted to ask, but she was afraid to talk about Ben.

Esther turns over and presses her face into her pillow. He'll ask around. Probably Mama and Papa will give people our address to give him. If only I could forget how Papa looked that day—like a ghost, his clothes all messed up, his eyes red and swollen. Papa screams and hollers, but he doesn't cry. Only that day I'm sure he did. She's got to stop remembering. She'll do what she did that day. She'll force herself to think about things that make her feel good—the picnic in Central Park, the pictures in the museum. As soon as her mother thinks she's old enough to go by herself, she's going to earn another dime and go back to the museum and see the pictures she missed and see the ones she saw, all over again. Esther lies in bed, smiling in the dark, seeing what she wants to see. Lila rolls over in her sleep and flings an arm across her. Esther doesn't remove her sister's arm or slide out from under it; she lies still so as not to disturb it. Her sister's face close to hers catches the light from the lamppost outside. Lila looks happy—she's glad about moving, especially because now Mama's going to let her work for Mr. Brenner this summer, helping out the bookkeeper. I only hope he doesn't get fresh like I told her he might. Lila said if he tried anything funny with her, she'd kick him you know where. Esther giggles, imagining the look on Mr. Brenner's face. Putting her arm very gently around her sister and still smiling, Esther falls asleep.